KILLER WEED

a novel by Michael Castleman

—ALSO BY MICHAEL CASTLEMAN—

FICTION

A Killing in Real Estate (2010)

Death Caps (2007)

The Lost Gold of San Francisco (2001)

NONFICTION

When Someone Dies: The Quick, Practical Guide to the Logistics of Death
(coauthor with Scott Smith, 2013)

The New Healing Herbs: The Curative Powers of Nature's Medicines
(2009, 3rd edition)

Building Bone Vitality: How to Prevent Osteoporosis—Without Milk,
Dairy Foods, Calcium, Estrogen, or Drugs
(coauthor with Amy Lanou, Ph.D., 2009)

Great Sex: The Man's Guide to the Secrets of Total-Body Sensuality (2004)

Blended Medicine: How to Combine the Best of Mainstream and
Alternative Medicine for Optimal Health and Wellness (2000)

There's Still A Person In There: The Complete Guide to Preventing,
Treating, and Coping with Alzheimer's Disease
(co-authored with Dolores Gallagher-Thompson, Ph.D.,
and Matthew Naythons, M.D., 2000)

Nature's Cures: 33 Natural Therapies to
Improve Your Health and Well-Being (1996)

An Aspirin A Day: What You Can Do To Prevent
Heart Attack, Stroke, and Cancer (1993)

Before You Call the Doctor: Safe, Effective Self-Care for More Than 300
Common Medical Problems (co-authored with Anne Simons, M.D.,
and Bobbie Hasselbring, 1992)

Cold Cures: The Complete Guide to Prevention and Treatment of the
Common Cold and Flu (1987)

The Medical Self-Care Book of Women's Health (coauthored with Sadja
Greenwood, M.D., and Bobbie Hasselbring, 1987)

Crime Free: The Community Crime Prevention Handbook (1984)

Sexual Solutions: For Men and the Women Who Love Them (1980)

E-BOOKS

Great Sex After 40 (GreatSexAfter40.com)

KILLER WEED

a novel by Michael Castleman

MP Publishing
6 Petaluma Boulevard North, Suite B6
Petaluma CA 94952

Killer weed : an Ed Rosenberg mystery / Michael Castleman.
p. cm.
ISBN 978-1-84982-240-4
Series : Ed Rosenberg mystery

1. Marijuana industry --Fiction. 2. San Francisco (Calif.) --Fiction. 3. Haight-Ashbury (San Francisco, Calif.) --Fiction. 4. Hippies--Fiction. 5. Reporters and reporting --California --San Francisco --Fiction. 6. Mystery and detective stories. I. Series. II. Title.

PS3603.A884 K55 2013

Manufactured in the United States of America

10 9 8 7 6 5 4 3 2 1

Book design by Dorothy Carico Smith

For my children,
Maya, Jeff, and Kristen

EARLY READERS CALL *KILLER WEED* A KILLER READ

"*Killer Weed* hooked me on page one and I savored the references to San Francisco in the 1960s. A fascinating story with a strong ending."
—**Grace Slick, vocalist, Jefferson Airplane**

"In *Killer Weed*, the rip-roaring '60's ride again. Hiyo cannabis! Away!"
—**Wavy Gravy, emcee at Woodstock,
founder, Camp Winnarainbow**

"I devoured *Killer Weed*. I loved the Haight-Ashbury history and all the tales of dope dealing. I read a lot of mysteries and *Killer Weed* smokes."
—**Joel Selvin, longtime *San Francisco Chronicle* rock critic
and author of *The Summer of Love***

"This tale shows a side of the quest for green gold that few people outside the isolated cannabis culture ever see. While presented as a mystery, it's a rare glimpse into the outlaw culture that prohibition created."
—**Ed Rosenthal, author of *Marijuana Grower's Handbook***

"*Killer Weed* is a delightful whodunit. A contemporary novel with an enticing infusion of 1960's San Francisco cultural magic. Castleman must have been there. The novel is just too dead on to have been written by anyone other than someone who lived through those unique times."
—**William G. Panzer, Esq., co-author of Prop 215
that legalized medical marijuana in California**

"Killer Weed is a magical combination of mystery, San Francisco history, and pot that grabbed me right away and never let go. Castleman skillfully blends an intriguing modern tale with the heady transcendence of the hippie period to paint a historically accurate portrait of the marijuana business in America, both then and now. The hard-boiled narrative makes the characters come alive and keeps you guessing until the end. So kick back, light one up, and enjoy this terrific page-turner."
—**Tony Bove, Producer/Director of Rockument's
Haight-Ashbury in the Sixties CD-ROM**

"Fast-paced and historically rich, a love letter to '60's hippie San Francisco couched in a fascinating mystery that reinforces the point that the problem is prohibition, not cannabis."

—**Doug Fine, author,** ***Too High to Fail***

"*Killer Weed* is a marvelous page-turner from compelling start to excellent finish. A real 'who-smoked-it' with a cast of unforgettable contemporary characters blended with colorful characters from yesteryear. I couldn't put it down."

—**Robert Altman, photographer, whose photos have appeared in** *People, Rolling Stone,* **the** *New York Times,* **and in his book of photojournalism,** *The Sixties*

"*Killer Weed* is a killer read, a fast paced murder mystery that illuminates forty years of the cannabis scene. And it's a pleasure to recommend a book that adds new meaning to the phrase, Prohibition Kills."

—**Chris Conrad, author of** *Hemp: Lifeline to the Future* **and** *Hemp for Health,* **curator of the Oaksterdam Cannabis Museum in Oakland, CA and the International Hash-Marihuana-Hemp Museum in Amsterdam, the Netherlands**

"Michael Castleman's fourth whodunit replicates the previous three with a fast-paced, gripping mystery, featuring San Francisco journalist Ed Rosenberg. *Killer Weed* not only tells a compelling story, but also beautifully captures both contemporary San Francisco and its complex, colorful, hippie past. I loved it."

—**Charles A. Fracchia, founder, San Francisco Museum and Historical Society**

"The sixties Haight-Ashbury shimmers like a psychedelic light show in this riveting tale of marijuana, mystery, and murder. Castleman throws protagonist Ed Rosenberg into a tangled web of interwoven lives across four decades—and then someone starts shooting at him. A great tale you're sure to enjoy. And after a few chapters, don't be surprised if you're rifling your cupboard for cupcakes."

—**Bill Yenne, author of** *San Francisco Then & Now*

Visit KillerWeedNovel.com

KILLER
WEED

1

A gunshot sounds distinctive, even over the phone, especially when followed by your wife screaming.

The sharp *bang* ricocheted around Ed Rosenberg's brain like a pinball on espresso. *Someone was shooting at Julie!* He felt unseen hands close around his neck and squeeze. "Julie! Are you all right?"

"It's Dave!" she shrieked. "Oh my God! *Dave!*"

"What?"

"He's on the ground! He's bleeding! Oh—! Ed, I can't talk. I'll call you back."

"Julie! Wait!" The line went dead. *Call Ended* flashed on Ed's screen. He jabbed Recents, then her number. Voice-mail. *Damn.*

Sitting parked between errands in the Mission, Ed realized he was holding his breath. He forced a long exhale and felt a sharp stab in his gut. He had only one thought: to fly to Julie, to be with her, hold her close, make sure she was all right. But *where was she?* He had no idea.

Ed stared through the windshield toward Twin Peaks. Wisps of fog blew over the ridge and somersaulted toward the Bay. He was also somersaulting—but it felt like being locked in a front-loader on high spin. First they get fired, now *this*.

Ed knew he had to calm down and remember where Julie was. Her face came to him first—her sparkling deep brown eyes, and her skin an alluring caramel mix of black and white. Her luscious lips formed a word. *Breathe.* Yes. Breathing was good—and even better after a hit, but what little remained of his stash was back home. That had been one of his errands, but now it would have to wait.

Ed rewound to breakfast, to their usual hectic flail. As he'd filled the dishwasher and readied Jake for daycare, Julie had hustled Sonya out the door to school and run down her plans for the day. But given what had just happened—*Dave Kirsch shot!*—her words disappeared, engulfed in fog.

Where *was* she? He slapped the steering wheel so hard his hand hurt. Then the fog cleared and it came back to him: Golden Gate Park, the band shell, some rally.

A spider of cold sweat scuttled from his armpit down his side. The shot, the hot *bam* of it, so loud, so menacing. It echoed between his ears and made the breath catch in his throat. He hadn't felt this frantic since his father's stroke. He could survive the *Foghorn* shoving them out the door—he could endure almost anything—but not losing Julie.

The curtain opened on *Hell: The Movie.* He slouched over an open grave, holding the kids' little hands as their mother was lowered into the ground. He opened his mouth and forcibly exhaled the nightmare. It was *Dave* who'd been shot—Dave. Julie was all right. Or was she? Someone was shooting and she was *right there.*

Ed texted her: On way 2 band shell.

He threw it into drive and stomped the accelerator. Tires screeched as he pulled out of the space by the cleaners' and headed from the lowlands of the Mission up to the hilly plateau of Noe Valley on his way over the ridge and down through the Haight to the park.

He hit the button for the news station. "Moments ago, San Francisco mayoral candidate Dave Kirsch was shot in Golden Gate Park. The Board of Supervisors member and marijuana activist was walking across the museum concourse when a single shot to the chest felled him. No word of his condition. Police are—"

Ed ran a yellow and hurtled across Valencia, narrowly missing two guys holding hands and walking a cocker spaniel. *Slow down. Get a grip.* But that was impossible. Someone was *shooting* and Julie was—

Ed held his breath. He was at the beach, his toes curling in warm sand, everything fine, and then the writhing Pacific reared up into a monster wave and raced right for him. He turned to run but could hardly move. He was standing knee deep in oatmeal. Their careers had been guillotined. Their finances teetered on the edge of the abyss. And now bullets were flying. *What next?* Shot in the chest. *Fuck.* If Kirsch died—! Such a decent man, the best advocate stoners ever had, and so good to Julie. What was the world coming to?

A red light stopped him at Market Street. He reached for his phone just as it chimed.

"Julie!"

"He's dead," she whimpered. "Dave's dead."

Ed didn't know what to say. "Sorry" seemed so feeble. His mind replayed their argument over her job. *Why give up steady work for the paper? Because I hate it. The gig's over on election day. If he wins, I'm the mayor's press secretary. Kirsch can't win. Yes he can.* Then a miracle, he was rising in the polls, he was number two and gaining, and then—

All Ed cared about was Julie's safety. "Are you all right?"

"*No!* Dave's *dead!* Didn't you hear me?"

The light changed. Ed crossed the wide boulevard and pulled up by Café Flore.

"I mean, are you *injured*?"

"No, no, I'm okay. But Dave—it's *horrible.* Blood everywhere, all over Cindy!" Cynthia Miller was Kirsch's campaign manager.

"I'm on my way. You're at the band shell, right?"

"Hold on—"

Ed heard muffled voices.

"I have to give a statement," Julie said, blowing her nose. "Ed, don't come here. You won't get close. They've got everything cordoned off. Cops everywhere." To someone else she said, "Julie Pearl, media…Yes… all right. In a minute." Then she returned to the phone. "I gotta go—"

"Wait! When will you be home?"

"No idea…I have to handle this. The first TV truck just pulled up. Oh, shit. It's my day to pick up the kids." Her voice caught. "Can you?"

"Yes, yes, don't worry about it." Ed heard a piercing siren. "What's that?"

"The ambulance." She sobbed once, then pulled herself together. "Oh, God, a body bag."

Ed's gut ached.

Julie said, "Don't forget the spoon." Their year-old son's security blanket was an old wooden spoon. He carried it everywhere and slept with it. If they left it at daycare, Jake bawled inconsolably.

"The spoon, yes."

"Now three TV trucks—and Wally." Police reporter Wallace Turner was one of the few *San Francisco Foghorn* old-timers who still had a job. "I'm in no shape for a press conference," Julie moaned, "but it's show time."

2

Ed felt like he'd been thrown into a pool of ice water. He was simultaneously shocked and numb. How could Kirsch be *dead?* Dave Kirsch of all people. He'd been a fixture in San Francisco for decades, first as the ex-hippie dope dealer turned guru of growing, then as the politician with the strong libertarian streak, and finally as the seriously lighthearted candidate for mayor. John Kennedy. John Lennon. Bill Graham. Some people are so embedded in your world, you take them for granted, and then *bang*, gone. Ed thought of how Julie must feel. All he wanted was to hold her as she cried, to feel her warmth, her heart beating. She was tough as steel, but even I-beams failed.

Ed knew he should return to the Mission, but his errands seemed so trivial now. He could barely breathe. Ever since the *Foghorn* had reamed them, he'd been waking up in the wee hours bathed in sweat from a recurring nightmare, the water rising, lifting him until his head bumped a concrete ceiling, the water up to his neck, his chin, his lips. Now the feeling of imminent doom had pursued him into daylight. What would become of them? He'd always considered himself nimble and shrewd, but he didn't know what to do.

A garbage truck rumbled by and startled him back to reality. He was in a bus zone in the Castro. Seagulls wheeled overhead under puffy clouds as an antique streetcar clattered by. His cheeks felt odd and he touched them. *Have I been crying?* He forced himself to breathe and worked his shoulders in circles the way Julie did to her yoga DVD. They'd been kicked in the gut and now Julie's Kirsch gig, their one candle of hope, had been blown out. But he wasn't a widower. Julie was okay. That was the main thing.

Still, his intestines cramped as though he'd been stabbed in the gut. It seemed like just yesterday he was a newly minted Berkeley Ph.D., with a job teaching history at Cal State East Bay. But after a few years, he and his department chair both decided that he was oil on the waters of academia.

Then Ed stumbled into a job writing for San Francisco's alternative weekly, and suddenly, much to his surprise, he loved going to work. Instead of lecturing gum-cracking kids who couldn't care less, he was reaching a hundred thousand people a week and occasionally even making a difference.

After a few years, he jumped to the *Foghorn* and fell in love with Julie, the daily's PR chief. Eventually, a new executive editor bought his pitch to write a column devoted to local history: San Francisco Unearthed, which became a modest hit. San Franciscans loved their city's golden, quirky, raunchy past, and Ed had a knack for making it come alive. Macy's noticed and started paying a premium for ad placement next to the column, and every few years, the *Horn*'s book division published collections that had allowed them to buy and renovate their modest Mission starter home, and now, a dozen blocks away, their second place, large enough for two kids. The new house needed more work than Jericho after the trumpets, but they hadn't worried—they had good jobs and assurances that they were safe.

Journalism. Ed felt acid burning his throat. As a young reporter, he'd reveled in working among the best and brightest. Now he realized that many journalists were dolts, with media pundits the biggest idiots of all. Not one had predicted that free classifieds on Craigslist would devastate newspapers. Not one had foreseen the Internet devaluing information to the point where Pulitzer Prize winners were groveling to get into law school.

Ed and Julie had survived two buyouts and three rounds of layoffs, but then the ax fell. The features editor had pushed open the glass door of his little office and said, "Sorry, Ed, you're history."

He called upstairs immediately. Julie had just gotten her pink slip— by e-mail. And what about management's promises? *That was then, this is now.*

As the sun set on their final day, Ed, Julie, and forty other newly laid off *Horn* folk gathered at The Poets, the venerable Irish bar down the alley behind the paper. Ed had written about the place, a fixture in the South of Market since the Civil War, when the neighborhood was Irishtown. He sipped one Guinness and stopped, but Julie lost count and had to be helped to the car.

Then they were offered their jobs back—freelance, at a third of their former salaries and no benefits. They'd been proletarianized, outsourced to themselves. They gnashed their teeth and cursed corporate America. Julie refused to crawl back to the paper, insisting she wouldn't be humiliated. Ed sympathized but implored her to reconsider. With young kids, a monster mortgage, savings depleted by renovations, and now paying out of pocket for health insurance, what choice did they have?

They sent out dozens of resumés and scrambled for work like pigeons pecking the gutter for anything that resembled food. *Nothing like self-employment to catapult you out of bed in the morning.*

In addition to his column, Ed picked up a California history class at City College, but it didn't pay much. The history chair at USF said they might have something down the road, but who knew when. The California Historical Society invited him to contribute to their magazine and web site, but they paid next to nothing. And the Bancroft Library at Cal hoped to launch a new California archive project, but in this economy…

Then a buddy on the board of the San Francisco Museum e-mailed him about a Silicon Valley zillionaire who was interested in funding an exhibit on the Summer of Love. Was Ed interested in compiling research for the curator? *Is the Pope Catholic?* But that was ten days ago, and no word since. Ed wasn't religious, but he found himself praying. *Please, God, I need a job.*

He drove down the hill to Rainbow Grocery, the Mission's worker-owned vegetarian supermarket. He pulled out Julie's list, hoping the routine of shopping would lift his spirits, but no such luck. He felt lost in a cold black cave. He also felt angry, which was nothing new. He hated the paper, and worse, hated himself for believing his editor's sweet talk and plunging blithely into renovations. But this particular rage burned with a special heat. By the dairy case, he realized why. He was furious with Julie.

When the Kirsch possibility bubbled up, she'd faced a conflict of interest. She couldn't represent the campaign while doing PR for the paper. Ed thought she should stay put. The Kirsch job was a short-term long shot, while the *Horn* was steady money. He'd begged her to be sensible, but she couldn't jump ship fast enough. Then Kirsch began rising in the polls, and Julie had embraced a rose-colored fantasy. The mayor's press secretary! Huge salary! Great benefits! Now Kirsch was on a slab in the morgue, and that dream was as dead as her employer.

Shoveling green beans into a plastic bag, Ed tried to look on the bright side. He was no longer in chains from nine to five. He could run errands on weekday afternoons when lines were short and parking plentiful. He'd gone to the bank, bought a hose, and dropped off the dry cleaning in just twenty minutes, half the time the chores would have taken on the weekend. On sunny days, he enjoyed lunch in their yard, inhaling the fragrance of the jasmine Julie and the kids had planted. And he could catch bargain matinées.

But the silver lining barely peeked out from under the coal-black cloud. Their severance was lousy and their savings were going fast. With newspapers in rigor mortis, no one was hiring, and hustling for freelance work made their former grind feel like a paid vacation. Who had time for bargain mats?

Ed filled his cart, finishing in the beer and wine aisle. Julie had written *Sauvignon Blanc,* followed by the number one, which she'd crossed out and replaced with a two. Since the big kiss-off, she'd been drinking more, but when Ed made the mistake of pointing it out, she'd retorted that he was smoking more weed, so there. He sighed and nestled two bottles into the cart.

As Ed hoisted the bags into the car, his phone chimed. He didn't recognize the number.

"Hello, Ed. Pat Lucas."

Pat was the principal at Sonya's school, and she sound perturbed. *What now?*

"I'm sorry to report that Sonya disrupted the DAP lesson and Jane sent her to me." Jane Dornacher was Sonya's social studies teacher. DAP was the Drug Abuse Prevention program that San Francisco Unified required in grades five, six, and seven.

This was a first. Never in all her years of school had Sonya ever been thrown out of class.

"Uh…" Ed slumped against the car. He couldn't decide which felt more inconceivable: Kirsch killed or Sonya busted. He wished he could start the day over again.

Pat said, "She ridiculed the DAP program's treatment of marijuana—and she wouldn't shut up." Then her tone became stern. "I detect parental influence."

Ed liked Pat and had every reason to believe the feeling was mutual. He was in no mood for a fight, especially not today, but he couldn't help himself. "I'm sorry Sonya got carried away, but you know the curriculum stinks." Ed wasn't the only parent who'd complained about DAP's contention that weed was as dangerous as alcohol, tobacco, heroin, crack, and meth.

"I know how you feel and you know I'm sympathetic. But I don't control the curriculum. What I control is the school, and we can't have disruptive behavior." Ed heard her sigh. "Now that she's been sent to me, I have to follow procedure."

"Meaning what?"

"A conference, the four of us, as soon as possible."

3

Ed pulled into traffic and found himself staring at a bumper sticker: *Unemployment Isn't Working*. He couldn't decide if he should laugh or cry.

He parked by The Healing Center and checked his wallet. He had just enough for a quarter ounce. From a dark corner of memory, a line he'd once read flashed like neon in the dark: *Addicts buy drugs instead of shoes for their kids*. He pushed the thought away. He wasn't an addict, just a long-time pothead who also had a nervous stomach, now more nervous than ever—and weed helped. His doctor, bless him, had written the letter qualifying Ed for a card. Buying at a store beat sending cash to his old high school buddy in Jamaica Plain and hoping the stuff was packed well enough that no one at UPS smelled anything and stole it.

The Healing Center occupied in a former shoe repair shop. The little storefront had a stout metal gate with barred windows and a sign, a bright green palmate leaf overprinted with the establishment's initials, THC.

Behind the locked gate stood a skinny white kid whose dreadlocks coiled down to a Kirsch For Mayor T-shirt. "Card?" he asked.

Ed slipped it through. He wondered if the people there had heard about Kirsch. The gate opened with a metallic click.

Ed stepped inside and discovered they had. Everyone was riveted to the flatscreen mounted in a corner of the ceiling. It cut from Julie, distraught but professional, to Cindy Miller sobbing inconsolably, to a bio of Kirsch, who'd parlayed legalization activism into fortune, fame, and elected office. The half-dozen people arrayed around the café tables shook their heads as they sucked on joints, bongs, vaporizers, and one-hitters. A few wiped their eyes.

A stereo playing reggae competed with the TV. Posters adorned the walls: Bob Marley, Legalize It, Visit Amsterdam, and the Fabulous Furry Freak Brothers, arm in arm, passing a doobie and proclaiming their signature line, "Dope gets you through times of no money better than money gets you through times of no dope."

Beneath the posters, display cases offered pipes, paraphernalia, spiked confections, and several books, including two by the late Dave Kirsch, *Grow It!* (sixteenth edition) and *Grow It Indoors!* (third edition).

Ed stepped to the counter in back. Behind it, a clean-cut young man smiled under a Giants cap. His lapel pin read "Pharmacist." Behind him, one whiteboard listed grades and prices, another a dozen brands of *sativa*, *indica*, and blends of the two. Ed was a *Cannabis sativa* man. *Indica* smelled skunky and gave him headaches.

"What'll it be?" the pharmacist asked. A Kirsch for Mayor bumper sticker was tacked to the wall behind him.

"A quarter," Ed said, "high-grade *sativa*."

"Any preference?"

Ed surveyed the list, then glanced at the kid, who had to be at least twenty-one but didn't look it. Ed realized he'd probably been getting high longer than this pharmacist had been alive. "Not really. I've been using Train Wreck."

"Like it?"

"Gets the job done…but—"

"What are you looking for? Pain relief? Sleep? Tranquilizer?"

"Upset stomach."

"Train Wreck's good, but have you tried Ambrosia?" The young man pulled a large Mason jar off a shelf, unscrewed the cap, and invited Ed to sniff. The buds, cherry-sized and bright green with golden threads, burst with fragrance. That was nothing new. Ed had to store his stash in the shed out back to avoid stinking up the house.

"Powerful healing," the pharmacist intoned.

Ed nodded and the kid weighed out seven grams plus a smidge more and scooped it into a plastic bag. "Free cookie? Papers? Lighter?"

Ed used a bong or one-hitter, so he didn't need papers. And he'd never liked eating marijuana. Dose control was a problem, and it took an hour to get off. "Lighter."

The pharmacist dropped a disposable into the paper bag and accepted a wad of bills.

On his way out, the gatekeeper said, "Feel better."

Ed sighed. He had problems not even his favorite medicine could cure, and now his hit would have to wait. He had to pick up the kids, make dinner, and call Julie. He pulled out his phone and held it, wishing he were holding her.

4

Ed tucked in Jake for the night, then poked his head through Sonya's door.

"Why do I have to be *up here?*" she whined, spreading her palms in supplication. "I want to be *downstairs* with *Mom*. She almost got *killed!*"

Ed stepped into her room, an increasingly alien realm where the floor was strewn with rumpled clothing and Barbie and Ken were being supplanted by hip hop icons foreign to her parents.

Ed groped for a reply, hoping to provide comfort while still insisting she finish her homework. "Your mother did not almost get killed. She was just nearby."

Sonya's eyes rolled in an arc so high Ed feared she might pass out. "There was *blood* on her *coat!*"

"Look," Ed said, striving for soothing, "I know you're freaked out. We all are. What happened is very upsetting, but—"

"If the *band shell* isn't safe, *what is?*"

They'd enjoyed many summer picnics there attending free concerts—rock, blues, jazz, and Sonya's favorite, big gospel choirs. The band shell had always felt like a sanctuary. Now Ed wondered if Julie would ever want to return.

Sonya stabbed a finger at him. "*Anyone* can get shot. You could, *I* could—"

"No—"

"How do you know?"

"Because," Ed said, "street shootings are pretty rare."

More eye-rolling. Ed was clearly the stupidest man alive. "They *are not*. They happen *all the time*. Tina's uncle got shot, and now Mom's boss and Mom—almost."

Tina Woods was a classmate. Her uncle had been killed outside the housing project where they lived, in what the *Foghorn* reported as a drug deal gone bad.

"What makes you think anyone can get shot?"

"I *see* it—"

"Where?"

"On TV, the news. People get shot all the time."

"Sonya," Ed pressed as insistently as possible, "listen to me, honey. You know I'm a newsman—"

"Yeah, till you got *laid off.*" Her words dripped scorn and anxiety.

"The news makes the world look scarier than it really is."

"But Mom could have been *killed!*"

They'd been riding this merry-go-round since Ed had picked her up, and now he felt motion sick. Someone at her after-school program had heard about the shooting and turned on the TV. Julie's face filled the screen, which made Sonya a momentary celebrity.

Ed had hoped she would weary of her tirade and knock it off, but no. Suddenly, he felt overwhelmed by a visceral need for contact with Julie. He had to touch her, massage her shoulders, loosen the knots he knew he'd find at the base of her neck.

Looking into Sonya's anguished face, he hated to play his trump card. The whole thing was silly, but under the circumstances, he had no choice. "You have every right to feel shaken up. Mom and I are, too. But the shooting isn't the only thing upsetting us. Pat Lucas called. Seems someone got thrown out of class today."

Eyes downcast, the juvenile delinquent replied, "Yeah, for saying what *you* said."

"There's a big difference, young lady, between conversation at the dinner table and disrupting school."

"But Jane said weed's as bad as *meth!*"

Ed reflected on the irony. Sonya's social studies teacher made no secret of her semi-hippie past. At school, she was as straight as a drug rehab counselor, but once Ed had run into her and her husband huddled in a doorway by the Fillmore before an Elvis Costello show. Jane looked embarrassed and mumbled something about the line for Will Call. Ed didn't need a calculator to do the math.

"Believe me, Jane's well aware that DAP's treatment of pot is nonsense. But if she doesn't teach it that way, she *loses her job*. She doesn't need you making her life harder."

"But you said DAP's a *lie*. Why are they teaching us lies?"

"Sonya, I hate to say it, but there's something you need to know about the adult world. Sometimes it makes no sense. But adults hate it when kids lecture them, especially when they're right. You're going to have to apologize. You know that. If I were you, I'd send Jane an e-mail tonight saying you're really sorry—and copy Pat."

Sonya frowned. She opened her mouth, then closed it. Her lower lip trembled. "I want to be with Mom."

"Finish your homework. E-mail Jane and Pat. Then you can come down and hang with us till bedtime."

5

Julie slumped at the dining room table, dabbing her eyes and sipping wine. A dozen friends were arrayed around her: neighbors, PR colleagues, women from her book group, former *Foghorn* staff, and a few of the paper's survivors. The table was littered with flowers, sushi, pizza, cookies, and beer and wine. A laptop displayed the *Foghorn's* obit. Several people told Kirsch stories.

"He was one of the first people I met in San Francisco," a former news editor, Ted Nello, reminisced. "He turned me on to grass." Everyone clamored for the details except Julie, who just sat there in a daze.

"It was '67. I was twenty-five and definitely not a hippie. I'd spent three years at the *Chico Enterprise-Record* reporting farm issues. I'd just been hired by the *Horn* and I was wide-eyed in the big city. Maybe two weeks into the job, I'm handed a release about a press conference for legalization on the steps of City Hall: Allen Ginsberg, the Dead, the Airplane—and someone I'd never heard of, Dave Kirsch. Ginsberg played a drum and chanted. When he spoke, he was incoherent. The bands weren't much better. But Kirsch's pitch was very together—less harmful than alcohol and tobacco, and the government could either legalize it and collect taxes, or waste millions trying to suppress it while gangsters made billions, like during Prohibition. I was impressed, so afterward, I buttonholed him for a quick quote and he invited me back to his place in the Haight, this big old Victorian by the park. When we got there, a bunch of people were passing a joint." He smiled at the memory. "I'd never seen one, but it felt impolite to refuse their hospitality." A few people chuckled. "I made my deadline—but I have no idea how."

Ed stood behind Julie and kneaded her neck and shoulders. She was a mess, but she was *alive*. Her skin had never felt so warm and silky, and Ed had never experienced such relief. He flashed on his momentary snit the previous evening when she'd left the garage door open. *What was I thinking?*

Loud ringing filled the room—the antique bell built into the front door. Sonya bounded down the stairs and opened it. A tall man with thin gray-blond hair greeted her by name. It was Wally Turner, the long-time police reporter who still had a job. He nodded to the group, kissed Julie's cheek, and accepted a beer. "Hell of a world, huh? Thank God you're okay."

"I'm not."

"So?" a recently laid-off sports writer asked, nodding to the laptop. "You know anything that's not on the site?"

"They recovered the slug," Turner said. "It's banged up, but they think they'll get ballistics. I swung by Kirsch's house hoping for a gravedigger, but the cops wouldn't let anyone near." A gravedigger was the obligatory interview with the family of the deceased.

"Suspects?" Ed asked, pressing his thumbs into the base of Julie's neck. He felt a strong urge to strangle whoever had fired that gun.

"None they're talking about," Turner said. "But he had enough enemies to fill the Cow Palace."

Several people nodded. Kirsch was nothing if not controversial. His marijuana activism had earned him the enmity of law enforcement and social conservatives. Property interests hated him for voting to strengthen rent control. Others thought he was a menace for wanting to legalize prostitution and raise money for education by letting Native Americans build a casino on Fisherman's Wharf.

"Any guesses?" Ed asked.

Turner shrugged. "In this town, who knows? He got more threats than the rest of the Board combined."

"And even more lately," Julie mumbled.

"He was moving up in the polls," Turner said. "It was starting to look like he might win. That always brings out the nuts. His campaign turned all the threats over to the cops, but the chief of detectives told me there was no pattern. They're following up, but they don't have much to go on."

"We hired bodyguards," Julie said.

"Yes, four of them," Turner said, "former state police. Two were walking in front of him, two behind. And there were six cops deployed around the band shell."

"A lot of good it did," Ed said.

"It's almost impossible to defend against snipers," Turner replied.

"I know his wife," said a neighbor, Betty Platt. "Olivia. Sweet woman. Her store's a few doors down from mine." Betty owned a chocolate shop on Union Street.

"His wife has a store?" one of the women from the book group asked. "Why? I thought his books made them rich."

"Yes," Platt replied, "but Olivia's owned Flower Child for, oh, five or six years—flowers, houseplants, and enough hydroponic equipment to keep the city stoned for ages."

"Vertical integration," someone quipped. "Dave tells 'em how to grow and his wife sells the gear. Neat."

"She's the former Olivia Tanner of Vichy Springs, near Ukiah," said a frizzy-haired woman seated in front of the computer—Roz Shapiro, a former *Foghorn* photographer and one of Julie's closest friends. After seventeen years at the paper, she'd taken a buyout. Now she shot weddings and bar mitzvahs. "They graduated from San Francisco State in '65, got married, and moved to the Haight."

She spun the screen around to reveal several photographs: the young, preppy bride and groom at their wedding, the hippie couple at the Human Be-In—long-haired Dave wearing a magician's cape and Olivia in a peasant dress—then the mug shot taken in '68 after Kirsch's one arrest for dealing; the young author hawking the first edition of *Grow It!* on Haight Street in 1971, and the middle-aged Kirsch campaigning for the Board in 2004 in front of a poster that read, "Elect the Candy Man."

"Great song, 'Candy Man,'" a former *Foghorn* illustrator said. "I always loved the guitar hook."

Several people who'd been around in 1967 spontaneously broke into the chorus: "Smoke, smoke, smoke, hey, candy man. I need some more, want to feel so grand. Smoke, smoke, smoke, hey, candy man."

"What?" someone asked.

"A local hit," Turner said, "by…" He shrugged. "I forget who."

"Magic Bullet Theory," said a yoga friend of Julie's. "Supposedly, it was about Dave."

"According to the *Horn*," Shapiro said, "it really *was* about him."

"Who believes that piece of shit?" This from an editor laid off with Ed and Julie. A few people smirked.

"Whatever happened to Magic Bullet Theory?" someone asked.

"Flamed out," Turner said. "They got a record deal but the album never happened. Their main guy, Tommy, forget his last name, got seriously messed up with drugs and alcohol. *Smith*. Tommy Smith. But for a brief moment, they were the hottest band in town. I went to a show once where Quicksilver and the Dead opened, and MBT headlined."

"You were a hippie, Wally?" Ed asked. It was hard to believe. Turner was a successful cop chaser largely because the police liked him, and they liked him because whenever cops became embroiled in controversy, he took their side.

"Not really, but I was young and had long hair and was into the music and—" He paused, then spread his arms and sang, "I need some more, want to feel so grand. Smoke, smoke, smoke, hey, candy man." He had a surprisingly good voice. Several people applauded.

"According to Wikipedia," Shapiro said, "*Grow It!* has sold more than four million copies and *Grow It Indoors!* a million. And get this: the current *Grow It!* is two hundred pages, but the first edition was a twenty-four-page pamphlet that Kirsch ran off at a copy shop. One of them just sold on eBay for *fifteen thousand dollars.*"

"Well, I can personally vouch for *Grow It!*" a PR friend of Julie's said. "I'm from a small town in Indiana. My high school boyfriend's family had a farm. He got the book and planted marijuana out in the cornfield. Grew more than we knew what to do with."

"After Kirsch got rich and famous from *Grow It!*" Shapiro read off the screen, "he always denied dealing, saying he was just a hippie gardener. But in 2007, for the fortieth anniversary of the Summer of Love, Grace Slick and Phil Lesh were quoted in *Rolling Stone* as saying that he *was* a dealer, *their* dealer—and he finally admitted to selling for two years, '66 to '68."

The doorbell rang again. Through stained glass, Ed saw a dark-haired middle-aged man in a suit. When he opened the door, the man flashed a badge and introduced himself as Detective Antonio Ramirez. He had the build of a fullback, with graying temples, hair swept back, and cheeks starting to form jowls. He said, "I need a word with Julie Pearl. Is that possible?"

"She gave a statement at the scene," Ed said, hoping to spare her further interrogation.

"I know. I read it. I just…a brief moment. Please."

Ed ushered him into the dining room. "Julie, Detective…uh—"

"Antonio Ramirez. Call me Tony." He directed a thin-lipped smile at Julie and nodded toward the others. When his gaze landed on Turner, his smile broadened. "Wally," he said, extending a hand to the police reporter.

"Tony." Turner shook it. "Anything?"

"Not much."

Julie took a slug of wine, girding herself for a grilling.

"I hate to barge in like this," Ramirez said. "I know you're shaken up. But if we're going to catch whoever did this—"

"Ask away," Julie said.

"Maybe we should talk in private."

"Actually, I'd rather…" She gazed around the table, drawing support from the dozen pairs of eyes focused on her. Ed stepped up and clasped her hand.

"All right," the detective said, launching right in. "Before the shooting, how long were you with Kirsch?"

"All afternoon. We had a lunch meeting, then a meet-and-greet with the Interfaith Council, then the Save the Parks rally at the band shell."

"Just the two of you?"

"No, lunch was with the staff: Cindy, Bo, Vladdy, a few others. After that, it was Dave, Cindy, and me."

Ramirez consulted a tablet computer. "That would be campaign manager Cynthia Miller, finance chief Bo LeBlanc, and pollster Vladimir Rostoff?"

Julie nodded.

"How did he seem to you? His mood."

"Fine. Great. Vladdy had new numbers. We were winning big in the Mission and closing the gap in the Sunset."

"He didn't seem tense? Nervous? Preoccupied?"

"No. He was happy, upbeat. Why?"

"The threats. Did he mention that someone had pushed a note under his front door saying that if he won, he'd never see inauguration day?"

"No, not a word. He always insisted all that stuff went right to the police."

"So you weren't informed of the threats?"

"Some of the real ones, but not all. Dave didn't want to scare us. But Cindy knew. Have you talked to her?"

"'*Real* ones?'" Ramirez repeated. "You mean there were *fake* threats?"

"Sure, jokes. The other day, Cindy showed me an e-mail. 'We're here. We're queer. We're going to kidnap Kirsch and fix his hair.'"

Around the room, several people chuckled, but not the detective.

"Since you gave your statement, has anything else come to mind? Anything at all."

Julie looked away. She inhaled deeply and exhaled slowly. "No."

Ramirez pursed his lips and ran fingers through his hair. He pulled out his wallet and handed her a card. "If you think of anything, please call."

Julie said she would. Ramirez nodded farewell to the group and Ed saw him to the door. As he reached for the knob, his hand trembled. Kirsch was dead. Julie was alive. And he felt somewhere in between.

"Political assassinations offend me," Ramirez said, handing Ed a card. "If your wife remembers anything...."

6

After everyone left, Ed and Julie cleaned up, and Ed caught himself following her from room to room like a puppy, reassuring himself that she was still in one piece. When she poured another glass of wine and headed for the back deck, he descended to his basement office and returned with the bong. He found Julie leaning over the deck rail gazing vacantly at the back fence. Ed held a lighter to the bowl. Exhaling a cloud, he offered the pipe. "Want any?"

She considered the idea. "Half a hit."

Ed reloaded and held the lighter as the water bubbled.

Julie exhaled smoke, then leaned against Ed and snaked her arms around his waist. "You okay?"

His mouth went dry, and not from the weed. He returned her hug, feeling her warmth, her heat. "I feel awful about Dave, but I'm *so* incredibly grateful you're okay."

"I keep seeing him spinning around, falling." She shuddered in Ed's arms.

"And I keep hearing the shot and you screaming over the phone."

"I hope I can sleep. I can't get it out of my mind."

"Well," Ed said, "here's something that might help. Jane threw Sonya out of class."

"What?"

Ed explained the tempest in a water pipe.

Julie withdrew from Ed's embrace and twirled the wine glass by its stem. "I thought you went a little overboard at dinner the other night."

"Yeah. On the phone with Pat, I flashed on what you said. 'You're not a lecturer anymore. Don't lecture her.'"

"Sonya acts like we're idiots," Julie said, "but everything we say, she soaks it up like a sponge."

"And here I thought she never listens to me." Ed explained that they had to schedule a conference.

Julie leaned against the rail and gazed around what she called "the estate." She was a New York City girl who'd never had a yard. Their first was tiny, but now, by San Francisco standards, they had a large one, and Julie loved it. The yard was her therapy and she was slowly transforming it from a wasteland into an urban Eden. *The Western Garden Book* had become her bible.

Without warning the wine glass slipped from her fingers and shattered on the brick patio. Suddenly, she was sobbing and reaching for Ed.

"I feel so *guilty.*"

Ed held her. "Why?"

"Dave's gone," she whimpered, "gone forever, and what am I thinking? That I just lost a great gig, and now we're up against it, and I better find another one fast or...."

"I've been caught in the same loop." Ed remembered his blaze of anger in the grocery store over her quitting the paper to work for the campaign. But the fire had burned out and the ashes had cooled.

Her sad, wet eyes peered into his. "Thanks for not saying I told you so."

He flashed a weak smile. "Hey, it was starting to look like you might actually become press secretary."

"I just couldn't stay at the paper. The way they screwed us."

"It's okay. You're the best and you're very well connected. You'll find something just as good."

"You will, too."

"Let's hope." But at the moment, he didn't feel particularly optimistic.

Julie gazed down at the shattered glass. Ordinarily, she would have jumped for the broom and dustpan, but she just stared. "One more thing," she said softly. "The detective asked if I knew anything else—"

"Do you?" This came as a surprise.

"I'm pretty sure I figured out Cindy's secret."

When Julie joined the campaign, Cindy had welcomed her warmly, and the two women had quickly become more than acquaintances—but less than friends. Cindy had a way of holding Julie at arm's length, opening one dresser drawer but leaving the rest firmly shut, and Julie couldn't understand why. As the months passed, she wondered if Cindy was feigning friendship while actually disliking her, but after a while, Julie decided that her new friend was sizing her up, trying to decide if she could share a big secret. But what?

"I thought you said it was about her marriage hitting the skids."

"That's part of it, but there's something juicier. I think she's having—*was* having—an affair with Dave." She threw Ed one of her searching looks, her brown eyes lustrous as polished mahogany. "You know Dave's reputation. And Cindy's an attractive blonde."

It was an open secret around San Francisco that Kirsch was a woman-izer. At the paper, people joked, "How long does it take Dave Kirsch to screw in a light bulb?" As long as it takes to stuff a woman inside.

When the campaign first approached Julie about handling his media, she and Ed feared Dave might hit on her, and worried about how she might fend him off while still keeping the job. Then Ed called one of the *Horn*'s political reporters and learned that Kirsch had a strong preference for milk-skinned blondes, which meant that he was unlikely to invite Julie for drinks, weed, and disrobing. Julie was the product of a Jewish mother and a black father. She'd told him her relationship with Dave had been completely professional, and Ed chose to believe it.

"What makes you think—?" Ed asked.

"There was a definite vibe," Julie said.

Ed didn't put much stock in women's intuition, but when Julie caught a vibe, she was almost always right. "And when did you figure this out?" he asked.

"This afternoon. She said she was involved with someone and loving it."

"Did she mention Dave?"

"Not by name."

"Did you ask?"

"Ed."

He glimpsed his reflection in her eyes. Ed was the nosy reporter who rarely hesitated to ask intimate questions, while Julie was the quiet hand-holder who listened patiently until people felt comfortable enough to spill the beans.

"So why do you think Dave?"

"As we walked to the band shell, I was a few steps behind them. They were laughing a lot and kept brushing up against each other. It reminded me of that Bonnie Raitt line."

Ed knew it well, from one of Julie's favorite albums. *We laugh just a little too loud, dance just a little too close. Let's give 'em something to talk about.*

"Are you going to tell the cop?"

Julie frowned.

Ed's eyes bored into hers. "Jealousy is a classic motive."

"Cindy said Al's clueless." Al Miller was Cindy's husband.

"What if he isn't? You figured it out. Maybe he did, too."

Ed understood Julie's reluctance to talk to the police. She'd grown up in the Bronx as her neighborhood completed its transition from white to black and Puerto Rican. At the time, the police were still overwhelmingly white and not well disposed to the new arrivals. Julie's late social-worker mother, for whom Sonya had been named, believed the cops caused more problems than they solved, and trained her daughter to keep her distance.

"Julie," Ed insisted, "a man's been murdered. If you don't call, I will."

7

Insisting she'd rather go blind than crawl back to the paper, Julie launched Julie Pearl Communications from their guest room. She moved the bed into a corner, consolidated the space devoted to her sewing machine, patterns, and fabric, and repositioned her computer desk to accommodate her new file cabinet. Then she worked the phone, e-mailed announcements to her list, and set up a web site. Years of activism in several PR organizations had graced her with a huge network. It didn't take long for her to hear from a friend down the Peninsula, who was planning a biotech conference and couldn't handle all the logistics. Was Julie interested in a four-month half-time gig?

Julie's fast start out of the gate impressed Ed. He knew she'd bounce back quickly, and the money would certainly help. But her success also made him feel worse about his own under-employment. She was smacking the ball for extra bases while he was, at best, getting walks.

He descended from the kitchen to his office behind the garage. On the way, he stopped to run his fingers along the exquisite felt of a regulation-size pool table, a lifelong dream purchased when they still had jobs. He racked up, imagining that the balls were the morons who thought that the way to publish newspapers on the Internet was to provide content for free. Smack! He ran five, missed, then ran six, and finally, the remaining four. Julie was doing the heavy lifting and his self-respect was suffering. He'd always carried his own weight but now he felt like a babe in arms.

Ed's office was larger than the cramped corner he'd used in their previous home, and he loved the intercom that connected his lair to the kitchen and second floor. But his new workplace was as dark as a subway tunnel, which did nothing to improve his mood. His lone window looked out through the forest of posts that supported the back deck. All he saw was a thin slice of yard, as if peering from a cell at San Quentin. The contractor had said the deck could be rebuilt to let more light in, but now, who knew when?

Ed sighed and opened his e-mail. A few students had questions about the midterm. A friend had scored an extra ticket to Dylan and wanted to know if Ed was interested. Another was organizing a surprise party. And his former editor, now his client, wanted minor changes in his latest column. Then an unfamiliar name caught his eye: Gene Simons. The subject line said "Summer of Love?"

Simons was the Internet wonder boy who was underwriting the museum exhibit on the Haight-Ashbury in the sixties. *Please God, I need this job.*

Ed clicked and his eyes raced over the e-mail. Simons wrote that he'd admired Ed's column for years, and was very interested in working with him; how about discussing the project over lunch at Farallon?

Yes.

Farallon was a four-star seafood place near Union Square. Ed had once taken Julie there for an anniversary splurge. Farallon, Ed replied, sure, great, love to, name your day.

Simons's e-mail included a P.S.: "You should know that I have a personal interest in our subject. My birth mother, Jackie Zarella, lived in the Haight during the summer of '67. She was a drug dealer—mostly marijuana and a little speed—who was just twenty-four in 1968 when she was shot to death in Golden Gate Park. Death of Hippie, indeed. I've moved heaven and Earth to learn who she was but I know very little and would love to learn more."

Ed kicked his feet up on the desk and gazed out the window through the posts. Shot in the park? Ed flashed on Dave Kirsch, and on Julie coming home spattered with blood. No wonder Simons was interested in the hippie Haight. But if Ed recalled correctly, the Death of Hippie parade happened the year *before* the death of Simons's mother.

In San Francisco, the summer of 1967 was known as the Summer of Love, but that was a misnomer—the Summer of Hippie Hype was more like it. The Haight-Ashbury wore flowers in its hair for roughly two years, 1965 through 1967, when young people disillusioned with *Ozzie and Harriet* began moving into the bohemian neighborhood by the city's premier park. They felt stirred by the civil rights movement and alienated from the Vietnam War, and hoped Mr. Tambourine Man would play a song for them. Then the media arrived and blared breathless reports of sex and drugs that were, at best, exaggerated, and at worst, fiction. But the publicity brought a huge influx, a second Gold Rush—only these miners were panning for Acapulco gold.

By the end of that fabled summer, the Age of Aquarius had devolved into a new Dark Age, as desperate kids loitered on every corner and the drugs of choice morphed from weed and acid to speed and heroin. In September 1967, a group of hippies who'd lived in the Haight for more than a few months became so disgusted that they posted flyers announcing a funeral, the Death of Hippie. On the appointed afternoon, eighty people marched down Haight Street in solemn silence holding lighted candles behind a cardboard coffin—a full year before Simons' mother died. But he could be forgiven his error. He wasn't a historian.

Ed had never heard of Jackie Zarella. His fingers tapped the keyboard, starting by habit with the *Horn*'s electronic archive. Then he remembered two details. The archive only went back to 1970. And he no longer had a password.

He Googled her name but didn't find much. The *Foghorn* described her as a small-time marijuana peddler who got caught in a crossfire between warring heroin dealers. The *Examiner* called her a major speed dealer's girlfriend, killed to intimidate him. The *LA Times* said she sold weed and speed and had stiffed her supplier, who'd killed her. None of the stories mentioned a son. Or an arrest.

Ed heard footsteps above. In their old house, he had to yell up the stairs; now he just pushed a button. "Julie?"

"Hi!" She sounded unusually bright.

"I might have some good news," Ed said.

He ran up the stairs. "That billionaire who's funding the sixties exhibit? He's taking me to lunch—at Farallon. Seems like I have a good shot."

"Great," she said, sorting mail. "Good luck." She handed him a stack, then opened the fridge and poured a glass of Sauvignon Blanc.

"I have news, too. Alice wants me to promote her new studios." Alice Starsky owned Yoga Breath, where Julie took classes. The business was expanding all over town.

Ed stared at the wine glass and frowned. "Do you really need that?"

Julie's face fell and Ed regretted the crack. After all, he was no paragon of sobriety, and at the moment, Julie was bringing home most of the bread, so who was he to question how much butter she spread?

She looked at him with the eyes of an injured fawn. "Do you really think I drink too much?"

"I don't know. What do *you* think?"

8

Sonya attended a sweet little public magnet school in the Excelsior, a hilly working-class neighborhood in southeast San Francisco far removed from the tourist orbit. The building dated from the 1920s, a boxy, three-story brick edifice built before anyone understood that brick was too brittle for earthquake country. A retrofit had encased it in a steel frame. Now it looked like a school behind bars.

Ed and Julie found Pat Lucas in the office. She was an attractive older black woman who favored pantsuits and pearls. She was on the phone finalizing arrangements for the all-school camping trip. Ed and Julie had chaperoned the annual three-day event since their little girl's days in kindergarten.

Sonya was seated in the Bad Chair, the perch reserved for kids in trouble. She fidgeted and hung her head, disoriented in delinquency.

Pat hung up and ushered them into the cramped conference room. "We are here," she intoned solemnly, "because Sonya disrupted class. We can't have that, we simply cannot." Pat was a charming woman who laughed easily, but her scowl could melt a glacier. "And I must say, young lady, I'm surprised at you."

"But DAP is *wrong*." Sonya muttered. "Isn't it, Daddy?"

Pat shot Ed a churlish look. "We're *not* discussing the merits of the curriculum. We're talking about *your behavior*. Which was *unacceptable*."

Ed opened his mouth, but Julie nudged him. They'd agreed that she would do the talking. The two women jumped into it, playing verbal tennis, lobbing soft shots back and forth. Sonya had to behave herself.

She certainly did—and she would. Sonya had every right to disagree with elements of the curriculum, but it was totally inappropriate to disrupt class by ridiculing it. True, but for an eleven-year-old, that's a subtle distinction...

Meanwhile, Ed feared he might bleed to death from biting his tongue. Pat was a native San Franciscan who'd grown up in the Fillmore a few blocks from the jazz clubs where Bird, Diz, Monk, and Trane played—and where reefer first appeared in the City by the Bay. Her father had spent twenty years as a cook at Bop City, a storied jazz club, so it was hard to believe that Pat was unacquainted with weed. But here she was getting all bent out of shape.

Of course, Ed understood why the district required the DAP program. San Francisco had been devastated by HIV, and even after gay men embraced safe sex, the AIDS numbers remained stubbornly high because of IV drugs. But was that any reason to lie to kids about pot?

Eventually, Pat and Julie agreed that during future DAP lessons, Sonya would be excused to the library, where she would work on a report titled, "Why the DAP Program Is Wrong about Marijuana." It would explore the curriculum's contentions that grass was addictive and that it caused lung cancer and motor vehicle accidents. Pat would send the paper to the superintendent, who had the power to alter the curriculum—if Sonya's arguments proved persuasive. Pat drafted a contract and everyone signed it.

Starting the car, Ed erupted like a sneeze that could no longer be stifled. "How's Sonya going to research all this? She's eleven years old."

Julie laughed. "Like she researches everything—with generous assistance from her loving father." Ed knew she was teasing, but she was shooting pins and he felt the pricks.

"Oh, great," he groaned. "Remember hermit crabs?" For that report, he'd taken her to the library, checked out a half-dozen books, read them with her, and practically spoonfed her the information. Then, the night before the thing was due, Sonya pretty much copied the article in Wikipedia, complaining bitterly that the subject was stupid and too hard.

"This isn't a project for Sonya," Ed said. "It's punishment for *me*. Pat's pissed that I told Sonya the truth, and now I'm being crucified for it."

"No comment," Julie cooed sweetly. Her opinion was as obvious as Bozo's nose.

Ed shook his head but couldn't help smiling. Didn't Pat have anything better to do? "And this shit about sending it to the superintendent. Like he's going to change the curriculum based on a report by a sixth grader."

"I don't like this any more than you do," Julie said, "but she *did* disrupt class and we have to keep the peace with Pat. Who knows? Maybe you'll learn something about pot."

"Yeah, like I should stick to inhaling it and otherwise keep my mouth shut." He reached over and gave her a playful pinch. "Just so you know, I'm not going to break a sweat helping her. If her report sucks, it's fine by me."

9

Every seat in Civic Auditorium was filled. Two huge banners flew over the podium: the Stars and Stripes and a bright green palmate leaf on a red field, emblazoned with thick black lettering: "Legalize It."

The mayor called Kirsch a dedicated public servant. The president of the Board of Supervisors reminisced about his great sense of humor. Ex-mayor Willie Brown said Dave was the main reason the state's medical marijuana initiative had passed in San Francisco eight to one. The executive director of NORML flew out from Washington to say that Kirsch was the single most effective advocate the legalization movement ever had. The head of the Tenants Union called him God's gift to renters. And the chief of police announced that the Bay Area Association of Medical Marijuana Dispensaries had offered a $25,000 reward for information leading to his killer's capture.

Then Robin Williams, a longtime friend, gently chided the multitude for being so funereal. "Dave wouldn't want long faces. Here's what he'd want, the answers to some *critical questions.* What do you get when you eat marijuana? A pot belly. And how do you know you're smoking too much weed? You study for the urine test." Then Williams choked up and, wiping an eye, said he still felt bad about the time he was responsible for Dave getting injured. "I rolled some bomb shit and he got so high, he burned his ear—answering the phone while ironing."

Julie had a backstage pass and Ed tagged along. On one side, amid old theatrical sets, he noticed Olivia Kirsch, a plump older blonde, crumpled in a chair weeping a river, while on the other side, Cindy

Miller, a thinner, younger blonde, slumped on a box doing the same. They were as far apart as physically possible while still inside the hall.

Cindy had come clean to Julie two days after the murder, confirming her suspicions. She and Dave had been hot and heavy for five months. Their favorite meet-up was the Fisherman's Wharf Holiday Inn—all tourists, so no one recognized them.

Ed figured that Olivia was painfully familiar with her late husband's reputation, but he wondered how much she knew about the specifics. Did she have any idea about Dave and Cindy? The seating arrangements suggested so, but perhaps the widow had just plopped down in the first available chair and the mistress had decided to keep her distance.

As a final gesture, Dave's campaign had asked San Franciscans to e-mail why they'd supported him for mayor. More than 22,000 people replied, and it fell to Julie to winnow the thousand finalists down to a few hundred to display around the lobby. She was up most of the night doing it and everyone agreed the posters looked terrific. A man in the Mission thanked Kirsch for spearheading the bike lanes on Valencia Street. A woman in Vis Valley praised him for saving her neighborhood library. A mom in the Marina said he'd arranged for more fruit in school lunches. A retiree credited him with protecting Muni's senior discount. And on and on.

Afterward, Ed and Julie stepped into the bright sunlight and saw Detective Ramirez striding toward them across Civic Center Plaza.

"Oh God," Julie said, clutching Ed's arm and huddling close. "He's going to yell at me."

"Why? You called. You told him."

"A day late and a dollar short."

In the glare of the afternoon sun, Ramirez looked like a Latino Joe Friday. *Just the facts, ma'am.* Instead of extending a hand, Ramirez folded his arms across his chest. Squinting at Julie, he said, "You were right. They were having an affair, Miller and Kirsch."

"Ah," Julie said, not mentioning any of the details Cindy had filled in.

"Doesn't that make her husband a prime suspect?" Ed asked.

Ramirez unwrapped a stick of gum and popped it into his mouth. "I can't comment on an ongoing investigation."

"Aw, come on, Detective," Ed snapped. He'd started at the *Horn* on the police beat and was practiced in the game of cops and reporters.

"Julie tipped you. And it's not like we can publish anything. We got fired, remember?"

Ramirez chewed, then stopped. "At the moment, I'd call him a person of interest. He and the campaign manager had been having problems. He started suspecting hanky-panky a month ago when she told him she was moving out. He was understandably upset."

"Enough to—"

Ramirez shrugged. "Possibly. But Alvin Miller's a professor at State. At the time of the shooting, he was teaching a class."

"Couldn't he hire—"

"A hit man?" Ramirez snorted and worked his face into a patronizing smile. "No."

"Why not?" Ed asked.

"You watch too much TV."

"Do you have a better suspect?"

"Not at the moment."

"The *Horn* said no on saw the shooter."

"Correct."

"Ballistics?"

"Not yet." Walking away, Ramirez turned and called over his shoulder, "Thanks for the tip."

10

South of downtown, across the filled marsh of Mission Bay, the north side of Potrero Hill offered spectacular views of the San Francisco skyline. Near the hill's summit on a rocky bluff, Dave and Olivia Kirsch had knocked down an old bungalow and built a wood frame castle with exposed beams and a tile roof that captured the casual elegance of a Spanish hacienda. From its glass-walled living room, across a flagstone patio bordered by tall bamboo, the towers of downtown looked so huge and close, you could almost touch them. After the funeral, a few dozen select mourners were invited up to the house, among them, Julie.

Ed recognized plenty of faces: the mayor, members of the Board, a state senator, media people, and even the young pharmacist from The Healing Center. But most people were unfamiliar.

Over four decades, the widow had morphed from hippie to hippy, but still looked younger than her sixty-odd years. Wearing a long black dress, her face blotched and puffy, she stood in the foyer and acknowledged the solemn parade of condolences, trying unsuccessfully not to dissolve into sobs. She was flanked by two women who might have been her sisters. They propped her up and offered tissues and solidarity.

Julie was surprised that Olivia remembered her. They'd met only twice at campaign functions. But good political wives make a point of recalling names. When Julie introduced Ed, Olivia said she enjoyed his column. The widow smelled of alcohol.

They drifted to the buffet and nibbled finger food. A glass wall offered a view from the Bay Bridge across downtown and the Mission up to Twin Peaks. At the bar, Ed asked for bubbly water. Julie cast a longing look at the wine, then glanced at her husband and also asked for water.

Ed scanned the crowd, nodding to those he knew. Then he noticed a tall, dapper man reaching the front of the receiving line. His charcoal suit fit exquisitely and his salt-and-pepper hair was impeccably cut in the style of the early Beatles. Face contorted in grief, he extended his arms to Olivia, clearly expecting her to fall into them. But she hesitated. Then she reconsidered and stepped into his embrace. They shared a long hug. As they separated, the man wiped his eyes.

Julie introduced Ed to Cindy Miller and her husband, Al, the professor. She looked like a woman who'd just buried the love of her life. He looked like a man whose wife was leaving him.

Julie tapped the shoulder of an older woman, a Pacific Heights matron who ran a prominent charity. The two women air-kissed, then stepped out to the patio to chat and savor the view.

Ed wandered back toward the foyer. A gnome of a man with a shaved head and a droopy white mustache stepped toward Olivia, leaning heavily on a cane. His old bomber jacket was too big. Its turned-up collar engulfed his head. His complexion was ashen and his skin was stretched so thin that it seemed translucent, waxed paper brushed with oil. Ed guessed chemotherapy.

As he approached Olivia, the man's expression said they were friends. Hers said she didn't know him. His smile resembled a skeleton's. He spoke into her ear and she rocked back on her heels, eyes the size of dinner plates. He folded his collar down to reveal a tattoo on the side of his neck. From where Ed stood, it looked like a pine tree. On seeing it, Olivia jumped into his arms and their embrace was so tight that Ed feared for their ribs.

Ed returned to the buffet and noticed the well-dressed man with the Beatles cut considering the brie. A stocky man of around sixty who sported short, curly blond hair and a gold post earring stepped to the table. Ed thought he recognized him—but from where? The man with the earring tapped the long-haired fellow on the shoulder, and grinning said, "Hey, sailor, new in town?"

The man in the suit turned and smiled. "Ken! I thought I might see you here."

"Hello, Owen. Long time."

Ed had always been an eavesdropper, more so since becoming a journalist, but standing on the other side of the buffet trying to be inconspicuous, he was surprised how well he could hear. *Love those glass walls.*

The two men hugged and kissed on the lips. The man with the Beatles hair, Owen, asked, "How *are* you? How's Chester's?" It was San Francisco's premiere blues club, and now Ed knew that the blonde guy was Ken Kelly, the club's founder/owner and a fixture of San Francisco's rock music scene for decades.

"Record income on record revenue," Kelly said. "Blues is more popular than ever. The investors are pleased." The investors, Ed knew, included Carlos Santana, Boz Scaggs, Huey Lewis, and members of Journey and Metallica.

"You've come a long way from taking tickets for The Family Dog," Owen observed. The Family Dog was the hippie commune that had promoted San Francisco's first acid-rock shows in the mid-sixties.

"And you," Ken said, "have come a long way from…living dangerously."

"What are you talking about?" Owen's mouth curled into a thin-lipped grin. "I'm a respectable businessman and always have been."

"Oh, yeah," Kelly smirked, "and I'm Liza Minelli."

They both chuckled, then stopped. It was a funeral after all. But around the room, many people were greeting old friends, smiling, and even laughing. Ed thought Dave would have wanted it that way.

"So," Kelly asked, "how's barbering treating you? What do you have, ten salons?"

"Fourteen. And very well."

Kelly slowly looked Owen up and down. "You coupled up?"

"Not at the moment, but I get my needs met. You?"

"As a matter of fact…" Kelly blushed. "A fire fighter."

Owen smiled. "You always *were* a sucker for men in uniform."

Then the shrunken man with the cane and neck tattoo approached. "Owen. Ken."

Their faces went blank.

The man dropped his collar. "It used to be a lightning bolt."

Owen's jaw dropped. "My God! Doug!"

"Shhh," the man said, raising a finger to his lips. "It's Joe now. Joe Bogen, solid citizen, businessman."

"I wouldn't have recognized you in a million years," Kelly said.

"You've lost weight," Owen said.

"Forty pounds. The one upside of prostate cancer."

"Oh man, I'm so sorry." Owen looked genuinely distressed.

"Fucking Agent Orange," Doug or Joe snorted.

"And your beautiful hair."

"Chemo. Not that I had much left. But I'm not dead yet. Chemo makes me nauseous. Guess what I take for it."

Owen smiled. "I can't imagine."

"It's funny," the frail man said. "I always figured I'd go first, not Dave, and definitely not *that way*."

"Uh," Kelly said, backing away. "I have to irritate the mayor. I'll leave you two to old times."

Owen shifted uncomfortably from one foot to the other.

"Thirty years," Doug-Joe said, "long time. I Googled you. Hair salons, huh? 'A Cut Above,' cute name." He worked his way up to another cadaverous smile. "And a nice cash business…as an old friend used to say."

"Nice and *legal*," Owen replied, "not to mention all the boys looking for a sugar daddy."

"And I bet you give them plenty of sugar, daddy."

"I'm…sorry you're ill," Owen said, adding tenderly, "I wish I'd known."

Doug-Joe took him in and asked, "Do you? That's a surprise."

Ed felt a little too conspicuous and wandered outside to collect Julie, who was holding one of Cindy Miller's hands in both of hers. "I'll call you," she promised.

Ed and Julie crossed the flagstone and headed for the stairs down the rock face to the street. One Rincon's sixty-five stories loomed over them, enormous and almost within reach. By a stand of bamboo, Owen, Kelly, Doug-Joe, and a few others passed a small brass pipe and toasted Dave.

Ed peered past them toward the leafy hedge. He realized it wasn't all bamboo. Here and there, hardly noticeable unless you looked closely, another plant was mixed in, a plant Dave Kirsch knew all about growing.

11

Ed was on his way out the door to take Jake to daycare when Wally Turner returned his call.

"Hey," Ed asked, "is Tony Ramirez an asshole? Or does he just act that way?"

The police reporter laughed. "Tony's old school. But underneath that armored exterior, he's a decent guy—you just have to dig down pretty deep to get there. Why?"

"Have you heard about Kirsch and his campaign manager?"

"He was fucking her. What else is new?"

"It went on for months, long enough for her husband's fuse to burn down to the dynamite—"

"*If* he knew."

"Did he?" Ed asked.

"According to Tony, no, but the guy's denial could easily be self-serving. Why do you care?"

"Because Julie's still beside herself. I want the killer caught. Soon."

"We all do."

"When Kirsch got it, Al Miller was teaching, so…" Ed summarized his speculation about a hit man. "Ramirez just about split his pants laughing."

"Let me guess. He said, 'You watch too much TV.'"

"How'd you know?"

"One of his standard lines—and he's right. Cop shows make cartoons look like documentaries, but people take them as gospel. Then real cops have to explain to lots of pissed-off people why the team from *CSI* isn't jumping all over their dipshit burglary."

"So, forget the hit man?"

"Think about it. How many marriages end in divorce? About half. How many of them involve a third wheel on the bike? So we're talking millions of affairs breaking up marriages. Now how many husbands kill the other guy? A few, but statistically, that's almost none."

"But it's still *possible*, and who's going to suspect a college professor?"

"Ed. Say Julie was having an affair and you wanted the guy dead. Could *you* hire a contract killer?"

"Well, no, but—"

"You can't Google 'hit man.' If you're a Mafia don or a big drug dealer, you have muscle on retainer. But regular people? Forget it. I know Tony ran a routine check of the professor's e-mails and phone records. *Nada*."

12

Ed checked his e-mail and saw one from Gene Simons. *Please, God.*

Their lunch at Farallon had been a treat. The seafood was terrific and Ed loved the light fixtures: elaborate plastic jellyfish suspended from the high ceiling with glowing tentacles that hung down ten feet.

But something other than sea bass had gone into Ed's mouth—his foot. Simons kept calling it the Summer of Love and at one point, Ed couldn't help mentioning that the term was a misnomer. The billionaire looked like he wasn't used to being corrected. Over dessert and decaf, Simons thanked him for his time and said he was considering one other candidate and would be in touch.

Ed kicked himself all the way home. This was a hand that might feed, and he'd nipped it. How could he be so *stupid?*

Ed held his breath and clicked.

"I'm pleased to offer—"

Yes!

Ed scanned the terms. The gig paid well, very well, and promised to be interesting. He could also double up, reworking what he did for Simons into columns, City College lessons, and maybe even a magazine article.

Simons wrote that Ed's point about the Summer of Love was well taken. Their subject wasn't just that summer, but the entire hippie period, and what did Ed think they should call the project? The Haight-Ashbury in the Sixties? The Hippie Haight? Hashbury? Love and Haight? Simons had also instructed his assistant to send PDFs of the thick file he'd amassed on his mother and her death: police reports, newspaper articles, and memos from the small army of private investigators he'd hired over the years. Finally, when could Ed have breakfast down the Peninsula to discuss things?

Ed exhaled luxuriously. This would be fun. But mostly it would be money, excellent money. It felt good to be a real breadwinner again.

Ed turned to his wall of bookshelves and pulled out several volumes on the hippie period. Time to bone up. When they had breakfast, he wanted to impress his client—without correcting him.

But first things first. He pulled out a fat history of the Gold Rush. Behind it, hidden from Sonya's prying eyes, was his one-hitter and plastic bag. He had a hit, exhaled out the window, and replaced everything behind the book, just as he heard footsteps on the stairs.

"Hey," Julie said, leaning on the door frame, "our Netflix came. Want to watch tonight?"

From the day they'd met, Ed had always loved looking at her. But flush with this success and in his current frame of mind, she appeared particularly alluring. He rose, embraced her, and shared the good news.

"Congratulations," she said. Then she held him at arm's length. "You're high, aren't you?" She had the nose of a bloodhound.

"One hit to celebrate."

"Did you really need that?"

Recalling their previous conversation, Ed just said, "*Touché.*"

13

"Daddy, it doesn't cause lung cancer!" Sonya exclaimed as Ed picked her up from her after-school program.

"What doesn't?"

"Marijuana, silly!"

They fastened their belts. Sonya hit some buttons and ten speakers blared hip hop.

Ed turned it down. "And how do you know this?"

"Google."

"Really." Ed sighed. This time, he'd sworn she was on her own, that he wouldn't be the helicopter parent, constantly hovering. But if he didn't teach her decent research skills, who would? "When we get home, show me."

They picked up Jake, smiling and squirming. As Ed buckled him into the car seat, the boy waved his spoon like a symphony conductor. At home, Ed plopped him into the wind-up swing as he and Julie prepared dinner. Ed was in the middle of chopping a red pepper when Sonya's voice came through the intercom. "Daddy! Come look!"

Ed found her pointing proudly at Julie's laptop. "See?"

Ed scanned the article. It was from a medical journal he'd vaguely heard of. Sure enough, the study showed no detectable lung cancer risk, even in people who'd smoked as many as *twenty thousand joints.*

Ed stared at the number and did a quick calculation. During his late teens and twenties, maybe four or five a week, then progressively fewer as weed became more potent, till today, a hit or two most days—

or maybe three, but even three was no more than half a joint. For argument's sake, say two joints a week for thirty years. That was about three thousand. Even if he'd underestimated by a factor of four, he was still way below twenty thousand. *Well, what do you know.*

"Looks good, honey."

Sonya beamed.

But on second thought, maybe it was too good to be true. Ed was no expert, but he'd read newspapers long enough to have a seat-of-the-pants credibility detector. UCLA researchers had compared lifetime tobacco and weed use by 611 Angelenos diagnosed with lung cancer and 1,040 similar folks who were cancer-free. Cigarettes showed the familiar pattern, but weed made no difference, none at all.

"Interesting. Very interesting. But one study doesn't prove anything. Keep looking and let me know what else you find."

After dinner cleanup, Ed found Sonya's lower lip protruding. "Why so glum?"

She thrust a sheaf of papers at him. "It does."

Reports from New Zealand and Tunisia said weed "significantly increased" lung cancer risk. Other studies showed that it impaired lung function and caused pre-cancerous tissue changes.

Ed leafed through the material, finally landing on a Case Western review of nineteen studies. Despite measurable lung impairment, pot appeared to play little if any role in lung cancer risk.

"It hurts your lungs," Sonya said.

"Well, you can't expect anything you smoke to be *good* for the lungs, can you?"

"And it causes cancer."

Ed flipped pages. "In some studies, yes. But the most believable studies are the ones with the most people. What do they say?"

"How should I know?"

This time, she's on her own. "Read them."

"But I *can't!*"

"Sure you can. I'll check with you in ten minutes."

When Ed returned, Sonya whined, "But if it *doesn't*, why do the little ones say it *does?*"

"Because, honey, life is messy. So you have to decide. What do you think? Does it? Yes or no?"

"I don't know…"

"Well, make up your mind and write it up."

His daughter might be confused, but Ed left the room with a spring in his step.

14

Ed's breakfast companion was clearly a regular at the exclusive Silicon Valley bistro. The hostess greeted him by name and led them to a corner table by a window hung with sheer curtains and ferns. Several diners waved. Gene Simons returned their acknowledgments with smiling nods at once regal and boyish. Speaking softly, he identified them to Ed: "CFO of Google…big venture guys…Facebook VP…Steve's trouble-shooter." As in Steve Jobs.

A boulevard away, the cylindrical towers of Yahoo reflected the morning sun. The hostess shook out a thick cloth napkin and covered Ed's lap. With a flourish, she presented the menu, a card clipped to a polished wooden plank. Ed's listed no prices.

The waiter arrived and touted the special, French toast smothered in brandied strawberries.

"My favorite," Simons said, ordering it.

Ed said, "Ditto."

"I've always liked the San Francisco Museum," Simons said, sipping orange juice and cappuccino, "but all they have is one little corner devoted to the hippie period. That's ridiculous, and I intend to correct it—with your help."

Simons explained that ever since his first company had gone public, he'd collected sixties memorabilia: Janis Joplin concert outfits, seats from the Straight Theater, a guitar Jerry Garcia had played in the Warlocks, the PA from the Matrix, the sign from the Drogstore Café, and posters for concerts produced by The Family Dog and the young

Bill Graham. One day, he might found his own museum, but in the meantime, he was happy to help San Francisco's do justice to its long-haired legacy.

"The thing is," Simons continued, "without context, without insight into that time and place, the artifacts are just curiosities that don't mean anything. Your challenge is to supply the meaning."

Ed asked what Simons had in mind. Captions for display cases? An introductory essay? A book? Something interactive?

"I wouldn't rule out anything. But at this point, I imagine something longer than an essay but shorter than a book—say, fifty pages that the curator can use to frame things."

"You realize," Ed said, "that fifty pages of text plus, say, two hundred captioned photos of your best artifacts would make a lovely coffee-table book. The gift shop could sell it."

Simons smiled. That hadn't occurred to him. He said their contract should include provisions for such a project, with Ed as the author.

Ed smiled. "I'd love to do a book. We could time the pub date to coincide with the opening of the exhibit." *And squeeze a few extra months out of this job.*

Simons saluted with his cup. "I like the way you think."

"But if I may, can we discuss the document? Do you want footnotes?"

Simons shook his head. "No need, but a bibliography would be nice."

"How about a discography? The bands, the music."

"Great. We can link to iTunes."

"And maybe add a CD or two to a deluxe edition of the book."

"Terrific."

"Now, would you like an overview of the era? The big picture? Or a microscopic look at a few key people and events? Or a combination?"

Simons' brow furrowed. "I'm not sure. What do you recommend?"

"For something open to the public, a combination approach usually works best." Ed explained that the river of historiography flowed in two channels—one focused on the person making the times, the other on the times making the person. The former produced biographies, the latter, *The Decline and Fall of the Roman Empire.* Simons had a warehouse full of memorabilia that automatically shone a spotlight on the people and places associated with them and provided the micro view—assuming effective captions. So the document should be more of an overview.

Simons nodded slowly. Then he asked what made good captions.

"Stories," Ed replied. "Anecdotes that give the objects—as you said—meaning. Take your PA from the Matrix. By itself, it's just an old sound system from a dead nightclub. But the caption could explain that Haight resident Martin Buchwald leased a pizza place in the Fillmore to create a club to showcase his act as folk-rocker Marty Balin. He asked some friends to back him up, and when the club opened, they became the house band. But they had no name. One night, they passed a joint and started satirizing the name of the old bluesman, Blind Lemon Jefferson. The take-off they liked best was Blind Thomas Jefferson Airplane. But after the club opened, they shortened it."

Simons's broad smile showed square teeth. "You certainly know the period."

"With so many artifacts spotlighting the details," Ed said, "I think people would want an overview showing how the times shaped the people involved. But it's your exhibit—"

"An overview sounds good. Complements the artifacts."

The waiter and another tuxedo-clad man appeared, each holding a plate. One stood behind Simons, the other by Ed. The plates landed simultaneously and Ed savored the most delicious strawberry he'd ever tasted. Then he said, "I'd suggest you also consider one other element."

Simons gestured. "Please."

"Oral histories. People love reminiscences." Ed explained that most former Haight-Ashbury hippies were now in their sixties and would probably jump at the chance to share their recollections. It shouldn't be too difficult to find, say, fifty or so—some notable, others obscure— and display then-and-now photos and vignettes. Their stories would enhance the artifacts and the overview, and add insight to both the exhibit and the book. "Then, at the opening, you invite all the vignette people, which creates buzz and generates media interest. With good PR, the opening could become a hippie reunion—and a national news item." *Maybe Julie could get a job out of this, too.*

"I love it," Simons said. "National news…that would be *fantastic.*" Ed could almost see him salivating.

"Tie the PR to a web site, and I bet the museum would sell a lot of books."

Simons touched the napkin to his lips. Was he drooling? "So three elements—artifacts, overview, and vignettes. I certainly hired the right man."

"An honor," Ed said, saluting with his last bite of French toast.

The waiter cleared the dishes.

"We should do everything we can to get national attention," Simons said. "The hippie Haight was more than just twenty blocks in one corner of San Francisco."

"Precisely," Ed said. "It was a microcosm."

Simons leaned forward. "Go on."

"The hippie Haight," Ed explained, "was actually a small town with only a few hundred key players: the bands, their fans, the Diggers, dealers, leftover beatniks, some shop owners, and the staff of the *Oracle*. It was the capital of hippiedom, but similar things were happening all over, wherever young people listened to rock, smoked pot, supported civil rights, and opposed the Vietnam War—which was why the media coverage resonated. Young Baby Boomers were hungry for group identification, for what became known as 'youth culture.' When the Airplane sang 'Feed your head,' kids everywhere knew exactly what they were talking about."

"I like it." Simons said. "I like it a lot. Sounds like we're in good shape." Then the Wizard of Oz stepped out from behind the curtain, just a man. "Now…about my birth mother. Did you read the file?"

15

Ed had spent two days perusing the more than three hundred PDF pages Simons had sent: newspaper clips, birth-registry documents, genealogy details, transcripts of dozens of interviews, police reports and mug shots from her two arrests, police photos and the ballistics report from her murder, and memos from a dozen private investigators who'd blanketed the country searching for any trace of her. When a billionaire decides to leave no stone unturned, he can trigger landslides.

"Yes," Ed said, "I read everything."

"And?"

"Heartrending. I'm so sorry."

"Thank you. I always knew I was adopted, but I had zero interest in my birth mother. Why should I care? She gave me up. But when I turned thirty-five, I got curious and my dad gave me the file he'd saved, the newspaper articles and police report. I was in a daze for a week."

Simons stared into space. "I have no memory of Jackie. My first memory is splashing in the kiddie pool my parents had in Palo Alto. But Jackie was my *mother* and she was *murdered.*" He hung his head. "When I read what happened, I felt terrible for writing her off. She *didn't* give me up. She was on a blanket on Hippie Hill holding me in her arms. She set me down, then stood up, and—" The wound was still raw. His voice cracked as he said, "She *loved* me."

"I'm sure she did."

"I'm under no illusions. I know I'm looking for a needle in a forty-year-old haystack, but I'm hoping someone might remember her—

another reason I love your idea about the vignettes. More interviews."

"No problem. I'll ask everyone—happy to." Ed smiled but his heart sank. After four decades, who would recall a little butterfly who'd flitted through the Haight for a brief moment before landing under the boot that crushed her?

Ed lifted his tea cup, but stopped before sipping. "I noticed that the police report carried a signature, Brendon O'…something."

"O'Hara."

Ed took a swig. "But I didn't see an interview. Did he pass away?"

"Alzheimer's. By the time we got to him, he was in a nursing home."

The police report contained little more than gruesome photos taken September 7, 1968, on the hill adjacent to Children's Playground near the eastern edge of Golden Gate Park. Jackie had been shot in the chest. The police recovered the slug, presumably fired from the thick shrubbery across the meadow. Witnesses said she'd been hawking quarter-ounce bags of weed. They'd seen her around, but didn't know much about her. She had no known address, just a New Mexico driver's license issued to Jacqueline Zarella. One prior in Albuquerque for shoplifting that brought a fine and probation. Then in San Francisco, two arrests for possession with intent to sell, the first for marijuana, the second, speed. The pot charge got dropped. The meth charge was pending when she died.

There were no suspects in the shooting. Witnesses told the story Simons had related. She was holding her son. She placed him on the blanket then stood up and—

The child, estimated to be three years old, was turned over to Child Protective Services. No one had claimed her body or her boy.

One private investigator had found a relative in Albuquerque, Angela Zarella, age seventy-nine, Jackie's aunt. She had no idea her niece had been dead forty years. The girl had taken her mother's last name because her father was unknown. Jackie's mother, Denise, had worked as a dancer and cocktail waitress at a titty bar that catered to truckers. She had two arrests for DUI and three for soliciting. The aunt said Jackie was a wild child who quit school and left town, never to be heard from again.

"The aunt's a real piece of work," Ed said.

Simons smirked. "The PI told her I wanted to fly down and see her.

She Googled me, and—"

"Let me guess. She wouldn't talk unless you opened your wallet."

Simons shrugged. "In my position, every waiter expects a big tip."

"Extortion is more like it."

"Yeah, well…it was real money to her and nothing to me. She lives in a ratty trailer park. I was happy to help. After all, she's my great-aunt, and she added a detail. Jackie got pregnant at fifteen and Aunt Angie helped her get an abortion. They were illegal then."

Simons sipped cappuccino, Ed tea.

"You moved heaven and Earth to find your birth certificate," Ed said. "Must have been frustrating."

"Very. We checked every birth registry in the country, using every conceivable spelling, for several years around my presumed birth date. Looks like she had a home birth somewhere and never registered it." He glanced through the window and sighed. "My parents had to jump through hoops to get me a birth certificate. They named me Gene. He was my adoptive mother's father. I like my name, but I'd *love* to know the name my mother gave me, my *real* name."

"I'm curious. What about your birthday?"

"Arbitrary. My parents decided on the day my adoption was certified."

"I assume you know that Sarah Herscowitz died." She was the matriarch of the family that, since shortly after World War II, had owned Mendel's Far Out Fabrics, an art supply store on Haight Street. The file contained an interview. Jackie fancied herself an artist, shopped there, and Herscowitz had remembered her.

"Yes," Simons said, "I saw her obit. Sarah took several hippie girls under her wing, especially if they had kids."

"After so long, I was surprised she remembered Jackie so well. I assume it was the shooting."

"Yes. Sarah said she opened the *Foghorn* one morning and saw the photo. It made an impression. She was so sweet, so glad to see me. She always wondered what happened to me."

"But she didn't remember your name."

"No."

"And that ex-dealer, Paul Nightingale—how'd you ever find him?" Nightingale had recalled Jackie selling baggies of pot in the park.

"A smart PI. He searched SFPD records for everyone convicted of dealing in the Haight from '65 until the day Jackie died. Nightingale popped up and we got lucky. The feds had an address."

"Really? The *feds*? And it was still good? I'd say you got amazingly lucky."

"Yes, because Nightingale *wasn't* so lucky. The arrest my guy found happened in the summer of '68. He got popped with five pounds and did six months in county jail. Eight years later, in '76, he took another fall—for possession of, get this, five *hundred* pounds, a mountain of cash, and an arsenal large enough to start a war. Beyond the drug and weapons charges, the IRS got him for tax evasion. He was sentenced to fifteen years, but got out after eight with four years of probation. That took him to '88. He's been off the radar ever since, but the last address the federal probation office had was an apartment in Oakland. My guy ran over there and found Nightingale sweeping up. Turned out he owns the place. After prison, he became a realtor and wound up buying his old building."

Ed shook his head in wonder. "Surprising how talkative he was. You'd think a big dealer would keep his mouth shut."

"I wondered the same, which is why I drove up there myself—to get a feel for him, and pump him for more about Jackie. He was happy to talk. He'd been out of dealing for thirty years. The statute of limitations expired long ago. And as he told me, 'What are they going to do? Put me in prison? I already did my time.' He was pushing seventy. He *wanted* to tell his story. He'd make a great vignette."

"I agree. I'll contact him. Did he say any more about your mother?"

"Just that I was always with her. And my clothes were clean." Simons set down his cup and signed the bill. "I'm under no illusions, Ed. She was killed a lifetime ago. But maybe *somebody* remembers *something*. I want you to find out whatever you can. Right now, the file is everything I know. I'd love to know more. Anything."

"I'll do my best. But realistically—"

"I know. We're in a dark room chasing a shadow with our eyes closed." He crumpled his napkin and dropped it on the table. "Now, do you mind if I ask you a personal question?"

That caught Ed by surprise. "Not at all."

"It's about drugs."

Ed gestured *go ahead.*

"Do you smoke weed?"

Ed hoped his smile didn't look nervous. What should he say? To potential employers, his knee-jerk response was denial—and the hope that they didn't test. What did Simons want to hear?

Before Ed could reply, his host said, "I get high every day. Have for almost thirty years."

"Really," Ed said, chuckling. "I wouldn't say *every* day, but…most."

Simons leaned forward. "How do you feel about it?"

"Uh…"

Simons said, "My wife has never been thrilled with my…habit."

Ed felt just a mite concerned about his. Since getting sacked, he was smoking more. While not exactly enjoying it less—or making moves to cut down—he was starting to wonder. But before Ed was even aware of speaking, something else slipped out. "When I get concerned, one hit usually takes care of it."

Simons laughed. "It's funny," he said. "I started in high school. Liked it better than getting drunk. By college, it was pretty much every evening—not a lot, just enough to take the edge off, like a beer after work. My original software? The idea came to me when I was stoned. My first company? I launched it, grew it, sold it, and got rich smoking every day. My second company, too. Then it turns out my *mother* was a *dope dealer.* I can't decide if I should feel appalled—or proud."

Ed smiled. "I guess the apple doesn't fall far from the tree."

"I'm fine with Jackie's dealing, at least the pot. About the speed, I give her the benefit of the doubt. She had a kid to support, and what did she know? She was trailer trash, a crazy young runaway in crazy times. Sex, drugs, and rock 'n roll." Simons licked his lips as if trying to taste the past. "I often wonder what her life was like…*our* life. I wonder where she lived, how she bought what she sold, if she had friends, and how she kept a toddler's clothes clean. You said the dealers were an integral part of the little village. Do you think you could devote some special attention to that?"

"To dope dealing? Sure. I'll ask everyone I interview."

Simons gazed out the window at a passing airliner. "People think I have everything—and I do. I count my blessings every day, especially my family. But there's something everyone else takes for granted that

I've been denied. My real name. I don't know the name my mother gave me. I'd love to know it. I *really* would."

Simons' eyes bored deep into Ed's. "If you discover it, I'll be happy to award you a sizable bonus." The figure he mentioned widened Ed's eyes. It wasn't a Lotto jackpot, but it would carry them quite comfortably for several years.

"I'll do my best," Ed said. Silently he vowed, *I really will.*

16

On the drive home, in the cool, clear light of late morning, Ed dismissed any fantasy of discovering Simons' birth name. A legion of PIs hadn't come up with it. How could he? *I'm more likely to find dinosaur bones in a burrito.*

But who cared? Ed cranked up an old Stones CD and reveled in a long, luxurious stretch of interesting work at a fee that promised sound sleep for the first time in months. And a book, too!

He did some arithmetic. This project plus their other gigs meant they were within shouting distance of matching their former gross. Of course, now they had to buy health insurance retail and Big Daddy was no longer contributing to their retirement, so they were still down a few rungs. But they could pay the bills, and if they were careful, slowly replenish their savings.

To prepare for the breakfast, Ed had reread his files and skimmed several books on the Haight-Ashbury. Once he got back home, he cast a larger net, pulling out everything he had on post-World War II California: Disneyland's creation in 1955, Haight residents killing the Panhandle freeway in 1959, the fracas over the House Un-American Activities Committee's hearings in San Francisco in 1960, the Free Speech Movement in 1964, and marijuana's slow spread from jazz musicians to the Beats to Baby Boomers.

It was history, time-lapse shots of buds opening to roses, and Ed loved it. But a career in newspapers had left him dubious of historians' zeal to impose order on the chaos. Yes, important trends could be identified: civil rights, Vietnam, and after the sleepy fifties, an upsurge in grassroots activism. *If we can put a man on the moon, we can do anything.* But historians' impulse toward order smoothed the rough edges, minimizing the complexities. *There's something happening here. What it is ain't exactly—*

Newspapers took snapshots of the whirlwind. Of course, newspapers were also superficial, biased, and rarely got their facts straight. But now that they were circling the drain, Ed felt nostalgic, and drawn to what the *Horn* and other papers had said about the Haight-Ashbury back when the Mamas and Papas were California Dreamin'. One cool foggy morning, he traversed the atrium of the Main Branch and walked up to the fifth floor.

The Periodicals Room was unusually crowded. Ed got the last reader. Oddly, as newspapers faded away, interest in old papers seemed to be growing. He started with the *New York Times*, January 1, 1965, and rolled through 1969, then did the same with the *Examiner* and the *Horn*. Their collective take on the hippie Haight bounced from surprise, to consternation, to alarm. The *Times'* coverage fell under the general rubric of California kooks, while the local papers reviled the hippies as dirty drug-crazed vagrants who preferred gloppy brown rice to fluffy Uncle Ben's and had more sex than any mortal deserved.

During the subsequent four decades, San Franciscans had folded the hippie era into the city's romanticized past, a time of innocent wonder, great music, kaleidoscopic light shows, and funny cigarettes. Since then, and partly because of it, San Francisco had become a bastion of liberalism, a town where the Sisters of Perpetual Indulgence, drag queens in nun's habits and glitter, elicited cheers with their signature blessing: "Now go sin, my children! Then sin some more!"

But it wasn't always that way. Back when Owsley was cooking up acid in his kitchen, the mayor was a conservative Republican, housing was segregated, and the cops regularly raided gay bars. The police and fire department were entirely white and male. Pressure from the Catholic Church kept San Francisco General from dispensing the new birth control pill. And city officials despised the hippies and torpedoed every boat they launched—notably, the Drogstore Café and the Straight Theater. Ed followed the venality on microfilm.

A hippie entrepreneur wanted to turn the old Haight Pharmacy into a café called the Drugstore. The *Horn*'s headline read: "Planning Commission Nixes Haight 'Drugstore.'" In the Commission's view, marijuana and LSD were plagues and a café by that name sent the wrong message to the youth of the City of St. Francis.

The entrepreneur appealed. No neighbors had filed objections and a drugstore in the Marina had become a café called The Pharmacy. "Planning Rejects 'Drugstore' Appeal." The Commission's chairman refused to approve a project that glorified immorality. So the café became the Drogstore, and the publicity made it an instant sensation.

Meanwhile, Texas transplant Chet Helms and his friends, The Family Dog commune, started producing dances featuring local bands, among them the Dead, the Airplane, Janis, the Charlatans, Moby Grape, and Magic Bullet Theory. But the dances and the wild light shows that accompanied them took place at Longshoremen's Hall near Fisherman's Wharf, miles from the Haight, where most of the bands and much of their audience lived. In late 1967, a trio of Haight-Ashbury hippies thought it would be cool to produce dances in the neighborhood's long-shuttered Haight Theater.

It was an ambitious fantasy that involved a million details starting with the name. "Haight Theater" felt obsolete. The dreamers rolled another one and envisioned a hippie community center, an artistic refuge from the corruption and hypocrisy of the straight world. "I know," one exclaimed, "the *Straight* Theater." His partners dissolved in giggles.

The Straight project quickly galvanized the neighborhood. Big Brother and Quicksilver Messenger Service each made sizable contributions. Moby Grape and Magic Bullet Theory offered to play benefits. A bucket at the Digger's Free Store collected hundreds of dollars. And Owsley promised to underwrite a state-of-the-art sound system.

But the project required a building permit. From the *Examiner*: "Permit Bureau Balks at Haight Theater Plan." For a year, the application followed a tortured course. The permit was finally issued in late 1968. The theater seats were removed and a dance floor installed.

From the *Foghorn*: "Fire Department Demands Changes at Haight Hall." Officials insisted on not just one sprinkler system, but two, one over the dance floor and another in the basement, adding considerably to development costs.

"Clash at Haight Hall Hearing." Fire officials said the department was simply trying to protect lives. The developers countered that no other dance hall had ever been required to install basement sprinklers.

Meanwhile, the Haight was fast becoming a mecca for runaway teens, hundreds of whom camped near the Haight Street entrance to Golden Gate Park, causing a sanitation nightmare that appalled longtime residents. "Haight Theater Permit Denied."

For a while, the Straight offered arts-and-crafts classes. The most popular taught a new way to make colorful T-shirts. Wavy Gravy wore one at Woodstock, and tie-dye entered the lexicon.

Finally, in early 1969, the Straight's doors were padlocked.

Ed was about to hit rewind, when, at the bottom of the page, a small headline caught his eye: "Draft Resister Gets Three Years."

A photo showed a bearded, angry young long-hair in a T-shirt proclaiming *Hell No, We Won't Go*. The caption identified him as Alvin Miller. The name rang a bell, but Ed couldn't place it. The article said Miller was a Stanford dropout, a former political science student. Then Ed knew. This was Al Miller, Cindy's husband. So he'd been a draft resister. Ed printed the article.

Back home, he Googled San Francisco State. Alvin R. Miller was a professor of political science, with a Stanford B.A. and a Yale Ph.D. One of his books was *Hell No: Draft Resistance During the Vietnam Years*.

Ed felt sorry for Miller. He was Othello, only he wasn't just imagining his Desdemona's infidelity. When Kirsch got shot, he was teaching, and Wally said the only people with access to hit men were Mafiosi and drug dealers. Now it turned out that Miller had served time in federal prison—no doubt with several big dealers. Of course, that was a long time ago, and he was a political prisoner, not a gangster, more Nelson Mandela than Al Capone. But if he'd kept in touch with anyone, an introduction might have been arranged.

Ed dialed the detective.

17

Sonya was at a sleepover and after fussing all evening, Jake was finally down for the night. A weary Ed chopped onions, carrots, tomatoes, and a potato for a pot of minestrone that would hold them for a few dinners. In the basement, Julie threw a load into the washer and pulled one out of the dryer. As Ed turned the soup down to simmer, Julie trudged up the stairs carrying a heavy basket and dropped it with a thud.

She always looked lovely to Ed, but even he could see the lines in her face and her regal posture slipping into a stoop. She was carrying too heavy a burden. When a job came up, she said *yes!* before figuring out how she'd manage it. Then she paid the price. When Ed had mentioned that, with his new job, they were climbing out of the hole and maybe she didn't have to take everything that came along, she'd snapped at him. The freelance viper had bitten and she was feverish from its poison. *If you ever say no, they'll never call again.* Ed embraced her and felt the swell of her breasts. "How about some ice cream? Or a cup of tea?"

Julie hugged him back and said, "Both. And a glass of wine."

Ed opened the freezer, Julie, the cupboard. A few minutes later, they sat at the table with hot mugs and cold bowls.

Ed looked at the stemware glass beside Julie's teacup. He wouldn't have filled it so full. Was it her second of the night, or third?

"I had coffee with Cindy," Julie said. "She's signed a lease, a two-bedroom near Laurel Village, but she feels miserable, depressed and weepy. This was supposed to be *their* place, her home with *Dave*. She feels like a widow, without being a bride."

"I don't know," Ed said. "Isn't that the philanderer's classic line, that he's going to leave the wife? Then he never does."

"All I know is what Cindy tells me, and she *swears* Dave promised that right after the election, he'd leave Olivia and move in with her."

"What about Ramirez? Did he ask Al about prison friends?"

"Yes, and Al threw a fit."

"So he's got a temper."

"He denied any involvement and accused Ramirez of harassment."

"What does Cindy say? Is Al still in touch with anyone?"

"One guy, his old cellmate. A big coke dealer who now has a motorcycle shop in Santa Cruz. But get this: during Vietnam, Al was a *pacifist*. Cindy says he doesn't have a violent bone in his body. She's convinced Al had nothing to do with Dave's death."

"Well," Ed said, "you know what they say: no atheists in foxholes… and maybe no pacifists when someone's fucking your wife into leaving you."

They sipped oolong and ate mocha fudge. They talked about the kids, social plans, and their vacation, car camping in King's Canyon. They agreed that freelancing sucked. It was hard getting work, hard completing it, and hard collecting the money.

"When you work for yourself," Ed said, "your boss is a slave-driver."

"I hate it," Julie said. "I want a real job, with benefits."

She poured another glass.

"Julie—"

She made a face. Now he knew where Sonya got her go-fuck-yourself expression.

Ed changed the subject. "Listen, you know those vignettes for the exhibit? They sounded great when I was pitching Simons, but now I have to find fifty ex-hippies. I'm thinking of Olivia Kirsch. Do you think you could…?"

"Ed, she just buried her husband. Have a heart."

"It doesn't have to be right away. Whenever she's ready. But I need people. And if I find Simons's birth name, we hit the jackpot."

Julie pursed her lips. "I'll call Sandy, see what she says." Sandra Selden had been Dave's chief aide.

Suddenly, Julie looked woozy. "I—I feel nauseous." Her caramel skin turned green. "I'm going to bed. Would you take the laundry upstairs?"

She pushed herself to standing and wobbled on her feet. "Oh, God—" She stumbled into the bathroom and shut the door. The sound was unmistakable.

"You need any help?" Ed called.

He could barely hear her feeble *no*.

"How about a glass of water?"

"Okay."

Julie drank it on her knees, her eyes watery, filled with confusion and shame. Ed helped her to her feet. She leaned heavily on him as he guided her up the stairs.

"I think I had a bit too much to drink," she said.

Ed started to speak but held his tongue. He helped her undress and tucked her in. Then he descended to his office, but couldn't concentrate on his lecture. His stomach ached. He loaded the bong, and exhaled out the window, wondering.

18

The Front Page Deli was the twenty-four-hour slide-your-tray place on the ground floor of the *Foghorn* building. All the sandwiches had newspaper names and a *Horn* ID got you a big discount, which meant that everyone at the paper ate there—some of the bachelors, three meals a day. It was also a magnet for cops, cabbies, musicians, politicos, night owls, and anyone who wanted a good meal at a decent price seasoned with potential access to newspaper people. Before the Internet, finding a seat was a challenge. But with the paper withering, the FP was hurting. Ed and Tim Huang had no trouble claiming a window table during the height of the lunch rush.

They'd met twenty years earlier at the karate dojo run by Tim's late uncle. Ed was into his dissertation and Tim was finishing high school. Ed made it to green belt, Tim to black. Then Ed quit and they lost touch. Years later, they ran into each on a story; Ed was a reporter at the *Horn* and Tim was working for Ed's former employer, the city's alternative weekly. Each was shocked that the other had wound up in journalism. Ed helped his old sparring partner move to the daily.

Over a decade, Tim worked his way from reporter to Metro editor. He still had a job, but with Metro down from forty reporters to eighteen, he found himself wandering among empty cubicles wondering what would become of him. On the one hand, he was fortunate: his wife, Kim Nakagawa, was the morning anchor on Channel 5 News. But the Internet was drawing eyeballs away from television, too, and the TV news audience was going the way of newspaper readers. Tim was taking antacids, Kim, antidepressants.

"So," Ed asked, spooning up black bean soup, "did your last paycheck clear?"

"Very funny," Tim replied, biting into a turkey club.

They chatted about what was left of the *Horn*. Rumors abounded. One day they were about to merge with the *San Jose Mercury-News*, the next, it was the *Contra Costa Times*. Meanwhile, if any of the unions stirred from their comas, management threatened to pull the plug and can everyone.

"Here we are," Tim lamented, "a talented group of professional news-gatherers, and we have no idea what's going on two floors above us. I'd send out my resumé, but what's the point? Everyone's laying off."

"So do what we did," Ed deadpanned, "go freelance—a real barrel of laughs."

"No thanks. I've thought about opening a dojo, but there are so many, and I'd have to work evenings and weekends. Kim would hate that. I've also thought about trying to become a plumber's apprentice. There's good money in plumbing." Tim knew more about home repair than several handymen Ed had engaged. "But I'm really hoping the newspaper business turns around."

"In your dreams."

Ed filled him in on Julie's clients, his class at City College, and his new Haight-Ashbury gig. All things considered, they were counting their blessings, but neither of them was sleeping well and their fuses were short. "I'm smoking more weed, and she's drinking more—too much. The other night, she wound up hugging the toilet."

"Not good." Tim sighed. "How much?"

"A glass of wine with dinner, sometimes two, then usually another one later. What she's sneaking, God knows. I don't get it. Julie was friends with Karen. She should *know better*."

Karen Arseth, a feature writer, had earned a Pulitzer nomination for a series about her journey to vodka hell and back. Then, after nine years of sobriety, she'd fallen off the wagon and smashed her car into a tree. The two couples had attended her funeral together.

"It's not a question of 'knowing better,'" Tim said. "It's a *disease*." Tim's brother was a recovering alcoholic and he'd seen more of the affliction than he cared to recall.

"I know that, intellectually," Ed said. "But when it's *Julie*…"

"She blowing any jobs?"

"No, everyone loves her."

"Any blackouts?"

"None that I know of."

"DUIs?"

"No."

"Empty bottles under the sofa?"

"I haven't looked. Maybe I should. What do you think? Should I be worried?"

"Well, getting sick once isn't—"

"*Twice.* The other night and the night we got fired."

"I'd say it's a yellow flag, but not exactly red…"

Ed frowned. "Not yet."

Tim worked on his sandwich and Ed spooned soup.

"What about you? How much are you smoking?"

Ed shrugged. "Couple hits a day. After work."

Tim smiled.

"All right, three or four. But that's less than a joint—"

"He said defensively."

"Hey, *you* try freelancing, see how *you* cope."

"It's funny," Tim said. "I *encourage* Kim to have the extra glass of wine. Boosts my chance of getting lucky."

"Yeah, but when women are drunk, the sex sucks."

Tim gazed into space. "I take it any way I can get it."

"You want hot sex," Ed said with a grin, "fire up some reefer."

"When Kim smokes, she goes right to sleep."

Ed smiled. "A hit on the bong, some scented candles, a Smoky Robinson CD—"

"Oh, to have a stoner wife."

"Speaking of stoners," Ed said, "anything new on Kirsch?"

"Not really," Tim said. "They got ballistics off the slug, but no matches, and most of the death threats have been ruled out."

"Most?"

"You can't track down every crank call. Bottom line, it doesn't look good. You know the stats."

Ed knew the police department's clearance statistics thanks to a four-month investigation Tim had spearheaded. The SFPD was very good at catching killers when someone told them who did it, but when no one stepped forward with a name and the detectives had to scuff their shoes, they nabbed about one in five for a batting average of .200.

"That sucks," Ed said.

19

Wouldn't you know, the library's complete set of the *San Francisco Oracle* had been stolen and the alternative press database only went back to 1969, the year *after* the *Oracle* had folded. Ed gnashed his teeth. How could he do justice to the hippie Haight and not read its newspaper?

He Googled *San Francisco Oracle* and found mostly junk. But several pages in, he stumbled on a quirky site called BADASS.org, the Bay Area Digital Archive of the Sixties and Seventies. Its "About Us" tab said it was a labor of love built by Allen Cohen, founder of the *Oracle*, and Carol Covington, an editor who'd worked at both the *Oracle* and the *Berkeley Barb*. BADASS indexed those two papers, plus a number of other flash-in-the-pan hippie-alternative publications. The site displayed big, colorful facsimile pages of the *Oracle*. Ed couldn't decide if they looked inspired or amateurish. He started with issue number one. By number three, he was kicking himself. He'd never written about the *Oracle*, and with all his scrambling for work, he'd let his column slide. His next deadline loomed.

THE *SAN FRANCISCO ORACLE*: SEX, DRUGS, AND THE UNDERGROUND PRESS

During World War II, the French Resistance mocked the German occupation with a clandestine publishing operation, the "underground press." Twenty years later, the term was applied to American tabloids produced by and for restive young

Baby Boomers. This new-wave underground press combined a love for rock music with left politics and drug-inspired spirituality. Among the nation's estimated 200 underground newspapers, one of the most prominent was the *San Francisco Oracle*, published in the Haight-Ashbury from September 1966 through February 1968.

The *Oracle* was not the first underground newspaper. The *Berkeley Barb, LA Free Press,* Detroit's *Fifth Estate,* and New York's *East Village Other* all launched a year earlier. And the *Oracle* was certainly not the longest-lived—it published only 12 issues.

Nonetheless, the *Oracle* was the most influential example of the genre. At its height, it printed 120,000 copies that circulated from coast to coast. It also defined the formula that most other papers embraced: support for the civil rights movement, opposition to the Vietnam War, and a cultural outlook that embraced peace, love, marijuana, and rock music. Its spirituality combined the Buddhism of Allen Ginsberg with Timothy Leary's vision of an LSD-infused utopia. Its design revolved around strikingly elaborate illustrations produced in bold colors, a first on newsprint.

Rolling Stone founder Jan Wenner called the *Oracle* "inspiring." The Grateful Dead's Jerry Garcia said it was "the heartbeat of the Haight-Ashbury." Novelist Ken Kesey insisted it was "more trustworthy than the *New York Times.*" Anti-war activist Abbie Hoffman called it "our version of illuminated manuscripts." And while playing the Fillmore one night, Beatle George Harrison distributed copies from the stage.

But the mainstream media held a different opinion. In 1967, the newspaper you are now reading sniffed that the *Oracle* was "a crude hodge-podge of drug-crazed nonsense over which someone spattered a dozen colors of paint."

The *San Francisco Oracle* was founded by editor/publisher Allen Cohen and art director Michael Bowen. Cohen (1940-2004) was a New York poet who moved to the Haight in 1964 for its cheap rents and post-Beat bohemian scene. One night he dreamed he was flying around the world. Whenever he looked down—on Paris, Tokyo, San Francisco—he saw people reading a tabloid newspaper decorated with rainbows. He shared his dream with friends, who said, "Let's do it!" In an interview shortly before his death, Cohen recalled, "The next thing I knew we were tacking flyers to phone polls up and down Haight Street asking for volunteers."

Bowen (1937-2009) grew up in Beverly Hills, the son of a dentist and a free-spirited mother who openly divided her affections between her husband and a long-term lover, the mobster Benjamin (Bugsy) Siegel, whom the young Michael called Uncle Benjie. Bowen became an accomplished painter and sculptor and felt drawn to Eastern religions. In the late 1950s, he moved to San Francisco, fell in with the Beats, and befriended Janis Joplin and Allen Cohen. His studio in the Haight became the *Oracle* office.

In October 1966, a month after the *Oracle*'s debut, Bowen and Cohen helped organize a rally in Golden Gate Park to protest the criminalization of LSD. Janis Joplin and Big Brother and the Holding Company played for free before an unexpectedly large crowd of 3,000.

The organizers were thrilled, and announced a more ambitious rally to celebrate the Haight-Ashbury's burgeoning counterculture. That event, the Human Be-In, took place on January 14, 1967. Jefferson Airplane and the Grateful Dead performed. Allen Ginsberg and Gary Snyder read poetry. And coining the phrase that became a hippie rallying cry, Timothy Leary urged the throng to "Turn on, tune in, and drop out." The Be-In attracted more than 10,000 people, and because of it, the media discovered hippies.

The Be-In also brought the *Oracle* dozens of new volunteers, who thought it was *their* paper. The staff quickly split into two factions. The new arrivals, political radicals, hoped to channel opposition to the Vietnam War into revolution against corporate capitalism. The founding hippies were more interested in getting high, dancing to the bands, creating art, and living on what they could scrounge at the Diggers' Free Store. The radicals eventually became disgusted and decamped to Berkeley, where the *Barb* was more their style. That left the hippies, including Cohen and Bowen, in control of the *Oracle*.

It was not a newspaper in the usual sense. It published little actual news. Instead, it styled itself a manifesto-in-progress, touting higher consciousness through love, drugs, music, meditation, poetry, and hippie tribalism. The paper's innovative design, wild illustrations, and bold use of color underscored its messianic vision. "The problem," Cohen recalled, "was that higher consciousness didn't interest advertisers."

The *Oracle* carried a few full-page ads for new releases by the Airplane and other local bands, and some smaller ads for Haight-Ashbury boutiques. But advertising brought in only a fraction of the print bill, and so many copies were given away free that circulation brought in next to nothing.

The problem was hardly unique to the *Oracle*. Every underground newspaper was based on strong convictions and weak finances. "We thought rock 'n roll would support us," Cohen said, "but it didn't. That left sex and drugs. The *Barb* chose sex—prostitution ads, hundreds of them. We chose drugs, and fortunately, the local dealers gave generously."

Why would marijuana and acid dealers bankroll a newspaper? "They were our friends," Cohen explained. "They had money and there was an ethos of sharing the wealth. They also wanted a sympathetic platform to organize support if they got arrested—and several did."

But after the Summer of Love came the long, cold winter when the Haight-Ashbury was flooded with heroin and methamphetamine. The Diggers' Free Store closed. Most of the bands moved to Marin. And Michael Bowen left for an extended trip to India. "In the spring of '68," Cohen recalled, "I looked around and everyone was gone."

Cohen moved to Berkeley and divided his time between preserving the *Oracle* (folio reprint 1991, CD-ROM 1996, New Human Be-In, London, 2002) and participating in cyber-culture (Digital Be-Ins, 1992-2002). Bowen resumed his art career. He died in Stockholm, Sweden, in 2009.

By the mid-1970s, most underground newspapers had

folded. They were replaced by today's alternative weeklies. These
tabloids, including the *San Francisco Defender*, owe less to the
underground press than to New York's *Village Voice*, founded
in 1955 by novelist Norman Mailer and friends. Compared
with the underground press, the *Voice* had a more realistic
approach to advertising (though it also has a long history of
sex ads). Less graphically flamboyant than the *Oracle*, the *Voice*
was nevertheless editorially similar: progressive politics, a focus
on the arts, and a libertarian streak—support for legalization
of marijuana and sex work.

Like the underground press, the alternative weeklies see
themselves as journalistic Davids hurling stones at mainstream
media Goliaths. Now, with the Internet threatening all print
journalism, some alternative weeklies appear to be in better
shape than many major dailies, thanks to "hyper-local" content
that readers can't obtain elsewhere. Wherever they are, the
founders of the *Oracle* are probably smiling.

Ed hit the Send button, reshelved some books, and tidied up his files.
Not long ago, his editor might have objected to his quoting the *Horn's*
ancient snootiness about the *Oracle*, but with the paper reduced to a
shadow of its former self, the few surviving editors were so overworked
he doubted anyone would notice, let alone care.

Noon was approaching and Ed's gut grumbled. From the fridge,
leftover pasta called, yet he remained glued to his chair. Gene Simons
was number 180 on *Fortune's* list of the 400 richest Americans, but he
didn't know his given name. It was clear that his mother had lived fast,
died young, and left no trace. But the clips in her son's file came only
from mainstream papers. Ed returned to BADASS and typed Jackie
Zarella.

Five hits. Two in the *Oracle,* two in the *Barb*, and a photo. The
Oracle called her a pot dealer and noted her arrest for possession. The
Barb said she'd become a speed dealer and had burned her supplier.

Ed clicked the thumbnail photo and his screen filled with a grainy
black-and-white snapped at the Human Be-In. A wisp of a woman
and a stocky long-haired man sat smiling in the foreground in front
of a field full of hippies. The caption identified them as Jackie Zarella

and Doug Connelly. Jackie was a petite innocent in a Minnie Mouse sweatshirt. Her arm snaked around her companion's waist and her head rested on his shoulder.

Looking at Doug Connelly, Ed did a double-take. On his neck was a tattoo of a lightning bolt.

Ed recalled the gathering after Dave's funeral. The skinny cancer sufferer with the shaved head and tattoo of a pine tree looked nothing like this husky long-hair. But he said his tattoo had once been lightning.

The photo was part of a two-page spread. The other Be-In shots included Ginsberg, Leary, the Dead and the Airplane—and that photo he'd seen after Kirsch was killed, of Dave in the magician's cape and Olivia in the peasant dress. They looked like young versions of their older selves, only she was thinner and he had a full head of long hair.

So Jackie had known Doug, or whatever his name was, and the photo implied they were more than friends. Meanwhile, Doug knew Olivia. Maybe Olivia could put him in touch with Doug. Maybe she also knew Jackie and her son. Maybe she'd remember his name.

20

Ed hadn't felt this feverish since his last bout of flu. After breakfast with Simons, he'd dismissed the man's fantasy as ridiculous. After forty years, who'd remember a waif like Jackie, let alone her little boy's name?

But the *Oracle* photos changed everything. Suddenly Ed had lines to three people who might recall the lost name: Doug with the tattoo, Olivia Kirsch, and that other guy…Owen. If any of them remembered—Ed's heart raced as he envisioned clanging bells, screaming sirens, and barrels of coins spewing from the slot machine.

He had to contact Olivia immediately, but the grieving widow was incommunicado. What had Julie said? That she'd approach Dave's aide about timing and an introduction, but so far, nothing. Julie was in Menlo Park working on her biotech conference. Ed whipped out his phone.

"Dave's aide?" he practically shrieked. "Did you ever contact her?"

"Why so excited? What's up?"

Ed told her.

"Oh, sorry, I meant to call Sandra, but it slipped my mind—"

"Sandra who?"

"Selden. Wait, I have her in my phone."

Ed e-mailed Selden and left a voice message. Of course, he understood that Olivia was still distraught. He didn't mean to intrude, but a guy with a tattoo on his neck had stopped by the house after the funeral and Ed *desperately needed* to contact him. Did Olivia know how?

Then the fever broke and Ed felt drained and spacey. Who was he kidding? He had trouble recalling the names of his cousins' children. How would a bunch of geriatric potheads remember one baby they'd known only briefly four decades ago?

Then Ed thought back to his teens, to his childhood home and the neighbors who paid him to shovel their snow. After thirty years, he still remembered *their* children's names. Maybe Olivia or Doug or Owen would, too.

Owen. Ed flashed back to the buffet table. If anyone had mentioned his last name, Ed hadn't caught it. But Owen owned some…what? Hair salons. Didn't Doug mention the name? He closed his eyes and conjured Owen and Doug chatting. They were old friends who hadn't seen each other in ages, and they seemed wary of one another, as if a falling out had never been resolved. Then the name materialized, A Cut Above. He knew the place—he drove by it all the time. Ed Googled it and found an e-mail address for the owner, Owen Pendleton. His fingers flew over the keys.

Ed felt like he had the hot hand at the craps table. *Baby needs a new pair of*— As the dice bounced against the wall, he envisioned new carpet upstairs, a new back deck, and maybe even a family trip to…Hawaii? No, *Bali.*

That evening, Ed found two e-mails waiting. Sandra Selden said Olivia was still in no shape to talk to anyone, but that at some point, she'd be happy to reminisce. Unfortunately, she had no contact information for Doug. She hadn't seen him in more than thirty years, and after the funeral, by the time it occurred to her to get his number, he was gone.

Owen's reply was less gracious: "I'm not interested in discussing the sixties. And no, I don't recall the little brat's name."

21

It was too long a drive north to Ukiah too early in the morning. Ed was at the wheel with Janis' *Pearl* on the CD. Julie sat beside him, alternately reading the *Horn* and doling out apple slices and baby carrots to the kids. Jake was strapped into his car seat, taking in the scenery, waving his spoon, and singing "Happy Birthday," though it came out "appy birdee." Sonya and her teammate, Carmen, were in their soccer uniforms. They whispered and giggled to each other while listening to iPods.

The tournament was some Northern California roundup thing. Ever since the end of Ed's stint as assistant coach, he'd tuned out the details. He simply transported Sonya to and from practices and games, wherever they happened to be, even halfway to the North Pole.

The park had three fields and Ed counted eighteen teams. It was shaping up to be a long day.

Julie stayed with the team and the gaggle of parents, while Ed took Jake to the little playground by an arched-roof hangar of a building that had to be a gym. Jake loved the swings, slide, and sandbox, and squealed with delight while riding the play horse on a big spring that bounced him every which way.

During Sonya's first game, Ed and Julie cheered themselves hoarse. With three years under her belt, Sonya understood the basics, but the game's fine points still eluded her, among them thinking twenty yards downfield. Fortunately for her self-esteem, she wasn't alone. Sonya logged her quota of minutes, made some decent passes, then flubbed one, but bounced back with a sweet running pass that wound up contributing to a goal.

The hot dog lunch broke up around one. Sonya's second game wasn't until three. The girls were in a meeting, and Julie took Jake back to the playground, which gave Ed a chance to stroll the grounds and have a hit to help him survive the afternoon.

The gym doors were open and he wandered in. It turned out this wasn't just a gym—the building also housed the offices of Ukiah Parks and Recreation. For a smaller town, they offered quite a program: all major sports for all ages, plus archery, riflery, ping pong, and several others.

Ed browsed display cases packed with trophies and a huge Wall of Fame, where photographs from as far back as the 1930s celebrated local, regional, state, and even a few national tournament winners. As a child of the suburbs who'd ended up in a city, Ed didn't have much experience with small-town America and, medicated as he was, he became mesmerized by the Wall—all those photos, all those brief shining moments of glory so meticulously collected and preserved for almost eighty years.

As he turned away, he noticed a name on the Wall: Olivia Tanner. Did he know her? He didn't think so, but hadn't he just heard about someone who grew up near Ukiah? Yes, Olivia Kirsch, Dave's wife. Ed took a step closer to the yellowing photo and saw a skinny, fresh-faced blonde girl of about twelve. The sixty-something widow he'd seen after the funeral looked nothing like her, but in the adolescent's features, Ed could discern the slightly older Olivia posing with her husband at the Be-In. The girl was up on the Wall because she'd won a local gold medal and regional silver for—Ed drew a sharp breath—*riflery.*

He found Julie and told her what he'd seen. It took her a moment to draw the inference, but when she did, her jaw dropped. She couldn't recall Dave ever mentioning his wife's early years, and considering Olivia today, a grandmother and businesswoman with half-lens glasses on a chain around her neck, it was hard to imagine her as a young Annie Oakley. But there it was.

Ed dialed Ramirez.

22

Ed loved their polling place, a neighbor's garage three doors down. The hominess of voting amid the clutter of bikes, skis, and gardening tools spoke to him of grassroots democracy. But this time, he couldn't muster any enthusiasm. All he brought into the booth was a heavy heart.

It was too late to print new ballots. As he stepped through the curtain, the name jumped out at him: David Kirsch, member, Board of Supervisors, author, lecturer.

They'd gone back and forth about it. Shortly after the funeral, Julie had announced that she didn't care if Dave was gone, he was her candidate and she was sticking with him. But Ed insisted it was silly to vote for a dead man, and as Election Day approached, Julie reconsidered. Why waste her vote? None of the other candidates excited them, but that was nothing new. Still, there were propositions they cared about.

As Ed scanned the ballot and began coloring in the broken arrows that pointed to his choices, he was filled with sorrow over what might have been—for the city, for Julie, and for them. A high-paying prestige job with great benefits, oh, how he wished he could have voted for that.

Ed stared at the candidates for mayor but suddenly found it hard to see. He wiped his eyes and flashed on his grandfather, dead thirty years, a corner grocer with the soul of a rabbi. What did he used to say about life and death? No, it was something else, the Book of Life? Ed couldn't remember. He colored in his last arrow and pulled the card out of the slot. Stepping out of the booth, he handed it to the polling person, an elderly Latina woman he'd seen around the neighborhood.

He found Julie sitting on the next-door neighbor's stoop, quietly crying into her hands. Ed coaxed her up to her feet and embraced her. "So?"

She choked back a sob and said, "Dave."

"Me, too."

They weren't the only ones. In a field of eight candidates, Kirsch came in third, only four hundred votes behind the second-place finisher. The *New York Times* was clearly amused: "Dead Candidate Takes 28% of San Francisco Vote." When Ed saw the headline, somehow his grandfather's words came back to him. "The Book of Life is written in invisible ink."

23

The apartment building overlooked Oakland's Lake Merritt, a dozen faux Tudor units that Ed guessed had been built in the 1920s. A short man with a full head of gray hair was pruning shrubs by the driveway. He wore a tattered flannel shirt distended by a potbelly that suggested the second trimester.

"Paul Nightingale?" Ed asked.

The man's face was jowly, but his eyes shone bright and impish. "Ed Rosenberg?" Nightingale wiped a hand on his jeans and extended it. "I've always loved your column. I hope you don't mind talking while I do chores. I own the place, which means I'm the gardener, janitor, and poop scooper."

The report in Simons's file said Nightingale had no recollection of Jackie until he was shown the newspaper clips about her shooting. Then he dimly recalled a sweet, artsy girl who held her little boy's hand while selling marijuana in creatively decorated baggies in front of the Straight Theater and in the park. But mostly he remembered her corpse.

He'd been passing a joint with friends in the meadow below Hippie Hill when he heard gunfire, followed by yelling and running and sirens. He saw Jackie crumpled on the ground, her chest looking like a watermelon dropped three stories. He watched the ambulance cart her away. He had no idea what happened to the boy and never caught the child's name.

Ed's e-mails had explained the sixties project, its vignette element, and the hope that during the year since his conversation with Simons, the ex-dealer might have remembered a little more. Ed produced a digital recorder, hoping Nightingale would recall that he'd granted permission.

"It's fine," Nightingale said with a wave of his hand. "I've been out of the business thirty-five years. It's ancient history." Nightingale raked up what he'd pruned and stuffed it into a compost container. "It's funny," he said gazing toward a sailboat on the lake. "When they contacted me—the PI and then, uh—"

"Gene Simons."

"Right, the wunderkind. I hardly knew Jackie and hadn't thought about those days in a long time. But lately, I've been thinking about them a lot."

"Really. Why?"

"Dave Kirsch," Nightingale said, his eyes turning sad as he produced a hankie and wiped his brow. Then he wheeled the big compost container to the back of the building. "A real tragedy."

Ed followed. "You knew him?"

"Oh, yeah." He nodded and smiled. "Back in the sixties, I knew him well. Guess who turned him on to pot?"

Ed cocked his head. "No!"

"Yes. I also introduced him to dealing, him and Owen."

He reached into a shed, pulled out a broom, and opened the building's rear door. Ed followed him down a hall to the lobby. Nightingale climbed the three flights to the top floor and began sweeping his way down, shepherding a growing pile of dust, dog hair, and bits of paper.

Ed pulled out a one-hitter, a baggie, and a lighter and held them out to Nightingale. "Care to?"

The ex-dealer smiled. "Don't mind if I do." He reached for the paraphernalia and blew smoke out of the window on a landing.

Ed unfolded a copy of the *Oracle* photo of Jackie snuggling up to Doug. "I thought there were three of them: Dave, Owen, and this guy—you remember him?"

Nightingale leaned on his broom and gazed at the image. "Son of a bitch, Doug! Doug, uh…Connor?"

"Connelly."

"Right! Sure, I knew him. When he first showed up, I hated him. He cost me a good customer. But a few years later, we got friendly. He was into the same Jesse James fantasy I was, the desperado dope dealer. Only he had a partner who kept his feet on the ground and his ass out of jail."

"Who? Dave?"

"No, Owen."

"How did he—"

"Owen was smart as a whip in business, but he was a strange guy, uptight and paranoid. Of course, in our business, paranoia was an asset. I was too caught up in being an outlaw to realize that. If I'd listened to Owen, I would have spent a lot less time in prison."

"Really. Do tell."

Nightingale raised his head from sweeping and stared at the recorder.

Ed read his mind, the ex-con intent on maintaining a low profile. But he'd agreed to be interviewed for a vignette, and Ed needed every ex-hippie he could find. "Dave's dead," he said softly, "and Doug's dying—"

"He is?"

"Yes. Prostate cancer. And Owen's owned a chain of hair salons for thirty years. Like you said, ancient history."

Nightingale shrugged. "All right."

Nightingale grew up in Altadena. His father was a jazz trumpeter who toured with Count Basie before settling into a career as a high school music teacher. Nightingale came of age listening to the Beach Boys, but jazz was in his blood, and when he entered San Francisco State, he obtained a fake ID and frequented the clubs in the Fillmore.

"I saw some great players," he recalled. "One night at Bop City, there were maybe a hundred people in the audience for John Coltrane and Thelonious Monk. Then for the encore, Monk invites this skinny guy with glasses to sit in on, of all things, bongos—Sammy Davis, Jr."

Dave and Owen were two years younger than Nightingale, freshmen roommates in the dorm. Owen was into Brubeck and turned Dave on to jazz with "Take 5." They joined the campus jazz society and met Nightingale, who introduced them to the art student who paid his tuition by forging driver's licenses. Nightingale took them to Minnie's Can-Do to see Coleman Hawkins, where they bought a couple joints from a waiter. For Dave and Owen, it was love at first toke.

"The first time Dave tried reefer," Nightingale recalled with a crooked smile, "it was like a cartoon—head exploding, lightning shooting out his ears. I can't say I've changed many lives, but I sure changed his. Once Dave got high, he was never the same. Owen, too, but he was very different, always wound up real tight. When he got high, he actually relaxed and became nice. I didn't care for him straight, but stoned he was cool."

Kirsch quickly decided that marijuana was more than just an intoxicant. It was a revelation, a sacrament, a gift from heaven, and he became an evangelist preaching the gospel, turning on everyone he knew. Around San Francisco State, Dave was the Johnny Appleseed of weed, and he acquired the nickname Johnny Appleweed.

After graduating in 1964, Nightingale moved to the Haight-Ashbury and fell in with some post-Beat bohemians who were into bebop and pot. Their weed came from Mexico via Los Angeles. Nightingale was soon buying a pound at a time and selling ounces to friends, including Dave and Owen.

"Compared with today's weed, it was weak and dirty, filled with seeds and stems. But I sold it cheap, and people kept coming back for more."

At the time, Dave and Owen were juniors starting to think about life after college. Neither was keen on the nine-to-five grind. Dealing seemed more attractive. Owen changed his major from econ to business and interrogated Nightingale about his operation, filling a notebook with calculations. If they moved to the Haight-Ashbury where rents were cheap, Owen figured the two of them could live comfortably if they sold ounces totaling three pounds a month. As an experiment, the two friends bought a pound from Nightingale and Dave offered ounces to friends. He sold out in a few days.

"Dave had a real talent for dealing," Nightingale explained. "Like every good salesman, he believed in his product. And he was charming and happy to provide free samples. As we used to say: Get 'em high, they buy."

Around the time Owen, Dave, and Olivia moved into a big dilapidated Victorian across the street from Golden Gate Park, Nightingale got bored selling ounces. He had dreams of becoming a major dealer, hauling it in by the truckload and wholesaling hundreds of pounds a month. He spent a few weeks in Baja and connected with the owner of a furniture company near Ensenada, who guaranteed him as much as he could move. When Nightingale returned to San Francisco, he handed his ounce trade over to Dave and Owen in exchange for their commitment to buy at least three pounds a month. A handshake and a hit sealed the deal.

"I had to hand it to Owen and Dave," Nightingale said. "They took the pipe and ran with it. Next thing I knew, Dave was buddies with Jerry Garcia and Janis Joplin, the go-to dealer for all the bands. They even wrote a song about him. You remember 'Candy Man?'"

Ed nodded. "In a special issue on the Summer of Love, *Rolling Stone* said Dave only dealt for two years, '66 to '68."

Nightingale made a face. "No way. He dealt much longer. He probably said that under orders from Owen."

"Orders?"

"In public, Owen always denied dealing and made sure that Dave and Doug did, too."

"When you went big time, how much did you sell?"

"We started at two hundred pounds a month, then more."

"'We?'"

"I was part of a group—a six-man partnership."

"And you operated from the Haight?"

"At first. Then we moved to Marin."

"Weren't you terrified of getting busted?"

Nightingale finished sweeping, filled the dustpan, and dumped it in the garbage. "A little, sure, but I was so deep into the outlaw fantasy that red lights looked green. And dealing on that level—what a rush! I had a big Chevy van with heavy-duty snow tires. We'd drive down with bags of cash stuffed under the seats and drive back at night off-road through the desert east of El Centro. We were young and stupid, and this was '65, '66. The border was still wide open. The cops were clueless or corrupt. And there was no DEA. The feds didn't get involved until the seventies."

Nightingale sold Dave and Owen a steady three pounds a month for almost a year. Then they bumped it up to four and then five—until one day Owen sheepishly informed their guru that they were switching suppliers.

"Doug?" Ed said.

"Right. He was an old friend of Owen's just back from Vietnam and hell bent on becoming *me*. He spoke decent Spanish and had a connection near Tecate."

"How'd you feel about that?"

"Royally pissed. We had a deal. I got them started and gave them dozens of customers. Of course, when it comes to money, a businessman's word is about as good as a politician's."

"But you were moving hundreds of pounds a month and they were only buying five."

"True, it wasn't all that much, but it was steady money from guys I could trust, and they betrayed me. I told Owen to fuck himself and didn't see him for a year." He sighed. "Then things changed, and I was *really glad* to see him."

24

Nightingale's reunion with Owen and Dave occurred in a place none of them ever expected to meet: the dining hall of the San Francisco County Jail. Nightingale had rolled through a stop sign on the Great Highway and the cop who pulled him over smelled something funny—a hefty load of primo Michoacan. Meanwhile, a few of San Francisco's finest had kicked in the door of the Victorian by the park, and found Dave and Owen sharing a doobie while watching *The Man from U.N.C.L.E.*

"I was still annoyed," Nightingale explained, "but in jail, the one thing you need is friends, and they were all I had."

Dave and Owen got released quickly, but San Francisco was drowning in weed and the DA was under pressure to make an example.

"They threatened me with hard time in state prison," Nightingale recalled, gazing toward the lake. "I was pretty scrappy, but I was small and skinny and had a boyish face. It didn't take a genius to see that I'd be turned out as a girl. I was scared out of my fucking mind."

That's when Dave and Owen visited and said their lawyer had waved a magic wand and made their charges disappear—for $15,000 in cash. They said he'd be happy to do the same for Nightingale, but considering the amount and the DA's mood, it would cost a good deal more.

"The lawyer *bribed the DA*?"

"No," Nightingale said, uncoiling a hose and watering thick shrubs. "Not even San Francisco is *that* corrupt. In their case, the cops went in without a warrant. Then they told the lawyer they could fudge one, or the case could get dismissed on a bad bust—for a price. In my case, they busted me with fifty pounds and the cops turned in five."

"The police *stole* the rest?"

Nightingale smiled. "Happens all the time. Cops don't make much. When opportunity knocks—"

"But wasn't it your word against theirs?"

"They pulled me over in front of a bar. With all the commotion, a dozen guys poured out and saw my van filled with the stuff. What the cops turned in wouldn't have filled the front seat."

"So?"

"So, the fuckers got forty-five pounds. My partners came up with $30,000 and the cops swore I was a solo operator, not part of a 'criminal enterprise.' But the five pounds was real weight, so I had to do six months in county jail."

"Ouch. Still, that beat prison."

"No shit. Dave and Owen saved my ass—literally. So I forgave them, and after my release I got to know Doug and we became friends."

One night in 1970, Nightingale and his partners drove into the desolate badlands of Baja an hour south of Ensenada with a thousand pounds of Oaxacan in fifty-pound bales. They'd arranged a rendezvous with a pilot from Tucson. They'd just lit flares, marking a makeshift runway, when a half-dozen pairs of headlights illuminated the night like a prison break in an old movie. Bullets started flying. One of Nightingale's partners was cut down and the rest of them fled into darkness. Crouched behind boulders, they heard laughter and cheers, followed by the drone of a plane overhead. But they couldn't signal the pilot. The aircraft circled a few times, then flew off. At dawn, when they crept back to the runway, the truck, their guns, and a half ton of weed were gone, and buzzards were well into the body. They walked thirty miles back to Ensenada under searing sun with no water. By the time they crossed the border, they vowed never to buy in Mexico again.

"Who were they?" Ed asked.

Nightingale shrugged. "Who knows? It could have been anyone. Maybe our connection fucked us. Or someone put a gun to his head. Maybe the *Federales* tracked us. Or maybe the pilot sold us out. You never know. But I'll say this. When Mexicans are nice, they're the sweetest people anywhere. But when they're nasty, they'd just as soon slit your throat as shake your hand." He pulled the hose out to the sidewalk and watered a gingko sapling. Over the lake, a flock of birds darted this way and that, as coordinated as a drill team. "The guy they killed was my closest friend, and I saw him being *eaten*. We threw rocks at the birds and buried him, but there wasn't much left." Nightingale hung his head. "As long as I live, I'll never forget—chasing off the birds, seeing Charlie like that."

Once he made it back to San Francisco, Nightingale recounted the disaster to Owen, who confessed that his trio had just survived something similar, and if he never again set foot in Mexico, it would be too soon.

"Wait a minute," Ed interrupted. "Owen went to Mexico? I thought Doug was the smuggler."

"He was, at first. But after they got busted, Owen decided to get out of ounces and into pounds, which meant moving more weight, so sometimes two of them went, or all three."

"Why'd they get out of ounces?"

"For the same reasons I did: more money with less risk."

"*Less* risk? But if you're caught with more—"

"True, but you're much less likely to get caught."

Ed's face wrinkled in skepticism.

"To make a go of ounces," Nightingale explained, "you need dozens of customers. It's a volume operation. You try to hold it to people you know and trust but inevitably you wind up dealing to friends of friends, people you hardly know, and if one of them is stupid, or gets pissed off, or has problems with the law, he gives you up. But when you deal pounds, you have a smaller network and your customers, dealers themselves, have more to lose. You can still get fucked—I did. But dealing pounds, you're safer."

"What happened to them in Mexico?"

"I don't know. They didn't say and I didn't ask. But eventually, Doug let it slip that after their last run, Dave and Owen stopped bitching about his 'gun fetish.'"

"Gun fetish?"

"That's what Dave and Owen called it. They hated guns but Doug was deep into AKs and MAC-10s. Part of it came from trying to stay alive in the Mekong Delta and part of it was his outlaw fantasy. This happened years before that song, but the singer nailed it: 'You got to carry weapons 'cause you always carry cash.' Dave and Owen were squirrely about outfitting their van with a weapons cache, but Doug insisted. Evidently, it came in handy."

Around the time the two groups of dealers soured on Mexico, Nightingale explained, excellent Colombian became available. Freighters loaded with legitimate cargo—coffee, bananas, textiles—steamed out of Cartagena and offloaded in U.S. ports. But at night in international waters, they transacted their real business. Boats approached flashing light signals, and buyers traded suitcases of cash for fifty-pound bales.

An Army buddy of Doug's worked on a fishing boat out of Half Moon Bay. Business was bad and the captain was scrambling for income. The three partners signed on for what they called "midnight fishing" and invited Nightingale's group in.

"I didn't care for the arrangement," Nightingale explained. "The Colombians had a dozen guys with AKs manning elevated positions around the superstructure. What was to stop them from slaughtering us and taking our money?"

"They'd lose customers."

"True, but at that level, customers aren't the issue. We were motoring out there with tons of cash."

"So what'd you do?"

"We all chipped in and bought the fishing captain a couple of World War II surplus M3 anti-tank cannons. We modified them so they could be mounted on the bow. Those puppies gave the Colombians something to think about. Any funny business and we could blow them straight to hell."

"Deterrence."

"In spades."

Nightingale and Doug, the swashbuckling pirates, were in their element—the high seas, secret rendezvous, light signals, M3s, AKs, and Uzis. Meanwhile, Dave and Owen couldn't stand all the testosterone, but what could they do? They needed product, and the Colombians arrived like clockwork with as much as anyone wanted.

"My group started with three hundred pounds a month and worked up to five," Nightingale said. "But Owen never went for more than one or two bales. I teased him that he'd never get rich. 'Maybe not,' he always said, 'but I won't go to prison either.'"

One night, Nightingale and company drove their big truck away from the dock and got stopped by agents of the new Drug Enforcement Agency. This time, the lawyer couldn't get them off. Nightingale was sentenced to fifteen years.

"You said that if you'd listened to Owen, you might have spent less time in prison. How?"

Nightingale dragged the hose back to the bib, recoiled it, and turned the water off. "What do you know about money laundering?" Then he pulled glass cleaner out of the shed and led Ed back to the lobby, where he went to work on the windows.

"Not much. Just that it hides illegal income."

"Yes. And if you do it right, the IRS can't pop you."

"You lost me."

"Get busted for weed by local or state police, and you're looking at state charges for possession and sale. But if you're moving enough weight to attract the feds, in addition to the criminal charges, the IRS comes after you for unreported income and tax evasion. The feds are hard to buy off. Owen set up a front business—I forget the name—but they imported houseplants."

"Really? They imported houseplants while importing pot?"

"Yes," he smiled, "at the same time, in the same truck. Nifty, huh?"

Ed's eyes widened.

"They bought an old UPS van and built secret compartments into the floor and walls. They filled the hidden compartments with weed and the rest of the truck with tropical plants. They got an agricultural import license from the USDA. At the border, they'd flash their documents, and if anyone got testy, they'd open the back and show a jungle of greenery and a list of plant stores around the Bay Area. They sailed right through."

"Amazing."

"It gets better. They funneled their drug money through the houseplant business. They reported it, paid themselves salaries, took out withholding, and paid their taxes like any working stiff. If they got busted, the IRS couldn't touch them the way they clobbered me."

"So you didn't have a front."

"Correct. Owen told me I was crazy, but my group? We were outlaws. We didn't need—" he affected a Mexican accent, "no *steenkeeng front.*

So, when we took our big fall, they nailed us for a couple million in unreported income and I peeled potatoes in Leavenworth for the better part of a decade."

"And after you got out, you rented a place here."

"That's right. I cooled my heels for a couple years selling cars for an old customer who had a dealership. I had some money stashed that the IRS didn't find. I got married and eventually bought this building and two others up the hill."

"Did you ever talk with Doug about Jackie?"

"Not that I recall. I didn't know they were an item. When did she get…?"

"September '68."

"Yeah, well, that was after my falling-out with Dave and Owen. I didn't get friendly with Doug until we started buying Colombian, around 1970. I don't recall him mentioning her."

"Or her son?"

"Right."

"I'm curious. If you had it to do over again, would you have been a dope dealer?"

Nightingale stopped rubbing glass and gazed past the mailboxes to a circle of potted ferns surrounding a fountain that featured a nymph pouring water from a pitcher. "I'd like to say no, but the answer is probably yes. I married a wonderful woman and feel very lucky. I saw my kids born and graduate college, which was incredible. But there's nothing like climbing a gangway armed to the teeth and opening duffels containing half a million in cash. On the other hand, I have no regrets about getting out of dealing. After prison, I wasn't about to risk going back. But if I ran my business the way Owen ran his, who knows? Maybe I'd still be in the game."

25

After dinner, Ed and Julie cleared the table and ran the dishwasher. Sonya trudged upstairs to do homework while Jake used his wooden spoon to play drums on a saucepan on the pantry floor.

Ed filled the kettle and asked Julie if she wanted a cup of tea. She declined and refilled her wine glass, paging through the *Foghorn*.

"You know what?" she said. "The *Horn* sucks. Who *are* these people? Wendell Grant? Greta Hernandez? Must be kids right out of J School."

"Try high school."

The stairs creaked and Sonya appeared, triumphantly waving a piece of paper. "Marijuana has the lowest addiction. See?"

She laid the page in front of Ed. In one enormous run-on sentence, she'd listed common recreational drugs and the proportion of users who became emotionally dependent or physically addicted. Tobacco was highest, marijuana lowest.

Ed smiled at his budding reporter. "Where'd you get this?"

"The Internet."

Ed sighed and Sonya noticed. "But Daddy, from that place you like."

"Where?"

"NewYorkTimes.com."

"Did you print the article?"

"Yes!"

"Show me."

Sonya scampered upstairs and bounced back with several disorganized pages topped by an Old English logo.

"See? You said this is good."

"It used to be," Ed deadpanned, glancing at Julie, whose expression said *lighten up*. "Good work, honey, good source, too. Let me see." He compared Sonya's figures with the newspaper's and they matched. "Using the *New York Times* is fine, and you got the numbers right. But the reporter who wrote the article—where did *she* get *her* figures?"

Sonya shrugged. "How should I know?"

"It's in there. Read it."

Sonya peered at the article.

"The National Academy of Sciences?"

"Right," Ed said. "So the National Academy report is the original source, the *primary* source. See the title?" He pointed to a line in the *Times* print-out. "Get that."

Sonya frowned. "Do I *have to*?"

"Do you want to convince the superintendent to change DAP? Or not?"

"Yes, but—"

"Then you need the most convincing evidence."

"But—"

"The *Times* is good, but the primary source is better."

"But—"

"It'll take you ten minutes."

"But—"

Julie chimed in. "What's the big deal? Just Google them, search the report, and print it out."

Sonya stamped her foot. "But that's *too hard!*"

"You agreed to do this report," Julie chided, hoisting a squirmy Jake and sitting him on her lap. "What do we say about anything worth doing?"

Sonya snorted. "That it's worth doing right." Then frustration got the better of her. She turned on her mother and snapped, "But alcohol is *really* dangerous and *you* drink it *all the time*."

Julie took a breath before replying softly, "I had one glass of wine with dinner."

"You had *two*—and now you're having *another*."

"Young lady," Julie retorted icily, "my wine consumption is not your concern. Did you finish your other homework?

"Yes."

"Then after you print out the report, you're free till bedtime."

Sonya retreated upstairs.

Ed tried to keep quiet, but couldn't. "From the mouths of babes...."

"Ed, don't start."

"Everything we do, she's watching, learning—"

"Enough!" Julie set Jake on her hip and headed up the stairs to bathe him, leaving her wine glass on the table.

Ed followed her and found Sonya huddled over the printer in Julie's office. "Here it is." With a flourish, she presented the National Academy report.

"Excellent. Now staple it together so you can clip it to your report."

Sonya scampered off. Ed crumpled the sheets of paper she'd left behind and faced the wastebasket across the room. Kobe Bryant stepped back behind the arc, set himself, and flicked his wrist. Swish, three points. His second shot hit the rim and bounced in. Six. The third hit the wall and missed. *Damn.*

Ed crossed the room, scooped up the errant paper ball, and flipped it into the can, but in the process, he tripped over his feet and kicked the wastebasket, toppling it. He was about to shovel the spilled contents back in when he noticed something under the trash. An empty bottle of Sauvignon Blanc.

26

"Interesting about the widow," the detective said when he finally called back, "but I like the professor better. His prison time."

"Why not Olivia?" Ed asked. "When Kirsch got shot, do you know where she was?"

Ramirez did not immediately reply. Ed could hear him breathing and considering how much to tell this civilian, weighing professional reticence against Ed's juicy tips. "As a matter of fact, she left work early and went home with a migraine."

"Home alone? Or can someone vouch for her?"

"She was alone."

"So she could have—"

"Maybe…" Then Ed heard the wheels spin as Ramirez turned a corner. "But she has a long history of migraines. And consider the weapon. Spousal killings account for almost half of all homicides, so I've seen plenty. Every now and then, a husband monkeys with the wife's brakes, or a wife convinces her boyfriend to kill the bastard. But when spouses kill each other, ninety-nine times out of a hundred they do it face to face: a stabbing in the kitchen, a shooting in the bedroom, or a wrench to the head in the garage. A rifle across Golden Gate Park doesn't fit the MO."

"There's always a first time," Ed said.

"Sure, anything's possible," the detective replied. "But with spousal homicide, you *always* see domestic violence beforehand. Pulling the trigger is the last link in a long chain. The husband's beating the wife.

She calls the cops a few times, then eventually she tells the guy, 'You ever do that again, I'll kill you.' He does, and then she does. When anyone married gets it, we always run a check. On the Kirsches, no police reports, no separations, no restraining orders—nothing.

"And did you see her at the funeral? Those didn't look like crocodile tears to me. She could hardly stand up without help. Either she deserves an Academy Award or she was devastated. The spousal killers I've seen have been cooler cucumbers.

"I appreciate the tip, I really do, and if you come across anything else, I'm all ears. But one trophy fifty years ago? No. I like Miller. He has a big fat motive and, with his prison connections, quite possibly the means."

27

The sun was dropping below Twin Peaks and fog spilled over the ridge like foam down the side of a beer glass. The street South of Market was alive with traffic, pedestrians, and a PG&E cherry-picker with a guy up in the basket, fiddling with a utility pole. Somewhere a sound system blared rap.

The thick blond man looked around fifty, but Ed knew he was sixty-three. He wore jeans, a crisp dress shirt, and cowboy boots, and had a diamond stud in one ear. They stood under the awning of Chester's Crossroads Lounge, named after Chester Burnett, the Chicago bluesman better known as Howlin' Wolf. The marquee announced: Tonight Only! 3rd Annual All-Star Benefit for Marriage Equality. The club's founder and owner, Ken Kelly, barked Spanish at a young man pushing a stretch hand truck loaded with beer barrels. He maneuvered it into the freight elevator and rode down to the basement.

"That's how I make my living, right there," Kelly said, sweeping an arm toward the silver barrels. "Beer. The bands get the door. I get the food and booze. I break even on the food. The money's in the booze, and most of that's beer."

The acne-scarred delivery man presented a statement on a clip-board. He wore a 49ers cap and a Giants jacket over a Sharks T-shirt. Kelly signed and took the pink copy. *"Gracias, Julio."*

A chilly gust blew fallen leaves, gum wrappers, and a page of tattered newsprint around Ed's ankles. Kicking the broadsheet away, he noticed the headline of his latest column.

"You wouldn't believe how much beer this place goes through," Kelly continued. "Surprises even *me*."

Inside by the stage, they sat at a small circular table beneath huge photos of Robert Johnson, Muddy Waters, Elmore James, and the club's namesake. Ed produced his recorder and pressed the button.

Kelly grew up in Detroit and attended the University of Michigan for two years, until a tab of acid and a dog-eared copy of the *Oracle* delivered a message from God that he should move to San Francisco. Hitting town in '66, he fell in with Chet Helms and The Family Dog. When they started producing dances, Kelly managed the box office, first at the Avalon Ballroom then at Longshoremen's Hall, which was larger and drew bigger crowds. But the high domed ceiling made the place feel cavernous and cold. What could warm it up? Helms, Kelly, and a few others were discussing possibilities when the lighting guy showed up in a purple haze. No problem, he exclaimed with wide-eyed passion. We paint Jimi Hendrix licks on the ceiling using colored lights. *Huh?* His friends were dubious but intrigued. What he came up with was strange but mesmerizing, and audiences cheered the rainbow kaleidoscope of bizarre images. Someone asked if the light show had a name. Kelly said, "Psychedelic."

"Wait. You coined the word?"

"No, no, it was floating around. I just used it."

"Whatever happened to The Family Dog?" Ed asked.

"Bill put us out of business," Kelly explained. "Bill Graham. Chet was a great guy—doesn't get enough credit. He knew Janis in Texas and convinced her to move to San Francisco and front Big Brother. But he wasn't much of a businessman. Bill's shows were better produced. They actually started *on time*—unheard of. And the bands made more money, so they gravitated to him. I did, too."

Kelly worked for Graham from '67 until the impresario died in 1991. He starting managing the box office at the Fillmore, then moved up to booking acts, producing shows at Wolfgang's, and eventually managing world tours for major bands and becoming a vice president with a piece of the company. After Graham's death, Kelly sold his interest and spent a year traveling. When he returned, he talked some rocker friends into investing and opened Chester's.

Ed thanked Kelly profusely, saying his reminiscences would make a fabulous vignette. "But if you don't mind," he said, "there's something else I'd like to discuss. Actually, some*one*."

Kelly gestured, sure.

"Owen Pendleton."

Kelly's eyebrows arched and he flashed a Mona Lisa smile. "How do you—"

"Up at the house after Dave Kirsch's funeral, I noticed the two of you talking. Seemed like you were old friends—more than friends."

Kelly leaned back in his chair. Ed wondered if he was stretching or trying to distance himself from this line of inquiry. "What about him?"

"Did you know him in '67, '68?"

"No," Kelly said, leaning forward, elbows on the table. "We met in the seventies."

"Did he ever mention a woman named Jackie Zarella, a hippie girl who had a little boy and got killed?"

Kelly looked at Ed, then at the long wooden bar where two women in Chester's T-shirts were setting up for the evening. He shook his head. "Not that I recall. Why?"

Ed explained about Simons funding the exhibit and searching for his birth name.

Kelly folded his hands and nodded at the recorder. "If we're going to talk about Owen, I have to ask you to turn it off."

Ed complied and promised absolute confidentiality, then asked why Kelly felt so concerned.

"Owen has a vindictive streak. You don't want to piss him off."

"I take it that once upon a time, you were lovers."

"Oh, yeah." He smiled and nodded. "I had some of the best sex of my life with Owen. Sometimes the guys who are the most uptight are the wildest in bed."

"How'd you meet, and when?"

"It was '73. I remember because I was managing Santana's world tour and our final show was at the Oakland Coliseum. I sent Dave two tickets. A thank-you."

"For what?"

"For weed. He'd been our dealer for years. I bought a pound or two every couple months to supply the musicians we managed."

"Really?" Ed's voice registered surprise, then he immediately regretted his naiveté.

"It wasn't in the contracts," Kelly explained, "but it was part of our deal. Wherever you have rockers, you have sex and drugs. The sex takes care of itself. Women throw themselves at musicians and you just have to make sure the dickheads use condoms. But drugs are a problem. See, musicians are flaky. They'll buy from anyone, including narcs, who love nothing better than busting rock stars. One arrest can destroy a tour, so we supplied them, which kept them out of trouble and got me all the weed I could smoke for free. So I knew Dave, but not Owen. He stayed in the background. I figured Dave would bring Olivia. But he showed up with this hunky guy who dressed real sharp. I was instantly smitten."

"You knew he was gay?"

"Well, it wasn't written on his forehead, but I've always had good gay-dar. The tight jeans, the perfect haircut, the bandana in his back pocket, the way he looked at me—it was as obvious as the sign on a men's room door."

"Did you know he was a dope dealer?"

"Not at first. Dave introduced him as a friend. Then we lit up and Dave started joking about their drip irrigation company. I like to think I'm not stupid."

"Drip irrigation? I thought they imported houseplants."

Kelly looked askance. "How do you...?"

Ed recapped his conversation with Paul Nightingale. Kelly said he'd heard Nightingale's name but never met him.

"So," Ed said, "the houseplant business?"

"That was their front when they ran it in from Mexico. But when they started growing in Mendocino, they folded that company and went into the drip business."

"To launder their dope income?" Ed asked, digging for details.

"That's right. It wasn't entirely a sham. They actually installed some systems. They did one for the Airplane, and other rockers. But most of the revenue came from pot."

"After they stopped going to Mexico, I thought they bought Colombian on the high seas."

"Oh, they did, but Owen never liked it, Dave either. But Doug *loved* it—you know Doug?"

"Sort of. Met him at the Kirsches."

"Doug was Captain Blood, the swashbuckling pirate swinging the big cutlass. You ever read any Rafael Sabatini? Growing up I loved those books—all those hunky guys in blousy shirts, and when they went after booty, all I could think of was *booty*. But Owen burned out on the Colombians, and so did Dave. Too many guns. Plus, Dave got horribly seasick, and the fishing captain kept raising his fee. So they started growing in Mendocino National Forest."

"Did Owen talk to you about dealing?"

"Not much."

"I'm surprised. You were lovers."

Kelly pointed at Ed's wedding ring and asked how closely he questioned his wife about her job. Ed realized he had a point—mostly he and Julie discussed the kids, bills, friends, and their Netflix queue.

"Owen had an aura of mystery and I'm a sucker for that. One thing he liked about me was that I was on the road a lot so I didn't pry. And it wasn't like he was getting his hands dirty. Doug did the growing. Dave did the selling. Owen was the bean counter. He managed the drip business, rode herd on Dave and Doug, and dealt with their salaries and taxes."

"Did they ever talk about why they stopped buying in Mexico?"

"No, just that things went bad down there."

"How long were you and Owen together?"

"Six years. Till '79. I remember because we had the Stones' tour, and there were problems in Chicago and I had to fly back and missed the opening of Owen's first salon. When I got back, he told me to move out."

"I thought he liked the fact that you traveled."

"When he was dealing, he did. But by then they'd stopped. They got out in '78."

"So just like that—you missed his opening and he kicked you out?" Ed never ceased to be amazed by the complexities of relationships.

Kelly smiled. "Well, that was the last straw, but the writing was on the wall."

Ed opened his mouth, but Kelly anticipated the question.

"By then, I was in my mid-thirties and I was a vice president of Bill Graham Presents. Owen likes his boys young and dependent, which wasn't me anymore. And our last year was rough. There was some major nastiness up north. Owen was a wreck but he wouldn't talk about it—not one word. It's one thing not to obsess about business when things are going well. But when you're hurting—and he was a mess—well, what's a lover for? Owen kept saying it didn't do either of us any good to make me an accessory. Well, thanks a lot. After six years, he still didn't trust me, which pissed me off. Meanwhile, without knowing what was eating him, I couldn't provide much support, which pissed him off."

"Major nastiness?"

Kelly waved a hand. "That's all I know. Whatever it was, it was bad. That's why they got out."

"So someone got robbed. Or maimed. Or killed."

Kelly shrugged. "Your guess is as good as mine. But they closed down pretty fast. Doug left the country. Dave had his book, and he toured colleges advocating legalization. Owen launched his salon empire."

Kelly's ice-blue eyes seemed sincere, but Ed wondered. You live with a guy for that long and then something life-changing happens, and he won't discuss it? Someone must have gotten killed. But who? And why?

"At the Kirsches', it looked like you hadn't seen him for quite a while."

Kelly smiled. "I've stayed friends with many of my exes, but not Owen."

There was sudden commotion at the door.

"Yo! Ken!" a voice called. "How's it hangin'?" Four men walked in, all wearing sunglasses, though it was dusk. The speaker was a tall, handsome man with dark, slicked-back hair. Ed knew the face but couldn't place it.

"Tommy!" Ken replied, rising to his feet and stepping toward them. "Welcome home. You want to eat now or after the check?"

"Both!" the man said, embracing Kelly warmly and patting his back. Kelly made the rounds, hugging all four.

Then Ed recognized the leader: Tommy Castro, San Francisco's blues-rock luminary, who'd jumped to the big time and didn't play much locally anymore.

Ed rose to leave and thanked his host. Shaking Kelly's hand, he asked briefly if he recalled Owen reminiscing about the period before the two of them met, the late sixties, his hippie days in the Haight.

"Oh sure, when he got high, he'd talk about the Be-In and hanging out with Janis and the Dead, that whole scene."

"I'd love to interview him, but he won't talk to me. Any chance you could…?"

"No way," Kelly said, smiling while shaking his head. "Owen's reclusive. He'd never want to be in any exhibit. You'll talk to Elvis before you talk to him."

28

"He's stealing from me, the prick. Twenty-four years of marriage and now *this*."

Ed didn't recognize the woman's voice as he climbed the stairs from the garage after dropping Sonya at soccer practice. Stepping into the dining room, he saw Julie at the table with Cindy Miller. Each held a glass of red wine, and from the look of the bottle, it was not their first.

A cardboard box sat on the table, its sides decorated with grape clusters and a glass filled with bubbly golden liquid. The box was open and Ed saw a dozen bottles, their caps held in place by wire keepers.

"What's with the champagne?"

Cindy stared grimly into space.

"Dave bought ten cases for the victory party," Julie explained. "Cindy's been dividing them among the staff."

"I told him it was too soon," Cindy said, her voice cracking, but not breaking. "Bad luck, counting chickens."

"Would you put it in the pantry?" Julie asked.

Ed hoisted the box and stashed it. *Just what we need,* he thought, *more alcohol.*

"Ed," Julie called. "Put one in the fridge, would you?"

"Why?" They rarely drank champagne.

"So we can celebrate when one of us gets a job with benefits."

Don't hold your breath. It was a waste of refrigerator space, but with company present, Ed wasn't about to argue. Returning to the dining room, he asked, "So Al's stealing from you?"

"Yes," Cindy hissed, her expression somewhere between a frown and a scowl, "the prick, $20,000. See for yourself." She pushed two sheets of paper across the table, then downed a slug of wine.

Ed had no interest in hearing a woman in mid-divorce railing about her thieving ex—and, no doubt, men in general. But to be polite, he glanced at the statements, murmuring sympathy.

Cindy's lawyer had requested all the financials. Al's attorney had produced a blizzard of paper, including documents relating to a dozen recent transactions. Al had shifted funds, closed accounts, and opened new ones, ostensibly to keep their division of assets as civil as possible. But buried deep in the paper avalanche were withdrawals totaling $20,000.

On each page, a transaction was highlighted in yellow: two withdrawals, $10,000 apiece. Cindy was right. Al was a prick. But divorce rarely brought out the best in anyone.

Ed was about to push the sheets back across the table when he noticed the dates of the withdrawals. The first took place two weeks before Dave was killed, the second, the day after.

Cindy had insisted there was no way Al could have killed Dave, that he was not a violent man. But some people kept their hands clean by contracting the dirty work.

29

Owen's e-mail said he didn't recall Gene Simons's birth name, but visions of the billionaire's jewel-encrusted bonus danced before Ed's eyes like the pumpkin transformed into Cinderella's coach, and he had a hard time letting it go. Kelly said his ex had enjoyed reminiscing about the Be-In, where Jackie and Doug were photographed with their arms around each other. Owen must have known her. Even if he didn't remember the boy's name, there was a real possibility that he'd recall details that might aid Ed in his quest. From what Nightingale and Kelly had said—and from the one e-mail he'd sent Ed—Owen was at best peculiar, and at worst, an ass. But during his years as a reporter, Ed had wheedled information from plenty of tough nuts who had no incentive to crack. He needed to pry Owen from his shell and find out what he knew—and now he had some leverage.

Ed clicked into SFGovernment.gov and meandered until he found the business license archive. In the search field, he typed Owen Pendleton. The name popped right up as the owner of A Cut Above, with a half-dozen locations around the city. The license listed the little empire's principal business address as A Cut Above: Castro, which turned out to be located across the street from the building that once housed Harvey Milk's camera shop.

Ed made an appointment and had his hair cut by a buffed young man in tight jeans and a tighter T-shirt that advertised his biceps and nipples, one of which was pierced. Like most stylists, Roger was friendly and talkative. It didn't take long for Ed to learn that the owner often stopped by in the late afternoon.

At a café that provided a view of the salon's door, Ed sipped tea as the warm afternoon turned cold and gusty with thick fog blowing over Twin Peaks. At five-fifteen, the man with salt-and-pepper Beatles hair opened the salon door. Ed gave him a couple minutes, then followed.

The young receptionist's T-shirt said Lock Up Your Sons. He gave no sign of remembering Ed from earlier. "May I help you?"

"I'm here to see Owen."

"He's in back," he said, reaching for the handset. "Your name?"

"No, please." Ed flashed his most ingratiating smile. "We're old friends. I'm visiting from New York. I want to surprise him."

The receptionist smiled and inclined his head toward a bead curtain behind the last station.

Ed passed a bathroom and a kitchen and knocked on a door marked Private.

"Who is it?"

He tried the knob. It turned and he stepped inside. Pendleton sat at a small desk and looked up from a laptop, a half-eaten brownie beside it. "I'm the journalist who e-mailed you about Jackie Zarella," Ed told him straight.

Owen regarded Ed the way Jews viewed Inquisitors. "I enjoy your column," he growled, "but as I said, I have nothing to say about Jackie. Or anything else. Now if you'll excuse me—"

Ed didn't budge. "Why not? I *know* you knew Jackie. Why won't you tell me what you remember? Her son is in pain—"

Owen waved a hand dismissively. "Everyone's in pain. Jackie was a stupid cunt who came and went in the blink of an eye. And when she went, I was *relieved*."

"Stupid? How so? And why relieved?" Ed hastened to add, "Everything you say is totally confidential. You have my word."

Pendleton's snort transcended contempt. "Your *word*? That's supposed to impress me? I've said all I'm going to say. Please close the door on your way out." He spun his chair and opened a file cabinet.

Ed's feet remained glued to the floor. "Look," he said in the tone reserved for his kids' scraped knees, "I don't care what you did back then. I'm not going to write about your houseplant business or the Colombian freighters—"

Owen whirled around, his face suddenly flushed. "How do you—"

"Or why you stopped buying in Mexico, or the nastiness in Mendocino—"

"You son of a bitch." Owen's eyes narrowed to slits.

"I totally respect your privacy. I'm only interested in Jackie. Just Jackie. Please."

Pendleton went from a simmer to a boil in seconds, his words exploding like firecrackers. "Get out!" And his eyes—Ed had seen such eyes before, but where? Then he remembered: in the reptile house at the zoo. Ed had held Jake in his arms as an alligator sized up the boy for dinner.

"Come on." Ed pleaded. "Can't we—"

"No. We can't. Now get out or I call the police."

30

For the project, Ed created a map of Haight Street and one by one located the hippie businesses. The first was the Psychedelic Shop near the corner of Haight and Ashbury, opened in January 1966 by Ron and Jay Thelin, two brothers who grew up in the neighborhood, whose father had managed the Woolworth's once located across the street.

The Thelins were spiritual seekers who embraced meditation and Asian religions along with rock music and Timothy Leary's vision of an acid nirvana. But the items associated with their diverse interests—books, incense, posters, candles, mandalas, Indian fabrics, and marijuana paraphernalia—were difficult to obtain and scattered among a dozen stores, if they were available at all. The Thelins decided to carry everything under one roof—a hippie general store. The shop quickly became an informal community center and a ticket outlet for Family Dog dances. When the theater seats were torn out of the Haight Theater to make way for the Straight dance hall, several found their way to the Psychedelic Shop's front window, where patrons could relax while watching the passing scene.

But as kids flooded the neighborhood, tensions flared with police. The Thelins tried to be a calming influence. They turned part of their shop into a meditation room and placed a sign in the window urging young people to "Take a Cop to Dinner."

The gesture became ironic when the SFPD raided the store, charging the brothers with peddling obscene material, specifically a collection of poems, *The Love Book*. The brothers were arrested along with *Oracle* publisher Allen Cohen, who happened to be working the register that day. *The Love Book* had sold only a few dozen copies, but the raid brought publicity and the brothers eventually sold thousands.

The Psychedelic Shop was in business for less than two years, closing in October of 1967. Ed wondered what had taken its place. He clicked to Google Street View, but felt restless and cooped up in the basement. It was a while before he had to pick up the kids. On a whim, he jumped in the car and drove over the hill to the Haight. Stopped at a light, he glanced to his right and saw a rare vision: a beautifully restored baby blue Thunderbird, the one with the porthole windows—a '56? He'd lusted after that car as a boy. A black man wearing a beret sat behind the wheel.

Ed lowered his window. "Great car!"

The man smiled and waved.

The Psychedelic Shop was now a pizza place. Returning to the car, Ed thoughts wandered to the word "psychedelic." Who had coined it? The Thelins? The derivation might make a nice poster at the exhibit. He could run home and click into the public library—its databases included the *Oxford English Dictionary* online—but that meant returning to his dungeon. The afternoon fog was rolling through the Haight, conferring a ghostly beauty on its century-old buildings. Gusts of wind made the trees in the Panhandle nod, as if to say yes, do it, so he did. He headed down to Civic Center to the Main Branch and its print edition of the *OED*.

It turned out that "psychedelic" was coined a decade earlier than Ed had guessed, in 1957, by Humphry Osmond, an English psychiatrist who used LSD in psychotherapy. Interested in a term for the visions produced by hallucinogenic drugs, he raised the issue with an acquaintance, Aldous Huxley, who'd taken acid and written a book about it, *The Doors of Perception*. Huxley had suggested "phanerothyme," from the Greek for "spirit revealed." He wrote Osmond a little ditty: "To make this mundane world sublime, take half a gram of phanerothyme." Osmond liked "spirit revealed" but found Huxley's term clunky. He played with Greek synonyms and replied with another couplet: "To fathom Hell or soar angelic, take a pinch of psychedelic."

Crossing Civic Center Plaza to his car, Ed felt pleased. The exhibit was shaping up nicely. Pulling into traffic, he glanced in the rearview and did a double-take. Right behind him was a classic baby blue T-bird. *Could there be two in San Francisco?*

He turned a corner and craned his neck. It had porthole windows. *Am I seeing things?* The black driver waved. *Am I smoking too much weed?* Ed's heart raced. *Is he tailing me? But why would anyone…?* At the next light, Ed looked around. No Thunderbird. *Maybe I should cut down.*

Ed dismissed the incident as a coincidence and drove into the Mission to pick up Sonya at aftercare and Jake at daycare. As he buckled his boy into the child seat, an ambulance screamed past and Ed glanced up at the blur of flashing lights. Parked across the street was a blue Bird with porthole windows and a black man in a beret smiling at him.

Ed didn't return the smile. He suddenly felt a stabbing pain in his gut.

31

Ed was slogging through a tome about the sixties counterculture when the daycare center called to say that Jake had a fever and could someone please pick him up, right now?

It was a delightful Mission afternoon, warm and sunny. Jake didn't seem ill and wasn't fussy, so Ed popped him into the stroller and wheeled him to Juri Commons, the pencil-thin park that ran on a cockeyed diagonal through a residential block near their home. It was the last remnant of the railroad right-of-way that, before the earthquake of 1906, had connected San Francisco and San Jose.

Ed had just strapped Jake into the baby swing when Ramirez returned his call.

"Very interesting about the timing of Al Miller's big withdrawals," he said. "Either he's stealing from his ex or he paid someone to do Kirsch."

The detective sounded surprisingly chummy. "So what do you think?" Ed asked.

"By themselves, the withdrawals don't establish probable cause, so I can't get a warrant. I could yank his chain, but why waste the time? If it's murder for hire, we'll find out soon enough."

"How?"

"Contract killers have a way of turning around and blackmailing their employers. When the shooter tells the professor, 'Pay up or I'll do you like I did Kirsch,' it's a convincing threat. So Miller pays for a while, then the killer ups his demands, and eventually Miller freaks or does something stupid, and I pop him. See, I can make a hundred mistakes, but bad guys only get one. Have you heard about any other big withdrawals?"

"No. You'll have to talk to Cindy."

Ed heard only silence, then Ramirez said, "I'm looking at fourteen open cases and I haven't had a full weekend in a month. For now, I'll let her lawyer scream about the money. If he hired a killer, the vise will close on his nuts, and I'll nail him."

32

Over the phone, the woman sounded vaguely African-American, so Ed wasn't surprised when she said she'd meet him in East Oakland. But he was startled to discover that Carol Covington, formerly of the *Oracle*, the *Barb,* and the Bay Area Digital Archive of the Sixties and Seventies, had directed him to the Union Baptist Church.

It was a modest, well-maintained wood edifice with a stout steeple topped by a cross, nestled in a quiet neighborhood of small well-kept homes fronted by postage-stamp lawns. As Covington directed, Ed entered through the side door and heard singing, a spirited call-and-response gospel number accompanied by a piano, a tambourine, and clapping.

Are you ready for a miracle?
Ready as I can be!
Are you ready for a miracle?
Spirit set you free!
Are you ready?
Ready!
Are you ready?
Ready!
Are you ready?
Yes, I'm ready!
Are you ready, are you ready for a miracle?

The rejoicing drew Ed to a multipurpose room where two dozen casually dressed choir members, teens to seniors, stood side by side on risers before a large well-dressed woman with a short Afro and gold hoop earrings. She conducted with her back to him.

Ed leaned against the doorframe as the choir took him in. White faces were apparently a rarity in this neighborhood.

"Better," the director said at the song's conclusion, "but altos, pick it up. The sopranos are drowning you out. And Tawana, how about a *smile*, girl? We're making a *joyful* noise." She glanced at her watch. "All right, one last time, with *spirit*." She nodded to the pianist.

Five minutes later, as the choir donned coats and filed out, the leader noticed Ed, and approached him with a radiant smile, extending a hand that engulfed his in soft warmth. "Mr. Rosenberg? I'm Carol Covington. Hope you haven't been waiting long."

"Not long enough. I love gospel."

"That last one is new. We're premiering it Sunday. It's still a little ragged, but Lord willing, we'll pull it off. Would you like some coffee?"

They sat on folding chairs by a children's mural of the Last Supper, only all the participants were black, including Jesus, who sported wild dreadlocks. Ed pulled out his recorder.

"I confess," Covington said in a rich singsong voice, "I was surprised to receive your e-mail. The Archive doesn't get much traffic." Ed gushed praise, calling it a historian's dream come true and a real boon to the museum exhibit.

Covington blushed. "Allen did most of it. I just helped out at the end when he got sick. It's a shame he didn't live to see it launch."

"Allen Cohen? Founder of the *Oracle*?"

"That's right. I worked on the first few issues, then moved to the *Barb*, but we stayed friends."

"What'd you do at the *Oracle*?"

"A little of everything. They called me an editor, but I spent most of my time on the phone nagging contributors to produce the copy they'd promised. Timothy Leary and Allen Ginsberg didn't understand the word 'deadline.'"

"Forgive me, but I didn't know there were African-American hippies."

She laughed and clapped her hands, and Ed felt powerfully drawn by her magnetism. "Hey, what about Jimi Hendrix, Sly Stone, and

Richie Havens?" She sipped her coffee. "I wasn't really a hippie. And you're right—I was the only black person on the *Oracle.*"

"How'd that happen?"

She shrugged. "Life. I grew up about a mile from here, graduated from Tech, and went to SF State. In high school, I knew this white boy, Tommy. We were friendly, but nothing more. Tommy also wound up at State, and we got involved. This was '65. Not many interracial couples back then. It felt weird, but we were active in the civil rights movement and San Francisco was pretty tolerant. But when we went to Mississippi, we were very careful. No public affection of any kind."

"What'd you do there? Black voter registration?"

"Yes, Hattiesburg, summer of '66. When we got back, Tommy became a radical with a rock band and they got popular in the Haight-Ashbury, so we moved there. I'd worked on the student paper and then I saw a flyer about the *Oracle.* Next thing you know, I'm an editor."

"Paid or volunteer?"

She laughed. "Oh, volunteer. No one got paid. To make the rent, I was a teacher's aide. Tommy split his time between construction and MBT."

Ed inhaled sharply. "Magic Bullet Theory? Your boyfriend was Tommy Smith?"

Covington's smile illuminated the whole room. "You know Tommy?"

"No, but he wrote that song, 'Candy Man,' about Dave Kirsch—at least, that's what people say. Was it about Dave?"

"Yes, it was." Covington's face fell. "Terrible about Dave, just awful. He was such a sweet man." She placed a hand over her heart. "I hadn't seen him in forty years, but when I heard the news, the memories came flooding back—the good times and that horrible night. I cried like a baby who lost its momma."

"What horrible night?"

"The night Tommy broke Dave's nose."

"What?" Ed couldn't believe his ears. "What happened?"

"The band was headlining at Longshoremen's Hall. Tommy saw Dave down front dancing with his wife—Olivia, Livvy. He jumped down and—" She mimed the punch.

"But *why?* What'd Dave do?"

"Nothing. And everything. Dave was a symbol."

"Of what?"

"Hip capitalism."

"You lost me."

Covington sighed. Her fingertips touched, forming a ball in front of her. "What do you know about the Diggers?"

Ed shrugged. "Just what I've read. They were a spinoff of the Mime Troupe, did political street theater in the Haight. Didn't they organize the Death of Hippie parade? Then they became the hippie Salvation Army with their Free Store and the forerunner of the Free Clinic."

"That's right." Covington smiled and nodded. "But back in the day, if you'd compared the Diggers to the Salvation Army, Tommy might have punched *you*. The Salvation Army is Christian. Now, I have nothing against Christianity—" She laughed and held her palms up, encompassing the church and the whole world. "But the Diggers were *utopians*. The name came from a group in medieval England, farmers who shared everything, no private property. The Diggers in the Haight wanted the same. They said America was becoming…what did they call it? Something about scarcity…a post-scarcity society." She smiled the way a teacher does for a good student. "They said we were so rich that only a small minority had to work, and they could support everyone. Everything could be free."

"Very utopian—and naïve."

"In hindsight, yes, but back then, we were pretty serious, especially Emmett."

"Emmett Grogan, the leader?"

"That's right. Officially, the Diggers had no leaders, but Emmett was the man."

"So…about Tommy punching Dave."

"Tommy and I lived a couple blocks from Dave and Livvy, so we knew them from around the neighborhood. Tommy and I also got involved with the Diggers, working in the Free Store and the soup kitchen. MBT became the Diggers's band and the boys played a lot of benefits. Dave dealt reefer to lots of bands and we bought from him, and Dave and his people gave money to the Store.

"But in the summer of '67, kids poured into the Haight and we were swamped. The merchants and dealers made donations, but we needed a lot more. Emmett asked and people gave, but it was never enough." Covington shook her head and scanned the room. "It all feels so far away now, another world, but back then, it was *huge…*"

"What was?"

"Everything!" She shook her head and slipped into the past. "The war was escalating. Black folks were rebelling. Detroit burned. The Panthers were picking up the gun. And the Diggers were completely overwhelmed. Tommy and I were young, idealistic—and, yes, naïve. We thought, wait a minute. We're working overtime running this soup kitchen, giving everything away free, and the merchants and dealers, they're making all this money. That's when Emmett started denouncing hip capitalists, and all of a sudden, Dave stopped being cool. It split the *Oracle.*"

"Hippies versus radicals."

She smiled. "We called ourselves 'revolutionaries,' but yes, the hippies wanted to smoke grass, eat granola, and dance to the Dead. We wanted to bring the war home."

"So you left and joined the *Barb.*"

"Yes, a dozen of us."

"And that was when Tommy broke Dave's nose."

Covington nodded and sighed. "Yes, Terrible Tommy." She saw the question in Ed's eyes. "There were two Tommys. When he was sober, he was the most loving man on Earth. But when he drank, he turned into Terrible Tommy. And he drank a lot. In his twisted mind, he saw Dave as a symbol of what the Diggers were denouncing. Not that Dave was a bad guy, he wasn't, but Tommy was drinking so much he didn't know what day it was.

"So that night, MBT was headlining. Tommy was so drunk and stoned and tripped out he could hardly stand, let alone sing and play. When he attacked Dave, for me, that was the last straw. That's what broke us up—that and Black Power, but mostly his drinking. I could have lived with a white guy, but not a white guy who was a violent drunk. My stepfather was a nasty drunk and no way in hell was I putting up with that. So I moved back to Oakland and started teaching."

"What about the band's name? Didn't it refer to the Kennedy assassination?"

"Yes. Anyone with half a brain knew the Warren Commission report was a lie." The Warren Commission had concluded that a single bullet had killed President Kennedy and caused the wounds suffered by Texas Governor John Connally. But critics pointed out that for this to be true, the bullet would have had to follow an impossible trajectory—a magic bullet.

"So Tommy was a conspiracy buff?"

"Not really. But MBT got together in '66, just a few years after the assassination. The magic bullet theory was on people's minds. It raised questions about the government's credibility, and we wanted to use those doubts to turn people against the war."

"How big of a hit was 'Candy Man'?"

"Not very. Tommy never quit his day job. But it got some radio play. First time we heard it on KMPX, we went *crazy*. We had this big ol' flat on Haight Street above the I/Thou coffee shop. I remember Tommy cranked up the volume and threw open the windows, and shouted at people below, 'Hey, that's my song!'"

"What'd you teach?"

"Reading. At the Panther Free School."

"The Black Panthers?"

Covington nodded. "After a while, I went back to State, got a credential, and—" She smiled and leaned back, spreading her arms wide. "Thirty-four years in Oakland Unified."

"Amazing. But the Panthers. How'd you feel about the militancy? The guns?"

Her eyes drilled into Ed's and her tone conjured a previous life. "People have a right to self-defense." Then her tone changed. "At our house, we didn't have guns. The police never bothered us. There are lots of ways to be political. I did what I could—and still do what I can." She took a sip of coffee. "Have you seen Livvy? How's she holding up?"

"Not well. I'd like to interview her, but she's in no shape."

Covington gazed out a window. "She worked at that café. Talked about opening a restaurant. She ever do that?"

"Not that I know of. But she has a store, Flower Child. On Union Street. Flowers, plants—and hydroponic gear."

Covington smiled. "I always liked her. I used to see her at the café… what *was* its name? Some flower…*Magnolia's.*"

Ed flashed on his list of lost hippie businesses. There was no Magnolia's. "Don't you mean Magnolia Thunderpussy?"

Covington started. "Excuse me, we're in *church*."

Ed raced to apologize, but Covington held up a hand. "Listen to me," she said softly. "I sound like one of the church ladies I swore I'd never become. Now here I am, conducting the choir, big hat and everything." Then she laughed. "But about Livvy. Magnolia's made these incredibly buttery croissants. Honey, let me tell you, this Oaktown girl never *heard* of croissants. But I tried one, and mm-mm, *heaven*. I knew Livvy through the *Oracle*. Dave wrote for us. I'd buy a croissant and she'd slip me a few extra for free. So sad about Dave. And now, with Tommy's relapse, I've been thinking a lot about old times."

"You're in touch with Tommy?"

"Oh, yes. He joined AA, cleaned up, and got a degree in computers. Works in Silicon Valley. He was sober for years. Then Rita—his wife—called to say he'd disappeared. We both knew what that meant."

"A bender."

"I was so worried he'd crash his car and die or kill someone. Rita was frantic. Then I heard about Dave and right after, Tommy got arrested for DUI. Now he's in rehab."

"Where? I'd love to talk to him."

"A place in Los Gatos."

Ed thanked Covington for her time and memories and was halfway across the street when he heard his name.

"Mr. Rosenberg!" Covington called from the door. "Have you heard about the Digger reunion? If you want people from the sixties, that's the place. There's a web site."

Later, as Ed approached the Bay Bridge, he scanned his mirrors to change lanes and froze. Behind him, in the next lane over, was a blue Thunderbird with porthole windows.

33

Crossing the bridge, Ed maneuvered so he was able to get a glimpse of the Thunderbird's plate. Back home, it took only a few clicks to determine that it was registered to one William Parker of Richmond.

Ed Googled the name, but it was so common that all he got was junk. He tried Facebook and found hundreds of William Parkers, with several dozen in California, but fortunately only four in Richmond. One of them had posed next to a classic car. He listed his occupation as private investigator.

Which meant he needed a license. It didn't take Ed long to find the state database. William Parker worked for Rubin and Wolper Investigations of Oakland. He'd been a PI eleven years, and for six of them, he'd had a carry permit for a nine-millimeter automatic.

Who'd hired him? Owen Pendleton was the obvious choice. Ed first noticed the tail shortly after Pendleton threw him out. Close personal surveillance didn't come cheap. Pendleton had presumably stashed a fair amount during his years as a dealer and now he owned a chain of hair salons. He could afford the luxury.

Which left only one question—why? What was Pendleton afraid of? There were the ugly incidents south of the border and in Mendocino, but Mexico was a million miles away, and whatever had occurred up north happened more than three decades ago. The statute of limitations had expired long ago, unless—

Ed's fingers flew across the keys. In California, there was no statute of limitations for murder. A compelling reason to keep your mouth shut and tell your lover you didn't want to make him an accessory.

Of course, Ed had no evidence that Owen's outlaw trio had been involved in anything like that, not even a rumor—just Ken Kelly's recollections that Owen had been very upset and wouldn't discuss it. But murder was the only crime that could come back and bite Pendleton now. Why else go to all the expense of a PI? Unless Pendleton was just being himself: paranoid and weird.

Assuming it was homicide, who'd gotten killed? Probably someone who'd threatened them or ripped them off. Soon after, Doug had left the country. Why? Wanderlust? They were out of business and he was no longer tied down by growing. He'd been to Vietnam. Maybe he wanted to see the world. Then again, maybe he'd killed someone and fled.

Ed thought back to the Kirsches'. Doug's presence had clearly surprised Owen. They hadn't seen each other in a long time. And Ed had sensed some wariness on both their parts, as if they still felt residual tensions.

But then, on his way out, he'd seen the two ex-partners in a circle, smiling, passing a pipe. Maybe no one got killed. Maybe they just lost one too many crops to thieves and decided to hang it up.

Or perhaps Owen put a tail on Ed not for who he'd been decades ago, but for who he was now. Ed noodled around the Internet. Pendleton might be a prize ass, but he was also surprisingly philanthropic. He served on the boards of several prominent nonprofits, among them the Stop AIDS Project and Boys and Girls Club. Maybe he feared that his beneficiaries might balk if they knew how he'd made his fortune.

Pendleton didn't talk to reporters, and Kelly had insisted that Ed turn off the recorder, saying he didn't want to risk irritating his ex. Evidently, the man had a vindictive streak. Stir it all together, and you could imagine a wealthy businessman with an image to protect hiring a PI to keep an eye on nosy vermin.

It would also explain why William Parker was being so obvious about his assignment—the distinctive car, the smiles and waves. Pendleton *wanted* Ed to know he was watching, which made the tail less menacing, but certainly not friendly. It carried an implied threat. Stop your snooping or else…what?

Ed leaned back in his chair and laced his fingers behind his neck. He raised his shoes to the desk and crossed his ankles, gazing out the window through the posts to the backyard. Splashes of red in a bush said some cherry tomatoes were ripe for salad. Sonya would be excited to pick them.

Should he be scared? Maybe, but on reflection, he wasn't. Parker seemed to be sending a message, not delivering a threat...at least, not yet. Should he tell Julie? No. Professionally, she was doing well—Julie Pearl Communications was thriving—but personally, she was as brittle as eggshells. She still got weepy at any mention of Dave, and Ed wasn't happy about her drinking. She'd undoubtedly blow this out of all proportion. For the time being, it seemed prudent to keep it to himself.

Ed saw Simons's golden carrot dangling just out of reach. He could almost taste it. Then he realized that the tail might actually be useful. He'd assured Pendleton that everything was off the record. Of course, talk was cheap and Owen had no reason to believe him. But if his very own PI reported that Ed had no ax to grind, Pendleton might change his tune, and maybe, just maybe, talk about Jackie.

Ed glanced at his watch. Julie and the kids would be home soon. In the kitchen, he pulled leftover soup out of the refrigerator and started making a salad, reminding himself to mention the tomatoes.

But *why*? Why have him followed? To protect his image? Perhaps. But while peeling a cucumber, Ed had another thought. After the funeral, he'd watched as Pendleton approached Olivia, arms open wide. He'd clearly expected to share a condolence hug with an old friend. But before stepping into his embrace, Olivia had hesitated. Was there bad blood between them? And if so, how bad? Bad enough for Livvy to think that Pendleton might have been involved in Dave's death? If that were true, the man had every reason to feel paranoid.

Ed wondered what Ramirez knew about Pendleton. He pulled out his phone.

34

The office of Rodney Wong Investigations was out Geary above a Korean barbecue and a Russian bakery. The reception area was decorated with posters of Hong Kong. Ed told the young Asian woman he had an appointment.

Ed had met Rodney years earlier through his *Foghorn* buddy, Tim Huang. They were old high school friends.

Rodney had come up in the world, literally, from the basement to the third floor. He was a fourth-generation San Franciscan whose grandparents had operated a sewing factory out of a cramped storefront in Chinatown, but made most of their money from the clandestine casino in the basement. Wong's parents turned the sweatshop into a video store, and replaced the casino with racks of Asian porn. When Netflix and online streaming killed DVD rentals, they sold the building and moved to Las Vegas.

Rodney had majored in computer science at UCLA but got bored developing software and signed on with a PI as a "computer researcher," a euphemism for hacker. A few years later, he went out on his own, setting up shop in the musty storage room beneath the family store adjacent to the porn. Now Wong had a five-room suite, a staff of six, and a view of the Kaiser Medical Center.

Wong greeted Ed with a warm handshake. Back in his basement days, he dressed in jeans and polo shirts. Now he wore a navy blazer, a starched shirt, and slacks. They caught up on each other's families and their mutual friend Tim's travails in the ghost town of the *Foghorn*.

Ed mentioned his close encounters with another private investigator.

"Rubin and Wolper, huh?" Wong said. "I know them. Good firm, quiet. They mostly nail Pacific Heights guys who cheat on their wives. But I don't know your William Parker."

"He's a pain, but he's not why I'm here."

Rodney opened a laptop and said, "I'm all ears."

"I hope you can find a guy. His name used to be Doug Connelly, but now it's Joe Borden, or Border or something, two syllables starting with a 'B.' He's white, in his mid-sixties. Served in Vietnam. Came back and started running Mexican weed. Lived in the Haight in the sixties with two other guys. One was Owen Pendleton, who now owns the Cut Above hair salons. The other was the late Dave Kirsch—"

Wong looked up from his screen. "The politician?"

"Yes. In the seventies, my guy moved north and grew pot in Mendocino National Forest. In '78, something bad happened and they quit the business."

"What?"

"No idea, but from what I can tell, it was nasty. He changed his name and disappeared for thirty years—until he made a surprise appearance at Kirsch's funeral. Neither Pendleton nor Kirsch's widow recognized him."

"How do you know they didn't recognize him?"

"Because I saw their faces when he told them who he was."

Ed placed a photo on Wong's desk, the *Oracle* portrait of Doug and Jackie at the Be-In. "This was taken in '67. He's bald now, with a white mustache. Oh, and he has prostate cancer. Looks pretty bad. Uses a cane. That's all I know."

"May I ask why you want to find him?"

Ed explained about the exhibit and the rich guy who wanted information about the girl in the photo and the name she'd given him. "She and Doug were an item before she got killed."

"Killed?"

"Shot to death in Golden Gate Park in '68."

"Did he kill her?"

"Possibly. It's unsolved. He knew guns and could have pulled the trigger, but as far as I know, our guy wasn't a suspect. The news reports are murky but they imply she was killed by her next boyfriend, some crazed speed freak, or by someone who wanted to send him a message."

"Any idea where your guy might be?"

"None. He could be anywhere."

"In the world?"

"I'm guessing this country. He heard about Dave and got to the funeral."

"What happened in '78?"

"No idea, except that it had to do with growing pot. I'm guessing someone stole their crop and Doug retaliated in some way."

"He killed someone?"

"Maybe. Whatever it was, it shook them up, because right after, they got out of growing and our boy left the country."

Wong picked up the photo, then pulled a magnifying glass out of his desk. "He's got a tattoo. Looks like lightning."

"Not anymore. It got altered. I only caught a glimpse, but now it looks like a pine tree."

Wong whirled around and slipped the photo into a copier. He hit a few keys and out came an enlargement. He pulled out a pencil, drew a mirror-image lightning bolt next to the tattoo, shaded it, and added a trunk. "Like this?"

"I think so. But I only saw it for a second."

"Presumably you asked Pendleton and Kirsch's widow where Joe Blow might be."

"They said they don't know, so I called you."

"All right. I'll look for him. What about their trouble in Mendocino? Want me to look into that?"

"Sure. Thanks."

"Mendocino National Forest, 1978, right?"

Ed nodded and Wong said he'd see what he could do.

35

Sonya was sick of her report, and teetered on the ragged edge of losing it. She was looking into marijuana's effects on driving and the research was more contradictory than an eleven-year-old could handle. Several studies agreed that when stoned, people drove slower and more cautiously but no less competently. Meanwhile, others showed that weed caused "significant driving impairment." Sonya was flummoxed. Ed advised her to summarize both sides and then declare which one she found more convincing.

"But *how*?" she whined.

In the kitchen, Ed and Julie sipped decaf while catching up and amusing Jake, who was becoming more talkative. Julie had been offered a lucrative gig managing logistics at the ballet's big-donor luncheon. But the same day, she was already committed to a save-the-coral-reefs event at the Academy of Sciences.

"So?" Ed asked.

"Zo?" Jake mimicked.

"I can juggle both jobs until the big day. Then the Ballet lunch is at noon and the Academy's at seven. I'm thinking I'll ask Joy to babysit the Academy until I get out of the Ballet."

Joy Gardner had been Julie's coworker at the *Horn*. She'd retired, but was happy to work on short-term projects that came her way.

"So Pearl Communications is hiring?"

"Hardly." Julie smiled. "But as my grandmother used to say, if we live and be well, we'll see. And you? What'd you do today?"

"I took the class at USF."

"Great!" Her smile broadened. "We're halfway there."

Ed had been dancing around teaching America in the Twentieth Century at the University of San Francisco. It was a lot of work for not much money. But faculty only had to teach two classes to qualify for subsidized health insurance.

"I also looked into the origin of the name the Grateful Dead."

"Really. I always wondered about that."

"A classic case of the drugged-out sixties. No one remembers."

There were, however, several stories. The most prominent had Jerry Garcia flipping through an encyclopedia and stumbling on the phrase, which referred to the medieval custom of the living contributing funds to bury indigents, who became the grateful dead. Another story had Garcia opening a dictionary and seeing the word "dead" directly across the spine from "grateful."

They heard feet stomping down the stairs. Sonya appeared at the kitchen door shaking a sheaf of papers. Her expression that said she wanted to throw them into a fire. "What's SDLP?" she demanded.

Ed and Julie looked at each other.

"Well, it's *important!* And they *don't explain it!*"

"Let me see," Ed said.

Sonya handed him one of the documents he'd helped her fish out of the Net, a National Highway Traffic Safety Administration report. It listed widely used medications—antidepressants, tranquilizers, muscle relaxants, antihistamines, alcohol, and marijuana—and for each presented something called "average SDLP," measured in centimeters. *Huh?* Ed flipped through the pages and discovered that it stood for "standard deviation of lateral position."

"It means weaving, honey, snaking back and forth instead of driving in a straight line like you're supposed to. The higher the SDLP, the more weaving, and the worse the driving. Now what does the report say?"

"Alcohol has the biggest SDLP. Marijuana is about the same as the rest."

"Correct." The chart showed that people who were completely drug free drove in almost a straight line. When legally drunk, they went all over the place. But on all the other drugs, including weed, they weaved a little, but not much. Marijuana was actually in the middle of the pack, causing a bit more weaving than antihistamines and cold formulas, but less than antidepressants and tranquilizers. "So, Sonya, what do you conclude?"

"It's not that dangerous?" Sonya's brow furrowed like a newly plowed field. "But that's *wrong*! Look at *this*." She held out a summary of a French study showing that recent cannabis use more than doubled the risk of motor vehicle accidents.

"Okay, cite that one, too. But it's just one study. How many studies show that marijuana is *not* a major cause of traffic accidents?"

"How should I know?"

"Count them."

Sonya shuffled pages. "Five." She looked from her mother to her father. "But I could *die!*"

"What are you talking about?" Ed asked.

"When you picked me up today, you were high."

"What?"

"I smelled it in the car."

"And how do you know what weed smells like?"

"Brittany's brother. I've smelled it in his room." Her friend's older brother was in college.

Across the kitchen, a throat cleared and one glance told Ed that Julie was enjoying this immensely.

"Sonya, this afternoon, I had an upset stomach, so I took a little pinch of weed as *medicine*. Just a pinch. Much less than they used in any of your studies. I was *not* stoned."

"Well, I don't think you should drive if you're high."

"Fair enough. Now go finish your report."

As Sonya scampered away, Julie said, "From the mouths of babes…."

36

Ed crested Pacific Heights and glimpsed a tongue of fog licking Alcatraz. He descended into Cow Hollow and parked by the Octagon House, the odd eight-sided museum open just three days a month. He'd written about it, the sole survivor of five octagonal mansions built during the 1860s in the belief that eight-sided homes enhanced virility. In the 1950s, when the house was turned into a museum of colonial Americana, a letter from 1861 was discovered sealed in a wall. In it, the original owner, William C. McElroy, railed against Chinese immigration, marveled at the speed of the Pony Express, and dismissed talk of a transcontinental railroad as ridiculous.

Flower Child was located around the corner on Union Street. The facade was framed in white Christmas lights that blinked day and night. A sign over the door said: OLIVIA AND DAVE KIRSCH, PROPRIETORS. On the sidewalk, a rack of bouquets burst with color. The window was filled with dazzling orchids growing hydroponically.

Ed stepped inside. A refrigerator case was stuffed with cut flowers. A gravel walk snaked through a rainforest of plants, some in pots on the floor, others hanging from the ceiling. The rest of the space was devoted to hydroponics: reservoirs, nutrients, pumps, fans, lights, reflectors, digital ballast, and books—including *Grow It Indoors!* by the owner's late husband.

Olivia emerged from the back and removed a glove. Shaking Ed's hand, she tried to smile but failed. She ushered him into the back room, where she was in the middle of creating two enormous bouquets.

"A wedding," she said, sounding funereal.

She was back at work, but not really there. Her shoulders were rounded, her expression vacant, her eyes dark and puffy. Deep creases extended from her nose to her jaw, making her mouth look like a marionette's. And perfume and lifesavers could not mask an odor of alcohol—at eleven in the morning.

Olivia pointed Ed to a stool next to the worktable. On a cabinet was a Kirsch for Mayor bumper sticker. As Ed produced his recorder, she snipped the stems of showy flowers he didn't recognize and arranged them in the vases.

"Thank you for seeing me," Ed said. "I'm so sorry for your loss. Dave was an original, a true San Franciscan. This must be a horrible time."

"Yes, it is, especially for the girls—" She clamped her eyes shut. When they opened, they glistened.

"If you don't feel ready to—"

"No, I want to help." Her voice was soft but resolute. "Dave always hated the little corner the museum devoted to—" Her fingers flexed air quotes, "—the hippies. Pathetic. He would have loved what you're doing and wanted me to tell our story."

"I didn't realize how much of the store is devoted to hydroponics," Ed said.

"Flowers and houseplants pay the bills. The profit's in grow gear."

"For growing weed, right?"

She pursed her lips. "I grow orchids. What other people grow, that's their business."

"As I mentioned," Ed said, "you'll have the opportunity to review anything attributed to you before it goes into the exhibit."

She waved a hand. "I don't care. I have nothing to hide. Dave stopped dealing thirty years ago. And now—" Her voice cracked and she wiped her eyes. "I just hope your exhibit mentions his legalization efforts. He would have wanted that."

She fussed with fern fronds and slipped them into the vases.

"I thought you might remember this." He produced the *Oracle* photo of the young newlyweds at the Human Be-In.

She rolled her eyes. "Oh, God, not *that* picture. I was thin then."

"How'd you guys wind up in the paper?"

"We were friends with the publisher—"

"Allen Cohen?"

"Yes. Dave wrote articles advocating legalization." She gazed out the window and back to a time when she was young and anything seemed possible. "The Be-In was really something. Allen billed it as a 'gathering of the tribes.' When I first heard that, I had no idea what he was talking about. Tribes? What tribes? But when we got there, we were blown away by the size of the crowd and how freaky everyone looked, and we thought, yes, we're a huge tribe. Then we ran into Allen and he told what's-his-name—the artist—to take our picture."

"The art director? Michael Bowen?"

"Yes, Mike. God, I haven't thought about him in a million years. Dave loved the *Oracle*'s wild graphics, all the color. Peter Max got rich off psychedelic art, but Mike invented it. And Dave's articles for the paper were his first steps toward writing *Grow It!*"

She picked some wilted petals off a huge purple flower and arranged it in the bouquet.

"And you? What did you think of the *Oracle*?"

"That it was hard to read."

"Tell me about it," Ed chuckled, "especially with these middle-aged eyes."

"But it was all so exciting. We were young and it felt like we were on the threshold of something big, something new and important. The *Oracle*, the bands, expanding consciousness—it was a whole new world." A hint of color returned to her cheeks.

"The Age of Aquarius," Ed said.

Olivia almost smiled. "Yes, though we didn't say any of that till later."

"Did you consider yourself a hippie?"

"Not at first. That was *Time* and *Newsweek*. We were 'freaks.' But after a while, the freaks became hippies."

"I understand that Dave dealt to several bands."

"Yes. The Dead, Moby Grape, Janis, the Airplane—they all lived in the neighborhood. The Dead had a house on Ashbury. The Charlatans were around the corner on Cole. Janis lived a few blocks away on Page. Dave was like the mailman making deliveries. And everyone came to our place, too. Somewhere I have a Polaroid of Jerry and Grace Slick and Dave and me in our living room sharing a doobie." The corners of her lips curled upward, then fell.

"In your big Victorian by the park?"

"That's right, the corner of Waller and Stanyan. It's not there anymore. It got knocked down for the McDonald's parking lot."

"Dave told *Rolling Stone* he dealt for only two years, '67 and '68. But other people have said he and Owen Pendleton and Doug Connelly were in business until ten years later, '78."

Olivia turned and looked Ed up and down, as if seeing him for the first time. "Who said that?"

"Paul Nightingale and Ken Kelly."

Her eyes widened. "I've seen Ken at Chester's, but *Paul!* What's he up to? I haven't seen him since…must have been his coming-out party from prison eons ago."

Ed caught her up on the dealer-turned-property-owner and then repeated his question. Why did Dave say he'd dealt for only two years when he was in business much longer?

Olivia smirked. "Because of Owen. Great businessman, but a strange guy."

"Yes, I know. I tried to interview him. He kicked me out of his office."

"I'm not surprised." She took a long look at the *Oracle* photo, at the young couple, happy and high, their lives unfolding like roses blooming. "Owen was with us at the Be-In, but he refused to be photographed. Owen never wanted any of them in the public eye—*ever*. He insisted that Dave deny dealing, especially after he started writing about legalization and growing. Dave was always security-conscious, but Owen was off the charts. He tried to convince Dave to write *Grow It!* using his *Oracle* pseudonym, Johnny Appleweed, but he refused. Then a few years ago, *Rolling Stone* showed up with statements from a dozen musicians swearing that when they lived in the Haight, Dave was their go-to guy for weed. He wasn't about to call Marty Balin and Bob Weir liars, so he admitted to dealing for two years. And you know what? Owen got pissed—thirty years after the fact."

"So how long did he deal, really?"

"From senior year, so '65, to '78. What's that? Fourteen years."

"What happened in '78?"

"Things got ugly and the boys decided to stop."

"Ugly?"

"Yes." Her tone said she had no intention of elaborating.

The young man who worked the register leaned his head through the door and asked if the bride's father could pick up the bouquets around three. Olivia said no problem.

"If you don't mind," Ed asked, "can we back up a bit? How did you and Dave meet?"

"In a class at State, Introduction to Horticulture. I didn't even want to take it, but it was the only thing that fit my schedule. And growing up on a ranch, I knew gardening. I figured it was an easy A. I noticed him right away—the cutest, smartest, funniest guy I'd ever seen. But he didn't notice me until we both got jobs at the bookstore. That's when we clicked. Owen worked there, too. I stayed till we graduated, but after a while, the boys quit and started dealing."

"Nightingale said he got them started."

"That's right. Paul was the original stoner. He used to brag that he smoked reefer with John Coltrane."

Ed chuckled. "Now he brags that he introduced Dave to weed."

Olivia snaked wide white ribbons around the vases and tied large perfect bows. Then she fluffed the bouquets, made final adjustments, and set them aside.

Removing her gloves, she pressed some keys on the worktable computer. "Fourteen corsages," she mumbled to herself. "Pins, not bracelets." She pulled white orchids from a small refrigerator and rummaged around the room for materials. "Where's the stem wire?" Then she found it and set to work, threading wire through the blossoms and around ivy leaves and strands of grass, then wrapping them in tape, and piercing the result with pearl-headed pins.

"Dave was all for dealing," she explained, "but Owen wasn't so sure. Great money, but risky. I remember one night the four of us were sitting around the boys' apartment near State, listening to music and getting high as Owen grilled Paul. Eventually, Owen said he'd go for it—on the condition that he run the business and set the ground rules for security. That was fine with Dave. He was the salesman, and later the author and poster boy for legalization. They bought from Paul for a while, then Doug showed up—"

"Doug Connelly."

"Yes."

"Was he at State?"

"Oh no, Doug didn't go to college. He and Owen were childhood friends, neighbors growing up in El Cajon. Doug was back from Vietnam. Said he never could have survived it without dope. He spoke some Spanish. Got into buying in Mexico and running it across the border."

Olivia recalled that Doug started with a single pound hidden under the back seat of a VW bug. But he had no head for business. Owen offered to buy everything he could haul to San Francisco. When Doug arrived with a load, Owen cleaned, packaged, and hid it, and kept accounts while Dave handled distribution. They started selling ounces to friends. By graduation, they were dealing several pounds a month. Many of their customers lived in the Haight, so they moved there.

"And you? I heard you worked at Magnolia Thunderpussy."

Her head snapped in his direction and ivy leaves scattered on the floor. Retrieving them, she asked. "Who told you *that?*"

"Carol Covington."

Olivia struggled to smile. "You spoke to Carol? God, what's *she* been up to the past…what, forty years?"

Ed told her, then asked, "Wasn't the café owned by some stripper?"

"Ex-stripper. Magnolia Thunderpussy was her stage name. Her real name was…oh, Lord, I'm getting old. Really nice woman. What *was* her name? *Patty!* Patty Mallon. I started out as a waitress. Wound up managing the place."

"Did you ever deal dope?"

"A little, but not much. An ounce or two here and there to friends as a favor. But I wasn't part of the business. That was the boys' thing."

"Didn't you worry? I mean your husband was a *dope dealer*. The cops hated hippies. The courts hated dealers. They could have sent Dave to prison and thrown away the key."

Olivia shrugged. "This might sound strange, but we weren't all that concerned. We were young and stupid. Everyone we knew got high. Pot was all over the Haight, and as far as we could tell, very few people got busted. Paul didn't go prison till much later. Smoking was a protest—against Vietnam, Jim Crow, and Lawrence Welk. The boys were careful.

They only dealt to good friends and we never kept much at the house. Owen stashed it."

"Where?"

"Different places. Storage lockers and eventually a warehouse in Hunters Point." She paused, then added, "We never got along that well, Owen and me. But the one time our house got raided, he saved our asses. The police tore the place apart, but found less than an ounce. Meanwhile, the boys had ten pounds at Self-Storage."

"When were they busted?"

"After the Be-In, so '67, maybe '68."

"Nightingale said they got off by bribing the cops."

She looked up from her workbench, then returned to wrapping wire around an orchid stem. "All I know is they got off. Illegal search. It helped that they found next to nothing."

Olivia recounted that by the end of 1966, Doug was running a dozen pounds a month and Dave and Owen started accompanying him to the hills outside Ensenada. They bought a VW van and fitted it with dual mufflers, only one was an empty shell that they filled with weed. The business took off and money started rolling in—but Owen got nervous and carped about tax evasion.

"I'd never heard of money laundering," Olivia said, "until Owen became obsessed with it. Dave and Doug never thought about the IRS but Owen kept saying, 'We need a story for the taxman.' One night, I'll never forget, Owen came home carrying an armful of library books about Prohibition. He lectured us on how the rum runners got put away—some for possession or selling, but most for tax evasion. Owen kept saying, 'We need to run our dirty cash through a legitimate business, report all of our income, issue W-2s, and pay taxes.' Dave and Doug mocked him, but I thought he was right, and I said so. Eventually Dave and Doug came around."

"So that's when they started importing houseplants." Ed saw the odd look in her eye. "Nightingale told me."

"Yes. Tropical Plants Direct, that was the name. Dave and I were into houseplants before they became popular. We had them all over the house—philodendrons, dracaenas, prayer plants. It was Dave's idea to sell them. He told Owen they could import houseplants along with dope. That's when Owen bought the truck and rented the warehouse.

They kept the houseplants up front and stashed the weed behind a false wall in back."

"How long did Owen and Doug live with you?"

"For a while. But after the business took off, they got their own places."

"I know Owen's gay—"

"Yes, the first openly gay person I ever knew."

"What about Doug? Did he have any girlfriends?"

"Some...."

"Anybody special?"

"Not that I recall."

Ed placed another photo on the worktable: Doug and Jackie at the Be-In. "Do you remember Jackie Zarella?"

"*Jackie!*" Olivia pricked her finger with wire and a spot of blood appeared. She shook it and pressed the wound with her thumb. "Now there's a blast from the past."

37

He'd been vague at first, but now Ed explained who was funding the exhibit and why.

Olivia's eyes widened and she shook her head in disbelief. "Jackie's *son?* A *billionaire?* Amazing! Last time I saw him, he couldn't have been more than three."

"Do you remember his name?" Ed held his breath.

Olivia made final adjustments on a corsage, focusing intently as if the answer might be hidden beneath the tape and wire. "Sorry, no."

"You're sure?"

She set the finished corsage aside and started the next one. "Yes. They weren't around long."

"How well did you know Jackie?"

"Not very. She mostly hung upstairs with Doug. She was the reason we got raided."

"Really? What happened? When was this?"

"I forget...after the Be-In, maybe '68. Yes, '68 because Nixon and Humphrey were running for president and the boys' lawyer wore a big Humphrey button."

Olivia explained that Doug had found Jackie and her son panhandling in front of the Drogstore and offered to buy them dinner. Doug and Jackie hit it off and mother and child spent a few months in the attic with him. Doug persuaded Owen to advance Jackie a pound, which she sold in ounces, eventually making enough to rent a room in a flat off Haight Street.

But Jackie was careless and got arrested. The boys bailed her out, but Owen insisted on cutting her off. With a police record, supplying her was too risky. To pay her legal bills, Jackie fell in with a speed dealer.

Then she got arrested holding a backpack full of methamphetamine. This time, the DA threatened to send her away and take her son. Jackie was desperate. The DA said that if she fingered a big dealer, she'd walk. She was afraid of the speed dealer, a violent man with bone-breakers behind him. So she gave the cops the Kirsches' address.

"How do you know all this?" Ed asked.

"Everyone said."

"'Everyone?' Who?"

"The boys, people on the street, at the *Oracle*...."

"When the house was raided, what happened?"

"I was at work. But the cops swooped in and took Dave and Owen away in handcuffs."

"What about Doug?"

"He was on a run to Mexico."

"What happened to Dave and Owen?"

"Like I said, the cops found very little. The lawyer got them off."

"What about Jackie? Did she ever admit—"

Olivia cut him off with a wave. "I don't know. After the bust, I don't think I ever talked to her again."

"You didn't see her around? She lived nearby."

"No, we didn't, and it was just as well. Owen said he was ready to strangle her."

"Do you think he was serious?"

She paused. "I didn't at the time…"

"But then she got killed."

"Yes."

"How long after?"

"I don't recall. Maybe a few months."

"Did you wonder?"

Olivia discarded a blossom with withered petal tips and reached for another. "Of course. Who wouldn't? He was so angry, he was spitting nails."

"So he might have—"

"He denied it, but maybe. Actually, at first, Dave and I were more suspicious of Doug."

"Why?"

"Because he brought her home. Started her selling. He felt responsible. And Jackie got shot. Doug was ex-Army. He knew all about guns. The rest of us were into peace and love. We hated guns."

"Really? But didn't you win that award for riflery?"

"My God, how did you ever—?" She snipped a stem too short and had to discard the flower.

Ed explained about the soccer tournament, Ukiah, and seeing the young Olivia Tanner on the Wall of Fame.

"That thing's still up there?" She rolled her eyes. "I grew up on a ranch near there. My father taught all us girls to shoot. Had to keep the varmints out of the vegetables. I stopped in junior high. By the time Jackie got killed, I was totally anti-gun. But Dave and I eventually decided that Doug didn't kill her."

"Why?"

"Because he was crushed by her death—devastated like I never saw him before or after. We didn't realize how he felt about her. Doug always played the outlaw. He never wanted to be tied down and didn't seem upset when she moved out. But when she was killed, he fell apart. He kept swearing he'd kill the speed dealer—what *was* his name? It's so long ago, I forget. A nasty man with a violent temper."

"And that was when they stopped selling ounces and moved into pounds."

"Right."

"Did they sell anything beside marijuana?"

"No, just pot. Bear had all the good acid—"

"Bear?"

"Augustus Owsley Stanley, the third. Everyone called him Bear. We did some acid and peyote and mushrooms, but not often. We were stoners. Owen used to say that acid was champagne and dope was beer. The boys liked beer."

"What about that song, 'Candy Man'?"

Another attempt at a smile that almost succeeded. "Magic Bullet Theory's one hit. It seemed like everyone in the Haight knew it was about Dave. We'd be walking down Haight Street and people would say, 'Hey, Candy Man.'"

"So Dave was moving, what, ten pounds a month?"

"More like fifteen."

"That's a lot. And then a hit song about him dealing? Weren't you afraid the police would swoop down, make an example of him?"

"Yes, we were—especially Owen. It drove him crazy. He made us leave town, Dave and me. We went to Hawaii for two months and Owen and Doug stopped dealing and focused on houseplants. Then the song faded and everything went back to normal."

"And the police?"

"They never noticed. They weren't into acid rock."

"I heard Tommy Smith broke Dave's nose."

Olivia organized the finished corsages in a box and pulled out more orchids, wire, and tape. "Yes, a sad chapter."

"Were you there?"

"Right next to Dave. Tommy almost hit me."

"What'd you do?"

"What *could* I do? Dave was flat on his back. His nose was gushing blood. I took him to the emergency room."

"Did you call the police?"

Olivia grimaced. "You're joking, right?"

"But I thought the Diggers were into nonviolence. How'd they feel about Tommy punching Dave?"

"Some were upset, but MBT played a lot of benefits. After that, we avoided the Diggers, and then the band fell apart."

"Nightingale said that at a certain point they stopped buying in Mexico. Why?"

Olivia folded leaves of grass and wrapped wire. "I don't know. They never told me—Dave said I shouldn't ask, that it was better for all of us."

Ed wondered if he should believe that, but let it go. After all, he was just collecting vignettes for the exhibit. "So they started buying Colombian."

"Yes. For a while."

"Why'd they stop?"

"Too many guns. And Dave had horrible sea sickness."

"So that's when they started growing?"

"Yes. Dave and I spent Thanksgiving at my family's ranch. It bordered Mendocino National Forest. A mile in, there was a spring and a creek and meadow."

"Just out of curiosity, where was this?"

"Synder Creek, above where it joins Waterfall."

From the start, Olivia explained, Dave had played with growing. He emptied joints he bought in the Fillmore and planted the seeds in milk cartons in his room. But it didn't work—bad soil and not enough light. He had better luck in their backyard in the Haight. But Owen was against it—security risk—and as soon as plants got to be knee-high, someone always jumped the fence and ripped them off.

But Mendocino was perfect for growing. Dave raised Colombian seedlings in peat pots and transplanted them to the forest. The meadow was too marshy, but its perimeter, where the wildflowers met the trees, provided a good mix of soil, water, and sunlight. With a couple buckets of ranch manure per plant, Dave could grow bushy giants in sixteen weeks and harvest a pound per plant, and later two pounds, without the risks of smuggling, without suitcases full of hundred-dollar bills, and without guns.

"Dave had a real gift for growing," Olivia said, "but he also considered pot a sacrament, and wanted it legalized. Owen hated the idea of legalization. He said RJ Reynolds would move in and they'd be toast. But Dave said if Anchor Steam could make it despite Miller and Bud, why couldn't they find a niche?"

"It sounds like Dave and Owen didn't always get along."

"They did and they didn't. They were like Lennon and McCartney or Jagger and Richards—bickering, yelling, doors slamming. But they made so much money, they were stuck with each other."

"Which meant *you* were stuck with Owen, right?"

Olivia sighed. "Yes. When it came to running the business and keeping Dave out of jail, he was great, but—"

Ed finished her thought. "If you were looking for a friend, you wouldn't choose him."

"No."

Owen wasn't the only person who scoffed at Dave's dream of legalization. All his friends—the bands, the *Oracle* staff, his customers—they all told him he was crazy, that it would never happen.

"One night," Olivia recounted, "Dave asked me if I thought legalization was possible. I said, honestly, no. He gave me a look right out of *Julius Caesar*: 'Et tu, Bruté?' Then he said, 'If everyone grew, there'd be no way to stop it.' And I said, 'Why don't you teach people how to grow?'"

Dave penned the first edition of *Grow It!* in a week. Owen screamed. If everyone grew, who was going to buy from them? Dave told him what he could do with himself. Then Owen implored him to use his pseudonym, but Dave refused. Johnny Appleweed was fine for little pieces in the *Oracle*, but not for a serious book that was destined to ignite a wildfire of legalization efforts from coast to coast. Doug supported Dave, so all Owen could do was throw up his hands and recheck the secrecy of the compartments in their van.

Dave and Olivia typeset the twenty-four-page booklet at the *Oracle*, then gave a hippie who worked at a copy shop a few ounces to run off a thousand copies after hours. Dave hawked them up and down Haight Street and Olivia placed a pile by the register at the café, cover price one dollar. The run sold out in a week. A second edition of five thousand sold out in a month.

Owen fumed. But when Doubleday offered Dave a big advance, he offered to split it three ways and Owen calmed down—on two conditions: that Dave never admit growing anything outside his garden in the Haight and that he never even *imply* that he had partners.

The book turned Dave into a minor celebrity. He was profiled in newspapers and magazines and appeared on radio and TV. College students flocked to his lectures. And visions of fat, resinous buds ripening from Nome to Key West drove the DEA crazy. Police agencies tried to entrap Dave into selling to undercover agents, but under Owen's watchful eye, Dave sold only to trusted friends.

Dave's book didn't do much for legalization, but it triggered an explosion of dope growing throughout Northern California. The area's traditional industries—lumber, ranching, and fishing—were all in decline, relegating half the population to food stamps. But weed put money in people's pockets. It also put ideas into the heads of thieves. "Your crop or your life."

Still, compared with the risks of buying in Mexico or on the high seas, growing in the national forest was fairly trouble-free. The trio's operation was small-scale and easily hidden. Farmer Doug moved north and enjoyed bountiful harvests. Owen laundered the money through the irrigation business. And Dave spread joy far and wide.

"Why'd they stop?" Ed asked. "What happened?"

"I don't know." Her fingers wrapped tape and inserted a pin. "They never said and I knew not to ask. All I know is they got out. Fast. And Doug left the country."

"When they were talking at your house, it sounded like Owen and Doug hadn't seen each other in a long time."

"I can't speak for Owen, but Dave and I never heard from him again. I didn't see him until…"

"Did you see Owen?"

"Hardly ever. He moved to Marin. Dave and Owen were more partners than friends. After they quit, we ran into him occasionally— like when Dave got elected supervisor, Owen stopped by the victory party. But that was about it, until *Johnny Appleweed.*"

Ed looked quizzical.

"Dave's memoir."

"He wrote one?"

"He was in the middle of it when—" She inhaled sharply, then exhaled slowly. "And, no surprise, Owen flipped out and insisted on veto power. Dave refused, but assured him that he wouldn't be named, that he wouldn't mention any partners. But that wasn't good enough for Owen. He barged into the house and started screaming."

"When was this?"

"Couple months ago. Owen and Dave had one of their worst scream-outs, and Dave threw him out. Next time I saw him was…after the memorial."

"You think Owen might have…?"

"It crossed my mind."

"Did you tell the police?"

"Of course."

"And?"

"They took the manuscript, then they returned it."

"And?"

"All I know is that Owen wasn't arrested."

"What about *Grow It Indoors*? If Dave got out of the business, how'd he write that book? And why?"

"He got out of *dealing*, not writing. He loved being Johnny Appleweed, the guru of growing. He hated paying for pot, so he grew some in our garden on Potrero Hill. But just like in the Haight, the plants kept getting stolen. So Dave started growing in the house in a closet, first using soil and then hydroponically. He really got into it. He loved hydroponics and always had a few plants going. The book was a natural."

"And the police didn't knock your door down?"

"No. By then the DA wasn't interested in people growing a few plants at home."

"So Dave's interest in hydroponics—is that how you got into selling the equipment?"

"Sort of. I always loved flowers. After our youngest left home, I got bored and wanted a project. Like I said, flowers and houseplants pay the bills. But the profit's in grow gear, and people have come from all over the world to buy from Johnny Appleweed. Dave isn't—*wasn't*—involved in the store, but when we opened, *High Times* ran a little article, and stoners started showing up asking about hydroponics. So I added it, and put his name on the sign. You wouldn't believe the number of tourists who have their pictures taken under it. Dave's name made the business—" She reached for a tissue and dabbed her eyes. "I like having the store. Especially now. Gives me something to do. Takes my mind off…things."

"For the exhibit, I'd love to interview Doug. You wouldn't happen to know how to get hold of him, would you?"

"Sorry, no idea."

Their conversation was drawing to a close. It was now or never.

"I'm curious about Mexico and Mendocino. Dave never told you anything? His wife?"

She finished another corsage and placed it in the box. "Owen strikes again. Courts can't make wives testify against their husbands, but they could have forced me to testify against Owen and Doug. So everyone was better off if I didn't know."

"One last thing," Ed said. "Jackie's son. If you remember his name, would you call me, please?"

38

When they'd had jobs, late-afternoon movies were out of the question, but now they were a perk. The theaters were never crowded at three on weekdays. They had their pick of seats. And they got out in plenty of time to pick up the kids.

This one was Julie's idea, a romantic comedy loosely based on *A Midsummer Night's Dream*, replete with mistaken identities, red-faced embarrassment, and a happy ending. They laughed and shared buttered popcorn. When the bag was empty, Ed licked Julie's fingers and she leaned over and kissed him.

During the two hours they spent in the theater, the sunny afternoon turned foggy and the temperature dropped twenty degrees on the wings of a stiff wind. They zipped up and huddled close.

It was rush hour and traffic was heavy. As Ed turned up Market, he saw something in the rearview. "Oh shit." Then he remembered he'd neglected to mention the blue T-bird to his wife.

"What?" Julie asked.

"Nothing. Just something I forgot to do for my class."

Julie didn't buy it and began probing. Ed felt like a frog on the dissecting table. Eventually, he revealed that a private investigator had been tailing him ever since Owen Pendleton had thrown him out of his office.

"You're being *followed?*" Julie said, her tone jumping from incredulous to alarmed. "And you didn't *tell me?*"

The movie's feel-good tenderness evaporated faster than a snowflake on a griddle.

"I didn't want to worry you—"

"Well, I'm *worried*. What on Earth were you *thinking?* We should call the police."

"And say what?"

"That this…*person* is stalking you! It's harassment!"

"No, it isn't. Harassment is calling someone every night at three in the morning. It's not stalking, either. He keeps his distance. He's never tried to talk to me or made a threatening move. He smiles—"

Julie whirled around. "Well, he's not smiling now. I can't believe you didn't tell me. This is creepy!"

"Yes, it is, but I'm playing a hunch. If he sees I'm no threat, Pendleton might feel safe enough to talk about Jackie, and if he can help me find Simons's name, we win the Lotto—and I can sleep again."

"I don't like it," Julie insisted. "Not one bit."

Ed turned up Valencia and the T-bird followed. A light turned yellow and Ed slowed to stop. The Bird pulled up next to them.

"Don't look at him," Ed said.

"Why not?" Julie demanded. "Christ! He's got a *gun!*"

Ed turned and saw Parker smiling as he closed his jacket over the holster in his armpit.

"Asshole," Ed muttered, resisting the urge to give him the finger.

"I'm calling the police," Julie snapped, pulling out her phone.

"Please," Ed pleaded, "*don't.*"

"Why not?"

"The police can't do anything. He's got a carry permit. I saw it on his license."

"He's *allowed* to wave a gun at us?"

"He didn't wave it. Let me handle this."

"How? What are you going to do?"

"I-I'm not sure, but don't you see? He must have told Owen that I saw Olivia Kirsch. Owen doesn't want me digging into his sordid past. He must have told the PI to turn up the heat a notch—"

"Which is *why* I'm calling the police."

As the light turned green, Ed proceeded up the street but the Thunderbird turned and disappeared. Ed grabbed the phone out of Julie's hand.

"Ed! What're you—"

"I asked you not to call the police. I'll handle it."

"What do they call it? Brandishing? Even with a permit, he shouldn't be allowed to—"

"It's not brandishing. He didn't point it at us. He didn't threaten us."

"When I see a gun, I *feel threatened*. What's wrong with you?"

"Owen knows something, something about Jackie. I can feel it. And if I find Simons's name—"

"Yeah, and if this guy shoots you, I'm a widow with two kids! Give me back my damn phone!"

She grabbed it from him as Ed had a thought.

"Tell you what, if you ever see that car again, call the police. But for right now, let me handle it. *Please.*"

Julie folded her arms across her chest and leaned away from Ed. When Sonya climbed into the car, she sensed the tension. "What's the matter?"

"Nothing," her parents replied in unison.

Back home, Ed pulled into the garage. Julie lifted Jake out of the car seat and stomped upstairs, closely followed by Sonya, who demanded to know what was going on.

Ed stepped into his office and grabbed his briefcase and laptop for his class. With a hand on the car door, he called upstairs, "See you later."

Silence.

He debated driving off versus trying to make things right with Julie. He climbed the stairs. She was ripping a head of lettuce with enough force to break fingers.

Ed tried again. "See you later."

She wasn't talking to him. His watch said this would have to wait. He descended the stairs and started the car.

When he returned later that night, the house was quiet, too quiet. Julie should have been in the living room watching one of her shows. But the TV was off, the room dark and empty.

Ed climbed the stairs and found Julie slumped over her desk, asleep and snoring with a trail of spittle extending from her mouth to her chin. Beside her stood a wine glass and an empty bottle of Pinot.

He nudged her. "Julie?" She was out cold. He eased her up to seated and shook her by the shoulders. "Julie!" She groaned and tried to lay her head back down.

"Great," Ed said as he pulled her up to her feet and half-guided, half-carried her to bed. She flopped down, moaning and burrowing into the spread. He pulled her shoes off and considered undressing her, then decided that drunks who pass out deserve to sleep in their clothes.

In the kitchen, he saw no wine on the counter. There'd been a bottle of red there earlier. So she'd downed all of it, five glasses.

Ed sought refuge in his office and returned to editing an interview with one of the partners in the Straight Theater project, now a lawyer in San Jose. But he couldn't concentrate.

Without really intending to, he reached for his bong and baggie. He exhaled a cloud out the window. He thought about the PI. He hated cat-and-mouse games, especially when he was the rodent. He thought about Pendleton. No question, the man was an ass. Then he thought about Julie. He regretted upsetting her. He sympathized with her distress. When he saw the Thunderbird, he should have kept his mouth shut. *Stupid.* But as he fired up his second hit, those thoughts were eclipsed by a question that grabbed his shoulders and shook him like an earthquake. *Could he stay married to an alcoholic?*

39

At a sidewalk café, Ed sipped green tea while keeping any eye on A Cut Above: Castro. Then his phone chimed.

"So," Ramirez said, "the widow thinks Pendleton might have done Kirsch."

"Yes. She said she told you they had a big argument over Dave's memoir like a week before he got it, and you took the manuscript, then said he wasn't a suspect. I'm wondering why not."

"And I'm wondering why I should tell you." His tone wasn't hostile, more like someone idly swatting a fly.

"You know why. I'm all the help you've got."

"Jesus," Ramirez chuckled, "reporters. All right, two reasons. First, Kirsch's book doesn't mention Pendleton. I went through it, not one word. So the book is no motive."

"But did Pendleton know that?"

"Doesn't matter because second, guess where he was when Kirsch went down—Ward Eighty-six."

It was the HIV floor at San Francisco General.

"He has AIDS?"

"He's been positive since the early eighties. He's in the long-term survivors study. He was having his quarterly check-up—all afternoon."

After the big argument, Olivia said Owen stormed out and slammed the door. Ken Kelly implied that Owen had a vindictive streak and Ed's experience with the gun-toting PI supported that. So what if Pendleton was at General? He was a dope dealer who still probably had connections to guys with thugs on salary…

But Ed's train of thought was derailed by a figure crossing the street—Owen Pendleton striding toward his salon. Ed jumped up and weaved through traffic.

"Remember me?" he asked.

Pendleton drew up short. "Unfortunately."

"Call off your goon," Ed said. "He's upsetting my wife."

"I don't know what you're talking about."

"Sure you do. William Parker of Rubin and Wolper, the joker with the classic Thunderbird and the nine millimeter automa—"

"Never heard of him." Pendleton moved to step around Ed but he blocked the door, leaving them standing chest to chest.

"So it's a coincidence," Ed said, "that he started tailing me right after you tossed me out of your office. And another coincidence that he flashed his gun right after I spoke with Olivia."

"Must be."

"Look, I don't care what you did forty years ago. I'm a stoner. I have nothing against selling weed. I'm just trying to find out about Jackie and her son. But your errand boy has upset my wife—and by the way, do you know who my wife is?"

"I couldn't care less." Pendleton said, trying once again and failing to shoulder his way around Ed.

"You should. She's the best PR person this side of New York. Very well connected with the media. I know you value your privacy. All she has to do is send a few e-mails and imagine the headlines: 'Prominent Local Philanthropist Made Fortune Dealing Pot.' Is that what you want? Your face plastered all over the *Horn*?"

"You fucker!"

Ed looked him in the eye. "Call off your goon, you hear me? If I see him even once more, you'll have satellite trucks driving up your rectum."

40

Ed drove south past Cupertino, turned toward the Santa Cruz Mountains, and near Los Gatos snaked up a narrow winding road through rugged hills and dense forest. Beyond a cemetery, he followed a stone fence to a pair of tall columns joined at the top by an elaborate wrought-iron arch that said SERENITY. A long tree-lined gravel drive led to a mansion straight out of *Gone with the Wind*. Nearly 150 years earlier, it had been the home of a Comstock Lode millionaire. Now it was a detox and rehab facility.

A nurse led Ed through the dining hall and across an outdoor patio to a sunny corner where a beefy man with thinning hair, formerly of Magic Bullet Theory, was stretched out on a lounge chair reading AA's *Big Book*. He wore jeans, flip-flops, and a T-shirt emblazoned with the Rolling Stones' big tongue logo. His arm was in a sling.

"Tommy," the nurse said, "your visitor."

For a guy arrested with three times the legal limit, Smith looked surprisingly good—no rheumy eyes, no ashen face, nor nose festooned with exploded capillaries. Of course, Smith was no stumbling drunk fished out of the gutter for the umpteenth time. Before his relapse, he'd been sober for twenty-plus years.

Tommy glanced at Ed but remained silent. He closed the book and, using his good arm, struggled to stand. Carrying a coffee mug, he shuffled to a patio table and motioned Ed to a chair, easing himself slowly into another. If the tales Olivia and Covington had told were true, Smith could be a prize jerk, but over the phone he'd sounded decent enough, open to reminiscing about old times as long as the interview didn't interfere with meetings or his chores. Seeing Tommy now, Ed pitied him. The look on his face said he'd never felt so ashamed.

"How are you doing?" Ed asked softly.

Smith shrugged. "It's a weird disease. I was sober for twenty-two years, eight months, and sixteen days. Then, I don't know…I barely remember what happened. I had a problem at work, not a big one, stupid really, a little screw-up, but it was my fault. I've dealt with similar problems a hundred times, but this time, I don't know, I flipped back into my addict mind and next thing I know…I only recall little snippets: buying vodka near work, driving past the airport, past Candlestick, buying more in the city, sleeping in Golden Gate Park, and then the police." He looked at Ed with sad puppy-dog eyes.

"But you're alive, and here. That's good."

"Yeah, alive." The words sounded dead.

"What happened to your arm?"

"Cops broke it. When they stopped me…I'm a belligerent drunk." Smith sighed. "Mr. Stupid takes that first drink." He downed a gulp of coffee with trembling hands. "Rita said you saw Carol. Or did you say that? How is she?"

"Good. Concerned about you. Her choir is fabulous."

Smith pursed his lips. "Never seen them. Never been into religion." He gazed down a gentle slope of lush lawn past the cemetery toward forested hills. "Neither was she way back when, but she grew up in church and always loved to sing."

"Carol said you knew each other in high school, but didn't get together till college."

Smith looked up at the back of the old mansion, partly covered in ivy. Ed could imagine Scarlett O'Hara stepping through the French doors and calling her guests to dinner.

"We knew each other's names and faces, but I don't think we had a real conversation until I ran into her at State. We were in the same Intro Psych class and had to read an article that was on reserve. They had only one left and we both asked for it. We recognized each other and wound up sharing it."

"How'd Magic Bullet Theory get together? Were you a musician in high school?"

.   "Second violin in the orchestra. My parents put me in lessons when I was eight."

Ed flashed on his own brief, dismal struggle with the clarinet. "You practiced?"

"Hated it." Tommy leaned toward Ed and became slightly more animated. "But my parents paid me a penny a minute. We had one of those wind-up kitchen timers. After dinner, my mother set it for twenty minutes. When the bell sounded, I got twenty cents—real money to a little kid in the fifties." He tried to smile and almost succeeded. "In junior high, I heard 'Johnny B. Goode' and picked up the guitar. I had a garage band, the Corvairs." This time, he made it to a thin-lipped grin. "We were about as good as the car. Then at State, there was this SNCC retreat—"

"Snick," Ed said, "the Student Nonviolent Coordinating Committee."

"Yeah, Carol and I were members—before they kicked out all the whites. A couple of us had guitars and somebody had a hand drum. We were singing 'We Shall Overcome,' and 'If I Had a Hammer,' when somebody said, 'Hey, want to play Chuck Berry?' We had a great time, three of us. After the retreat, we became the core of MBT."

"So you were all political."

"Oh, yeah. We weren't into silly love songs. We wanted to change the world."

"So you moved to the Haight and became a member of the Diggers."

"It wasn't like they had *members*. But we hung with them. When they rented space for the Free Store, I pounded nails and helped paint the place."

"And you knew Dave Kirsch. Tell me about 'Candy Man.'"

His weak smile morphed into a smirk. "Carol and I lived around the corner from Dave and his wife."

"Olivia."

"Yes, Livvy. She was hot. Worked at a café. I saw them around and heard Dave dealt reefer. When we were building the Free Store, he came by and passed out joints. I went home and wrote the song in like five minutes. The guys liked it and audiences *loved* it. So we pressed a single and dropped one off at KMPX. First time I heard it, I went nuts. They were playing *my song* on the *radio*."

"I heard you got a record deal, but then MBT broke up and the record never happened."

Smith frowned. "MBT broke up because I broke down. I was drinking, and…" A sweep of his hand encompassed Serenity. "Now here I am, working my program, trying to get back on track."

"Did you go to the Be-In? MBT didn't play, did they?"

"We were supposed to, but a couple of our guys were away, so I sat in with Quicksilver on a few songs. I loved it. The Diggers did their Frame of Reference puppet show. Carol was in it. There were so many of us. And when Leary came out with his famous line, I thought: Whoa, this could be big."

"And then the hippies were on Walter Cronkite, and kids flooded the Haight, and the Diggers were overwhelmed and started denouncing 'hip capitalists.'"

Smith sighed. "Looking back, it all seems so trivial—the political battles, the litmus tests, who's with us, who's against us. But in those days, it was intense. We were young and brash and full of ourselves and the revolution was just around the corner."

"Then you jumped off the stage and slugged Dave."

"That's what they tell me. I have no memory of it—none. I was so drunk and stoned, I couldn't find my dick in the shower."

"Does the name Jackie Zarella mean anything to you? She sold weed and speed. Cute brunette, petite, with a toddler."

"I don't think so. No."

"What about Owen Pendleton? Dave's partner."

"Maybe. I don't know."

"After MBT broke up, and Carol left, what'd you do?"

"Drank and kept drinking. Not that I remember much. I was out of it. Carol was gone. I lost my job. I lived in a shithole in the Tenderloin—junkies shooting up in the stairwell."

"Did you—"

"No. I was all about booze. I smoked reefer if somebody offered, but mostly I drank, day and night. Then, in the spring of '68, Martin Luther King saved my life."

"How?"

"By getting killed."

"I don't understand."

"When I heard the news, I was in my room, drunk out of my mind.

But somehow, that tragedy, the enormity of it, got through to me, and I started crying. I bawled like a baby. I must have cried for hours. Then I was on the street. I ran into a guy I sort of knew, an ex-addict who was clean and sober. I asked him to take me to AA."

"And you cleaned up?"

"Started to. The first year, I relapsed a couple times, but eventually I got sober, went back to State, finished up in computers. Got a job in medical software, been at it ever since."

"Your time in the Haight, many people called it a magic moment—the Summer of Love and all. What about you?"

"When MBT was hot, when I was a celebrity on Haight Street, that was great. But the rest of it, for me, was bad, very bad. Everywhere you looked, people were doing drugs, and drugs are a plague."

"All drugs? Even marijuana?"

"Absolutely. People draw a distinction between pot and everything else. But that's wrong. Pot's a gateway."

Ed flashed on Sonya and took a deep breath. "That opinion puts you at odds with all the experts."

"Maybe so, but that was my experience."

"You tried marijuana, then started drinking?"

"No, I drank first. Booze was always my main drug. But pot was part of what kept me drinking. I'd get high and think, 'What the hell, I'll have a drink,' then a couple of fifths later, I was on my ass."

41

Ed stood next to Julie behind the smoothie table at the school math-a-thon, each of them working two blenders nonstop. The smoothies were a big hit—oranges, strawberries, bananas, and crushed ice with a dollop of yogurt and a dash of cinnamon. The line of kids stretched almost to the door, and many returned for seconds.

The math-a-thon was an annual fundraiser. The kids solicited donations to spend an evening solving a hundred grade-appropriate problems while gorging on pizza and ice cream. As activist parents, Ed and Julie were happy to help, but Julie had a problem with the menu. *Couldn't we serve something nutritious?* She was invited to bell the cat and came up with smoothies. A local produce market gave her a break on the fruit, and several parents loaned blenders.

Ed worked his machine, stuffing fruit and ice into the pitchers, watching everything whirl, and pouring the concoction into the plastic cups kids thrust in his face. At first, he felt heartened by the smoothies' popularity. Julie was a genius. The kids were eating fruit and loving it. But after a while, the clamor got tiresome and the whole enterprise became irritating. *I could be home working, making money.*

Meanwhile, Julie was cranking just as hard or harder and serving as many kids or more, but no clouds obscured her sunny disposition. She bantered with the kids and seemed to be having a great time.

It didn't take long for the tabletop around Ed's blenders to become a fruity, yogurty mess. But on Julie's side, the table was almost spotless.

Is she or isn't she? Ed had been all over the Internet reading up on alcoholism and came away more confused than ever. Since they'd been laid off, she was definitely drinking more, and who knew what she was sneaking. But here she was, sober and working happily under pressure while he wished he'd had a hit before the hordes descended. She'd passed out drunk, a definite danger sign, but she hadn't had any DUIs, her mind never seemed fogged, her speech was never slurred, and she was more patient with the kids than he was.

Toward the end of the evening, Ed caught the eye of another stoner parent and they ducked outside behind the play structure for a quick hit. Returning to the cafeteria, he found that someone had uncorked a few bottles of wine and a dozen parents, Julie among them, held glasses as Pat Lucas added up the last-minute pledges and announced the grand total, a new record.

As the weed worked its calming magic, Ed snaked an arm around Julie's waist. He smiled at her, but she saw a different expression. "What's with the disapproving look?"

"What look?" he countered. "I'm not—"

"Yes, you are. I don't need your permission to have a glass of wine."

They helped the other parents clean up, then saw Sonya off to a sleepover at a classmate's and headed to the car. It was a chilly night. They turned up their collars and slipped hands into pockets. The happy Julie of earlier in the evening was gone, replaced by a woman who seemed somber and subdued.

"About the other night," she said, "when you found me...*asleep*—"

"Is that what you're calling it? A nap?"

"He had a *gun!* I was *scared!* I had some wine to calm down."

"You had the whole bottle."

"What? You measured?"

"You won't see him anymore."

"How do you know?"

"I had a little talk with the guy who hired him. It's over."

"Good. Now what about us?"

Ed bit his lip. "I'm concerned about your...health. And I'm concerned about the kids, what they see, what they absorb."

"So you think I'm a bad mother?"

He glanced at her. "No! I think you're a great mother."

"But?"

"I wish you didn't drink so much."

"I can stop anytime."

"Really? Prove it. Stop for one month. Can you?"

Her expression radiated shame and indignation. "All right—if *you* stop smoking for a month. Can you?"

"Uh—"

"I didn't think so."

Ed drew a breath, his mind shuffling notes for another lecture about the relative hazards of the two drugs. Then he exhaled. What was the point? They'd been over it a hundred times. She was teetering on the edge of the precipice, and nothing he said could pull her back. How could such a wonderful woman—? He knew her better than he'd ever known anyone, yet she remained a mystery. He'd sworn till death do us part, but now he wasn't so sure.

42

Ed suggested lunch at The Front Page, but Tim didn't want to be any-where near the paper. They wound up on the seventh floor of the San Francisco Shopping Center at the Nordstrom café, in a secluded booth overlooking the Powell Street cable car turnaround.

"Let me buy you a drink," Ed said. "Beer, wine, booze, you name it."

"I can't," Tim said. "You know the rule."

The *Foghorn* expressly prohibited consumption of drugs or alcohol during the workday, and employees were subject to random testing. A positive result got you a warning and a four-week, drug-dependency-prevention class. A second positive, goodbye.

"Fuck 'em. You're laid off. What can they do? Fire you?"

"I don't want to screw up my severance."

"Suit yourself. But lunch is on me."

Tim had been Metro editor for a dozen years. He'd gotten the news that morning in an e-mail from the executive editor, who just happened to be out of the office for a few days. Metro, National, and Features were being merged into a single department to be managed by the Features editor, Trudy Hammond, who was widely rumored to spend lunches in hotel rooms with the publisher. Tim had two weeks to hand off his job. Adding up his severance, accrued days, and management incentives, he was looking at almost a year of income before he faced the abyss.

Only for Tim, there would be no cold-sweat wake-ups at three a.m. His wife, the TV news anchor, made twice what he did. The station was also laying off, hurt by eyeballs migrating to the Internet, but the focus groups loved Kim, and so far, so good.

When the ax fell, Tim wasn't surprised. After all the buyouts and layoffs, the newsroom was virtually deserted, with only the faintest sound of keyboards clicking. Still, it was shocking to be pushed out the door.

"So," Ed asked, "what about the next two weeks?"

Tim stared at his burger but wasn't interested. He stabbed a French fry and took his time chewing. "Be professional. Do my job—what's left of it. Fill out the forms. Bring Trudy up to speed."

"And then?"

"I don't know…some projects around the house. I want to reroof the garage and plant some fruit trees behind the swing set."

"What about sending out your resumé? You're very impressive."

"What's the point? Newspapers are graveyards."

"What about that plumber's apprentice idea?"

"Yeah, maybe. I've made a few calls, but so far, nothing."

Tim asked the waiter to wrap up the burger and half the fries. "Actually, I've been considering something else, but Kim's not happy about it."

"What? A barista at Starbucks?"

"Worse. Oaksterdam U." It was the school in Oakland that offered courses on all aspects of medical marijuana, from growing high-quality buds to managing dispensaries.

"Really? Would you grow? Or open a store?"

"I don't know. Probably a store."

"You're not much of a stoner."

"That's *good*. Preserves the inventory."

"You'd be looking at a lot of competition." San Francisco already had thirty stores, Oakland twenty.

"True, but not one is run by an Asian American. I checked. Thirty percent of San Francisco is Asian, and fifteen percent of Oakland. Design it to appeal to Asians. Call it something like Jade Wind Healing. Set it up like a Chinese pharmacy."

"But you've never run a business."

Tim shrugged. "I could learn…or not. I don't know. I don't know anything anymore."

On the way back to the paper, Tim looked old. At the corner, Ed extended his hand, but Tim hugged him. "Thanks for lunch, for coming down, for caring."

As Ed watched his friend trudge into the building, his phone rang. It was Rodney Wong.

"His name is now Joe Bogen, B-o-g-e-n. Lives in Reno, owns laundromats."

"Great work! How'd you find him?"

"You said he was a Vietnam vet, so I figured he's getting his cancer treatment from the VA. I got into VA records, searched for prostate cancer and a pine tree tattoo. Two guys, but only one matched your description. And you were right. He's in bad shape. Stage four on the cusp of five. Next stop, hospice."

"You're amazing."

"Hold your applause. I struck out in Mendocino. You said the incident took place sometime in '78. I checked the local cops, the county sheriff, state police, DEA, and CAMP. No warrants, no arrests, no citations, not even a parking ticket—nothing. I thought maybe you got the date wrong, so I checked from '76 to '80. Nothing. Then I checked Synder Creek and the neighboring counties: Humboldt, Glenn, and Trinity. Zip. I don't know, man, but as far as the police are concerned, whatever happened up there…it never happened."

43

Ed waited outside the small seminar room until the dozen students filed out. Then he greeted the professor, who was sweeping books and a laptop into a briefcase. Al Miller had a horseshoe ring of long gray hair pulled into a ponytail. Faded jeans, cowboy boots, and a corduroy sport jacket completed his geezer hippie look. Miller extended a hand. He didn't seem like a person who would order a contract killing. But you never know—the guy next door might be a serial killer.

"I liked your piece on the underground press," Miller said, "especially the politicos getting fed up with the *Oracle* and going to the *Barb*. I tried to interest the *Oracle* in a piece on draft resistance, but they blew me off. Guess where I took it." He glanced at his watch. "I have an hour till my next class. We can get coffee."

They descended wide stairs noisy with students to a café on the ground floor. Glass doors opened to tables on a deck that led to a lawn surrounded by academic buildings, but it was foggy and cold so they stayed inside. A young woman with braces filled two mugs. Ed carried them to a table made from an old cable spool under a poster of a sea otter and the words: Reduce. Reuse. Recycle.

"Remind me what this is about. A museum exhibit?"

Ed explained about the hippie Haight and the vignettes.

"You're Julie's husband, aren't you?"

Ed hadn't mentioned it when he e-mailed asking for the interview. Now he hoped he wouldn't be judged guilty by association. But there was no rancor in Miller's voice, just wistfulness.

"She's friends with my ex."

"Ex?" Ed asked, striving for a tone that combined empathy with distance from the cat fight. "Last I heard you were in counseling."

Miller blew on his coffee but it came out more like a snort. "That was a charade, so she can say she tried. Let's talk about the sixties, okay?"

Miller explained that he'd grown up in Santa Monica, the son of an accountant and a librarian. He attended Stanford, opposed the Vietnam War, and became active in the Draft Resistance, founded by Stanford student body president David Harris and publicized by his then-wife, Joan Baez. In 1967, Miller dropped out of Stanford, moved to the Haight, and launched Resistance San Francisco. That summer, he and seven other young men burned their draft cards on the steps of City Hall, triggering a brawl between their supporters and members of the American Legion, who were beefier and more numerous. The police were in no hurry to break it up. Miller suffered a concussion and broken ribs. Eventually, he served twenty-six months. After his release, he earned a Ph.D. in political science. He'd taught at State for twenty years.

"I have to ask. What was Joan Baez like?"

Miller smiled. "I haven't seen her in years, but back then, she was a delight: smart, charming, funny, totally committed—and her voice, magnificent. It gave me chills."

"When you left Stanford, why'd you move to the Haight?"

"I wanted to organize young men facing the draft, and in San Francisco, they were in the Haight."

"Were you a hippie?"

"No…and yes. I was an activist working full time to end the draft and the War and U.S. imperialism and racism. I considered myself a communist. I read Marx and Mao and Ho Chi Minh. I wanted a revolution—not like Russia or China, or God forbid, East Germany or North Korea, but a new *American* revolution inspired by the Wobblies, Norman Thomas, and Noam Chomsky by way of the anti-war movement and the Panthers. So I was no hippie. But I also had long hair and smoked pot and read Ken Kesey and loved rock music. I saw the Stones at Altamont and I adored the Airplane. I wore out two copies of *Volunteers*. I looked and dressed like a hippie, but I was under no illusions about peace and love. While they were braiding flowers in their hair, I was getting tear-gassed at the Oakland induction center."

"In the Haight, do you recall a young woman named Jackie Zarella?"

"No. Was she political?"

"Not that I know of. She was a dope dealer. Had a little boy. Hung out on Hippie Hill."

"No. My pot connections were at Stanford."

"Did you ever visit the Diggers Free Store?"

"Once or twice, just to see it. They were fools, a bunch of airhead utopians who didn't need acid to be totally out of touch with reality."

"So you didn't view America as a 'post-scarcity society'?"

Miller snorted. "Hardly. The summer of '67, Detroit went up in flames. The privileged children of the upper-middle class talked about post-scarcity, but for black people and the white working class, the kids who did most of the fighting—and dying—in Vietnam, that was beyond ridiculous."

"You mentioned a new American revolution, but the Draft Resistance wasn't revolutionary. It was classic civil disobedience. You didn't call the government illegitimate—just the War. You willingly allowed the feds to put you in prison. You courted it."

"True enough. Resistance leadership was committed to nonviolence and civil disobedience, but personally, I felt ambivalent. I mean, say you were Vietnamese, with bombs raining down on your fields and napalm incinerating your family, how far would nonviolence get you? I didn't feel ready to pick up the gun, but the machine was so odious, I had to throw my body on the gears. So I chose civil disobedience and saw it as a prelude to revolution. Of course, that was hopelessly naïve, but what did I know? I was barely twenty-one."

"What was naïve? The idea that you could change the world?"

"That and everything else. We really believed—deeply—that stopping the draft would end the War. What it did was cut the heart out of the anti-war movement. Without the draft, the middle class no longer felt threatened, and everyone went back to watching *The Smothers Brothers*."

Ed couldn't tell if Miller truly believed what he was saying or if his shattered marriage had brought out the cynic in him. "That's a bit harsh, don't you think? Plenty of people remained active, and there's all sorts of progressive activism today."

Miller smirked. "You been to any demonstrations against Iraq or Afghanistan? You see a few kids, but it's mostly gray-hairs, and not many. Compare that to the Vietnam protests that brought out millions."

"What about environmentalism? Aren't kids into that?"

"They *say* they are, but for the vast majority, environmentalism isn't a commitment, it's a fashion statement. We're 6 percent of the world's population using 40 percent of its resources. Real environmentalism would mean a substantial drop in our standard of living—and kids today, my students, they don't want that, no way. What they want is a cool loft South of Market and a $100,000 electric hot rod to commute to the big job at Google."

"But—"

"The other day, I was at Safeway. They have Muzak. You know what was playing? 'Street Fighting Man.' That's activism today, an insipid version of the real thing. When I tell students I spent two years *in prison* for what I believed, they look at me like I'm from another planet. And you know what? I am."

"If we could go back to the Haight for a moment…I don't want to pick any scabs, but back then, did you know Dave Kirsch?"

Miller made a sour face. "I knew who he was—the Candy Man, a local notable. But we weren't friends." He drained his coffee and the mug hit the table with a loud smack. "It's funny. There was a time I actually felt sorry for that fuck."

"Why?"

"I was at a concert where he got beat up."

"You were at Longshoremen's Hall when Tommy Smith—"

"I was. MBT was political. I was trying to get them to play a benefit for us. They played 'Candy Man' and Tommy jumped off the stage and wailed on some guy. I had no idea who. He was just standing there and *pow!* Of course, now I can't help wishing he'd killed him. But someone else did." He gazed out the window and muttered under his breath, "That's consolation."

44

The *Ukiah Mirror* had modest offices just east of 101 in the sleepy downtown of Mendocino's county seat. Ed said he had an appointment and flashed his *Foghorn* ID. The receptionist was texting and didn't notice that it had expired. She pressed a button on her console.

A young editor materialized, gushed about Ed's column, and led him down to the basement. The morgue was housed at the end of a long hall in a cramped, windowless room whose mustiness revealed that few people ever waded this deep into history. Rickety metal bookcases held bound volumes of the paper starting in 1861, when it was the *Gazette*, through 1985 when the archive went electronic.

Ed had searched the database from home and found no mention of Doug Connelly or his partners, and only four of Synder Creek. One described a landslide after a week of rain that washed out thirty yards of logging road. The second covered a DEA sweep that netted six hundred plants. The third noted placement of a bronze plaque on a boulder above the ravine marking the approximate location of the home of the forest's first white resident, Josiah Synder, a failed miner turned trapper, who erected a crude, one-room shack in 1855. The fourth lamented environmental degradation of Synder Ravine because of water diversions by pot growers.

Ed pulled out the bulky volume marked January 1978 and placed it on a small table. The rusty desk lamp still worked. He flipped through the pages. Synder Creek wasn't mentioned the entire month: no pot seizures by the authorities, no shootouts, no bodies, nothing.

Ed replaced the volume and pulled out February. Again, no mentions. Month by month, he ran through the year. Right after Christmas, a huge front-page headline blared news of shootings near Las Pulgas Creek. Ed unfolded a topographic map and located it, a rugged mile and three ridges over from Synder. Men with guns had attacked backwoods growers, killing two and wounding two others. But there was no mention of Doug Connely. All the victims were longtime locals, former loggers and fishermen. A survivor said the attackers wore DEA jackets and flashed badges, then started shooting. A spokesperson for the DEA vehemently denied that agency personnel had anything to do with the attack. He said thieves were counterfeiting badges and uniforms. The thieves made off with a truckload of mature plants whose street value was estimated at seven figures. The article concluded: "With marijuana cultivation increasing in remote parts of Mendocino County, officials have been predicting violence. Now those predictions have come true."

Now? Ed reread the final graf. Its implication was clear. This late-December 1978 incident marked the first documented firefight associated with national forest growing. So maybe Doug hadn't shot anyone. But if not, what had sent him abroad? What had driven Owen to distraction and made the partners quit the business?

Only one explanation made sense. Doug had killed someone—maybe more than one—and his victim or victims probably carried badges. The cops, thieves, and thieves disguised as cops were all heavily armed, so Doug must have been, too. He must have killed them and disposed of the bodies—and evidently, no one knew.

Ed flipped more pages. By 1980, firefights in the national forest had become routine. Hikers and bird watchers stopped using the trails for fear of getting shot. Schools canceled camping trips. Churches with backcountry camps abandoned them as too dangerous. Fewer loggers ventured into the forest, and those who did went armed. Forest Service costs mounted as the drug war escalated, and cultivation took a toll on the fragile landscape. Meanwhile, as logging and recreational use declined, Forest Service income plummeted, prompting cries in the legislature and Congress for CAMP and the DEA to get serious about eradication.

Ed kept reading. Months passed, then years. By the mid-1980s, the old Mendocino of ranching, logging, and fishing was largely a memory.

A new county was emerging, a land of recent arrivals in tricked-out four-wheel drives who drank espresso, slept with *Grow It!* under their pillows, rooted clones, and grew them all over the backcountry.

By the time Ed hit 1984, he'd had enough. He was about to close the February volume when a headline caught his eye: Skeletons Found on Waterfall Creek. Ed checked his topo map. Waterfall was the next creek over from Synder. A landslide above the falls had exposed a new section of bank. A forest ranger had spied what looked like a leg bone sticking out of the debris. Forensics determined that it was human. Digging turned up three skeletons, men aged twenty to thirty. They'd been shot—in the chest, shoulder, and pelvis—then executed with single shots to the head. Their clothing had rotted away, except for worm-eaten hiking boots and a moldy leather belt with a horsehead buckle. The pathologist estimated they'd been buried five to eight years earlier, between 1976 and 1979. But a search of police records—hunting accidents, missing persons, escaped convicts—provided no clue.

Ed copied the article and reshelved the book. Who knew if these were Doug's victims, but the date and location looked about right. Clearly, this was no hunting accident. They'd been wounded and then dispatched by someone who was taking no chances. Only one thing was certain. These men had died as far under the radar as they were buried under the blackberries.

45

Ed spotted the bald, emaciated man with the white mustache and neck tattoo through the window of the Lost Sock Laundromat in a Reno strip mall not far from Harrah's. Moving slowly and leaning on a cane, the man gathered newspaper pages strewn around the plastic benches and stuffed them into the trash. He refilled the vending machine with little boxes of detergent and bleach, then very gingerly climbed three steps up a ladder to replace the sputtering fluorescent over the half-dozen slot machines by one wall. Finally, he traded his cane for a broom and swept the place. He had difficulty crouching with the dustpan, and more trouble standing up. It was an effort for him to push the glass door open and step into the afternoon sun where Ed was waiting.

"Joe Bogen?"

The man looked him up and down. "Do I know you?"

"Sort of," Ed replied, smiling brightly. "We met at Olivia Kirsch's after Dave's funeral. Out on the patio, you and Owen and a bunch of us passed a pipe." That wasn't exactly true, but Ed figured that between the chemo and his prognosis, Bogen wouldn't remember. Ed radiated friendliness but felt a surge of desperation. This might be his last chance to hit Gene Simons's jackpot. "I came up here because of an old friend of yours, Jackie Zarella."

Bogen's eyes became Frisbees. "*Jackie?!*"

"Actually, her son sent me." Ed explained how the little boy had grown up and was sponsoring the exhibit, hoping to learn more about his mother.

"*Jackie's son?* For real?" Bogen shook his head in disbelief and a bit of color returned to his cheeks.

"Can we talk?"

Bogen didn't budge. Squinting, he searched Ed's eyes. "How'd you find me?"

Ed flashed his most ingratiating grin. "I knew three things about you: Vietnam vet, prostate cancer, and neck tattoo. Let's just say the VA could use a better firewall."

"Well, I'll be damned." A woman pushing a stroller and pulling a laundry basket approached. With obvious difficulty, Bogen opened the door for her, then turned to Ed. "Now, who *are* you, man?"

Ed explained his wife's connection to Dave's campaign, and his own to Jackie's son. "His adoptive parents named him Gene. But he'd love to know the name Jackie gave him. Do you remember?"

Ed held his breath, envisioning the wheels spinning and hitting three cherries. Bogen gazed past Ed toward Mount Rose as if the boy's name might be carved into its ski slopes. "Uh…no."

Shit. "You're sure?"

"Sorry. That was a long time ago, and the damn chemo's messing with my mind. Something with an F, maybe. Freddie? Frankie? I don't know. Jesus…*Jackie.* I haven't thought about her in…a while."

Ed mentioned his conversations with Paul Nightingale, Ken Kelly, and Olivia Kirsch—and Owen Pendleton's flat refusal to discuss anything.

Bogen shook his head. "Good old Owen." His tone was a thick stew of resignation and disdain. "But Paul, God, I haven't seen him since he…went away. What's he up to?"

Ed told him, then asked, "Can I buy you a cup of coffee? A beer?"

Bogen was about to reply when a phone chimed. Pulling his out, he held up a finger and said, "Yes," and "Okay" a few times, and then "When?"

Bogen said he had to run home and take delivery of a dozen new machines. He invited Ed to accompany him and nodded toward a pickup truck. "We can talk on the way."

Climbing into the driver's seat left Bogen momentarily breathless. He dialed his phone and told someone named Pedro to meet him "at the barn." As he pulled into traffic, he explained that he'd listed his five

laundromats, and to dress them up, the broker had suggested replacing
the older equipment.

They drove to the outskirts of Reno, where subdivisions gave way
to a mix of car repair shops and old farmhouses on acreage. Joe's home
was a craftsman bungalow in need of a paint job. Its wide veranda had
once held a porch swing, but all that remained were two lengths of
chain. An overgrown lawn, tall pines, and thick shrubs made the place
look spooky, a house kids would avoid on Halloween. He turned into an
asphalt driveway that quickly became a rutted gravel track. The gravel
became dirt and led twenty yards through a field of knee-high weeds
to an old barn that had been transformed into a towering three-car
garage. A short Hispanic man in jeans and a cowboy hat stood beside a
dusty motorcycle.

Bogen pressed a remote and one garage door lurched upward.
Climbing out of his truck, he leaned on his cane and introduced Ed
to Pedro, then spoke rapidly in Spanish. Pedro slouched into the barn
and rode out driving a small forklift as a six-wheeler wheezed up the
driveway, crunching gravel. The truck's liftgate unfolded and rumbled
down to the ground. Pedro drove onto it and the gate rose. The big
appliance boxes sat on pallets that Pedro moved from the truck to the
garage.

The sun shone bright and hot. "I have to sit down," Bogen said, "in
shade."

Moving slowly, he led Ed inside the barn. The two side walls had
high transom windows front to back that bathed the interior in light.
The rear wall was hung floor to ceiling with magnificent Persian carpets.

"I'm a collector," Bogen said. "Got 'em when I lived in Iran." He
pointed to a worn nine-by-twelve. "That one's three hundred years old."

Washers and dryers in various states of disrepair occupied much of
the floor. A Coin-O-Matic sat on a table, for counting the quarters that
came out of the machines. A desk, computer, and file cabinet occupied
a far corner next to another pickup, a flatbed trailer, and a pile of old
pallets.

"When did you live in Iran?"

The driver presented Bogen with a document. He signed it and the
man withdrew. As the truck drove off, Bogen tossed Pedro a set of keys
and said something in Spanish. Pedro climbed back into the forklift and

maneuvered two of the new machines into the back of the other pickup. Then he hitched up the trailer, drove the forklift onto it, and secured it with rope.

"Fall of '79 to the end of '83."

So that's where he went.

Pedro drove off in a cloud of dust. Bogen rose slowly and led Ed to his truck, teetering on his cane. "About that beer…how about a pizza to go with it?"

"Great," Ed said. "It's on me."

As they headed back into town, Bogen suddenly slapped the steering wheel, shaking his head in disbelief. "Jackie's son! Sounds like he's done all right."

"Much better than all right," Ed said, mentioning Simons's rank on the Forbes 400.

"I'm glad. I always liked him—cute little guy—but I was never much for playing with kids. Not like Dave. Dave played with him a lot."

"Really?" Ed hadn't expected that.

"Children's Playground in the park was just a short walk from the house. Dave took him there."

The freeway stretched out before them. Ed reached into a pocket and pulled out a one-hitter, baggie, and lighter. "Care to sample some of San Francisco's finest?"

Bogen smiled. "Don't mind if I do. Grown in the city?"

"That's what they said."

Ed loaded the hitter and passed it to Bogen, then held the lighter up to the barrel.

"Smooth," Bogen said, exhaling out the window.

"I'm curious how you met Jackie. Olivia said you found her panhandling in front of the Drogstore."

"Not quite." Bogen smiled, remembering.

He'd driven all night from Ensenada carrying twenty pounds. The three of them—Doug, Owen, and Dave—cleaned it and moved it to the warehouse. Back in the Haight, Doug was exhausted but too wired to sleep, so he went looking for bacon and eggs. He noticed Jackie and her little boy hawking the *Oracle* in front of the Drogstore, but ignored them and had breakfast. "When I came out, the kid ran up to me and held out a paper. His mother was cute, so I bought one."

The next day, the little boy toddled up to Doug again and waved the paper. His mother said, "He bought one yesterday." Doug noticed that Jackie looked gaunt and hungry. After eating, Doug emerged from the café with a burger and fries. Mother and child sat cross-legged on the sidewalk and dug in. Jackie called Doug a saint between ravenous bites. A couple days later, he invited them into the café with him. "They were crashing in the park. I thought, that's no place for a little boy. And they needed baths. So I brought them home. It was supposed to be just temporary, but then—"

"You and Jackie became lovers."

"For a while."

"You said she was cute. Is that what attracted you?"

"Sure, but she had a good heart. And she was smart and I felt sorry for her, trying to support herself and the kid selling the paper. And she was sexy. She didn't wear a bra. Dave really liked that."

"Dave? Did he—"

"Get it on with her? Oh, yeah."

"You weren't jealous?"

"Nah, I was in Mexico a lot. When the cat's away…"

"But Dave was married." Knowing now that Dave had fooled around with Jackie, Ed thought it odd that Olivia didn't remember the boy's name—but as she'd mentioned, Jackie and her son were in and out of her life in a flash, and forty years was a long time.

"It was the sixties, man—free love. Dave and Olivia were solid. There was never any question about that. But they weren't exclusive. Dave couldn't keep it zipped. Made Mick Jagger look celibate. And Livvy wasn't just pining when he was away. She and I got it on a couple times when Dave was delivering, and she was a bit of a groupie. Had a fling with Jerry Garcia."

Ed's eyebrows arched. "The Grateful Bed, huh?"

"Once or twice."

"But wasn't it uncomfortable, you and Dave and Olivia all in the same house?"

"No," Bogen explained. "Livvy and I were basically friends. Today they call it 'friends with benefits.'"

Bogen pulled into the parking lot by his laundromat. Pedro was using the forklift to pull the machines off the truck. Then he strapped them to a big hand truck and maneuvered them inside.

Bogen nodded toward a pizza place a few doors down. "That's some fine weed. I'm starved."

Bogen wanted mushroom and pepperoni. Ed ordered a large and a pitcher of beer.

Doug had never viewed his relationship with Jackie as anything deeper than a casual affair. But it turned out she felt differently. The single mom was shopping for a husband and stepfather. If Doug wouldn't play ball, Dave looked like a good prospect, and she wasn't about to let a little detail like his marriage deter her.

"The thing was, Dave liked the kid more than he liked Jackie. And while Livvy was okay with Dave's adventures out of town, she wasn't too keen on hearing him and Jackie moaning in the next room while she was trying to eat breakfast. So after a couple months, Jackie moved to a flat a few blocks away."

"What about the bust? Olivia said Jackie ratted you out."

Bogen made a sour face. "That's the story."

Ed looked into his eyes. "Are you saying the DA *didn't* threaten to take her son unless she gave him a 'big dealer'?"

"It's possible, but Jackie swore she didn't finger us, and I believed her."

Ed had feared that Bogen would be as skittish as Pendleton, but the ex-dealer took a gulp of beer and leaned back in his chair, serene as a purring cat.

When the police kicked the door in, Doug was on a run to Mexico. By the time he returned, Owen and Olivia insisted that Jackie had betrayed them, and she was *persona non grata*.

"But," Bogen explained, "it was their word against hers, and both of them had issues. Livvy wanted her away from Dave, and Owen was all over Dave and me to tighten up."

"On the business, you mean. I heard the bust marked the moment when you got out of ounces."

"That's right. Dave and I weren't stupid. We followed Owen's lead. Dave only sold to trusted friends, but sometimes we made exceptions…" He smiled and chewed a bite of pizza. "The bust shook us up. That's when we got out of ounces and started dealing pounds—fewer customers, safer. And the bust broke us financially. It took everything we had and more to get the charges dropped. That's when Owen insisted we set up a front, a story for the taxman. Next thing you know, we're importing houseplants and Owen has us on salaries paying taxes."

"Tropical Plants Direct."

"Right. That one bust was the only time we ever had a problem with the law, and we moved thousands of pounds—always staying in the sweet spot. Owen kept us out of prison. Hell, I've never even been arrested."

"Sweet spot?"

Bogen smiled, recalling the time shortly after the bust when Owen spent several days at SF State's library, reading voraciously about drug arrests. The vast majority of border busts involved fifty pounds or more. Owen concluded that they could minimize their risk by not getting greedy, by limiting themselves to, say, twenty-five pounds per run. That weight was easy to hide and it kept them under the radar because the law was looking for bigger loads.

Meanwhile, dope dealers were typically arrested selling either an ounce or two or five pounds or more. Owen said they'd be safest if Dave distributed amounts between those two figures, staying in the sweet spot of a pound or two per sale.

"Olivia said Owen was furious at Jackie," Ed prompted.

"Like I'd never seen him."

"Furious enough to kill her?"

Bogen sighed. "Maybe, I don't know. Owen swore he didn't. He was never partial to guns. But I'd known him since we were kids, and like I say I'd never seen him that angry before, so who knows? On the other hand, I never believed that nonsense about Jackie getting killed for stiffing the speed dealer. She dealt a little speed, but she made her nut selling our weed."

"Really?" Ed's eyes widened. "Even after the bust? Olivia said Owen—"

"Cut her off? He did…and he thought we did, too. Actually, Dave and I kept supplying her, a couple pounds a month."

"About the bust. You said you didn't blame her, so who—"

"Somebody else. When we sold ounces, we had dozens of customers. We were careful, but with so many people, you can't be *that* careful."

"So you and Jackie stayed friends—with benefits?"

Bogen smiled. "Now and then. Dave and Jackie, too. She lived close by—in the flat that became the Haight-Ashbury Free Clinic. When she got killed…" Bogen inhaled deeply and exhaled a long sigh, "it really tore me up." He opened his palms and gazed upward. "It took her death to make me realize how special she was, how attached I felt to her… that I loved her, I really did. I remember a few days after, going over there, packing up her stuff and crying like I never have before or since. Everything she had fit in a couple boxes. I took them back to the house, laid everything out in my room. I must have spent a month just staring at her things, kicking myself for being such a fool, for keeping her at arm's length."

"What happened to her stuff?" If Bogen still had it, perhaps he'd give it to Simons.

"Gone. Who knows?" He shrugged. "I moved around a lot."

"If she wasn't killed by Owen or the speed dealer, you have any idea who shot her?"

"Her cops."

Ed cocked his head to one side. Did he hear right?

"Two of them, partners."

"Wait. You're saying *police* killed her?"

"I wouldn't be surprised. See, the cops hated dealers and loved busting guys like us. But if the dealer was a sweet young girl, then they were open to other arrangements."

"They blackmailed her for sex."

"Once a week. One of them would play with the boy while the other had his fun, then they'd switch, a nasty little tag-team. Jackie turning us in—it didn't make sense. We were supplying her. She *hated* doing the cops, but what choice did she have? They could have taken her downtown anytime and she would have lost her boy. She felt trapped and wanted out. I remember one night not long before she got killed, she was talking about moving back home, going to community college, maybe nursing school. She also talked about telling the cops to take a hike or she'd spill to the *Foghorn*. And then—" Emotions Bogen hadn't felt in years broke over him like surf in a storm and he wiped his eyes.

"It's funny," Ed said. "Olivia thought *you* might have killed her. She got shot. You knew guns. And you felt guilty that your girlfriend got your partners busted."

Bogen's eyes flashed. "Livvy can go fuck herself. I *loved* Jackie. I just didn't realize it. I was young and stupid and totally caught up in being an outlaw."

"Olivia said she suspected Owen more, but he hated guns."

Bogen chuckled. "Oh, yeah, Owen and Dave, all peace and love—until things changed…"

Ed gazed across the table and appraised the elfin man, who looked like a cadaver with a white mustache. A string of mozzarella hung from the corner of his mouth. He seemed surprisingly relaxed, evincing none of the grieving widow's brittleness nor his former partner's paranoia. He seemed eager to talk, almost as if he'd been waiting for Ed to find him.

Then Ed realized why. Bogen was heading for his last load of laundry. He was selling his business to get his affairs in order. But before checking out, he wanted to tell his story. Ed decided to take a chance.

"So their feelings about guns changed…maybe after that business in Mexico."

Bogen's mustache framed a crooked frown. "What do you know about that?"

"Not much. Nightingale said you had problems down there and stopped buying Mexican. Olivia wouldn't talk about it."

Bogen asked, "Any guesses?"

"You ran into police or thieves or men who were both. Then I see only three possibilities—you outran them, or bribed them…or killed them."

Bogen took a swig of beer and swallowed hard. "We outran them—thanks to my AK."

Ed averted his eyes and cut a slice in half, sliding one piece onto his plate. Years of reporting had taught him that in situations where people have every reason to clam up, it's a mistake to churn the waters. Best to wait and let the shell open on its own.

Bogen leaned closer and lowered his voice. "Our connection told us he was getting out, but offered to introduce us to a new guy in the hills. That was the first tip-off. No one gets out, especially not Mexicans. Once a dealer, always a dealer.

"Dave and Owen were all, 'Oh, you're getting out, that's cool, man, whatever, and hey, thanks for the new connection, and how do we get to his place?' But our guy—what was his name?" Bogen shook his head. "I forget, but he wouldn't look me in the eye. Of the three of us, I spoke the best Spanish. I knew him best and he wouldn't look me in the face. That's when I knew.

"Dave was driving. I begged him to turn around, forget it and head for home. Meanwhile, he's giving me shit: 'Don't be so paranoid. We're steady customers. Why would he fuck us?' Because we're dipshit gringos and there's plenty more like us, that's why. Meanwhile, Owen felt torn. His gut said I might be right, but his head couldn't figure how Dave was wrong. We were buying a steady twenty-five pounds a month. Why kill the goose laying those eggs?

"So we're out in the middle of nowhere. It was a classic setup: high desert hills, no one for miles, a long dusty road. We pass a sign. It's shot full of holes. I say fuck it, and pull my AK out of the stash. I'm checking the magazine while Dave's telling me I'm more paranoid than Owen and I'm going to scare our new guy to death.

"We round a bend and there they are, up ahead, a Jeep with guys in uniform pointing weapons. Soon as I see them, I scream, 'Stop!' And thank you, Jesus, Dave slams on the brakes. I'm yelling, 'Turn around! Step on it! And get ready to drive with no windshield!'"

"No windshield?"

"Right. In an ambush, it's not the guys in *front* of you, it's the guys *behind*. Dave does a one-eighty and we're burning rubber, bouncing all over the road, and I'm hoping the damn tires don't blow, and through the dust, I see another Jeep roaring down a hill, heading right for us, more guys and more weapons."

"So you were caught between them."

"That was their plan, only they didn't count on the AK. With all the dust, I couldn't see too good, but their weapons looked compact, like Uzis or MAC-10s. AKs have twice the range. Suddenly, I'm back in the jungle."

He scratched his cheek and his breathing turned shallow and quick. "You know, Nam wasn't about big armies facing off across the fields of Gettysburg. It was about small squads in vicious firefights. And in that kind of war, it's less about who outguns who than who's got the range and shoots first."

"So you killed them? You said you outran them."

"I opened up, blew out our windshield. Love those AKs—a thousand rounds a minute and noise to wake the dead. Glass everywhere, and dust like you wouldn't believe. I couldn't see a damn thing. I was scared shitless and shooting wild and I've got a lap full of glass and I'm choking on dust and Dave's flipping out and the van's bucking like a rodeo bull. I didn't hit them, but I came close, kicked up dirt around them, and they stopped, which was all that mattered. They didn't expect an AK. Dave floored it and we zipped past them."

Ed realized he'd been holding his breath and forced himself to exhale. "And then?"

"Dave pissed his pants and Owen shit his. They realized how stupid they'd been, how we came *this close* to being buzzards' lunch. 'We don't need AKs.' Fucking hippies. That AK saved our asses. By the time we reached the border, we agreed our days of running Mexican weed were over."

"So you started dealing Colombian."

"Couple months later."

Doug related that he'd called an old Army buddy, Artie, who'd been running Mexican from Oaxaca to El Paso, asking if he'd share his connection or wholesale to them. It turned out that he too had encountered problems south of the border and was looking for another source. An old friend of his crewed a fishing boat out of Half Moon Bay.

"Nightingale said you guys teamed up."

"Yes, his group, us, Artie, and a couple others."

Late one night, the consortium of buyers motored out to a rusting freighter. In one hand, they held suitcases stuffed with Franklins, and in the other, automatic weapons.

"Wait," Ed said, "Dave and Owen were armed?"

"Oh, yeah. AKs and Uzis. They didn't like it, and wouldn't train for shit, but after Mexico…"

As things turned out, the Colombian connection lasted only two years, 1970 to '71.

"The Colombians had fine weed and never shorted the weight, but they were nasty fuckers—made the Viet Cong look like choir boys. Not to mention that after a few trips, the fishing captain doubled his fee, and a while later, bumped it again. Meanwhile, Dave started experimenting in the forest near his in-laws' ranch."

46

"So," Ed said, "you dumped the Colombians and started growing in Mendocino."

"Well…" Bogen made a face. "It wasn't that simple. I almost bailed."

Owen and Dave were enthusiastic about backcountry growing. Weed grew in the national forest like, well, a weed, and compared with smuggling, cultivation was easier, cheaper, and safer. But Doug was dead set against it. The pirate had no interest in trading his cutlass for a hoe.

Owen was incredulous. He sat Doug down and ran the numbers. At a pound per plant, they could easily grow as much as they were buying from the Colombians, with much less risk and tons more profit. All they needed was someone in the woods to tend the plants. With Owen running the business and Dave handling distribution, there was only one choice.

"The thing was," Bogen said, swallowing pizza, "I *hated* gardening. Growing up, my family had a big lot, and my dad made my brothers and me spend two hours a week doing yard work: weeding, watering, raking, mowing the damn lawn. I couldn't stand it—and they wanted to make it my *career.*

"Meanwhile, I *loved* smuggling. What a rush! Sure, the Colombians were sick pricks, but so were the Mexicans. Everyone was. I was hanging with Paul and Artie and their people, and we all loved midnight rendezvous on the high seas. So when Owen and Dave said they wanted to grow, I told them go ahead and good luck, but I'm throwing in with Artie—goodbye."

Dave's reaction had been largely philosophical—it was a shame Doug wanted out, but he was a free agent. Meanwhile, Owen felt betrayed and told Doug he never wanted to see him again.

Then the DEA arrested Nightingale's group. It wasn't clear how they got nailed. Fingers pointed in all directions. The fishing captain disappeared. His crew evaporated. And no other captain could be trusted. Meanwhile, Artie never liked trucking loads from California all the way to Texas, and arranged to buy off a freighter in the Gulf. When the dust settled, Doug had only two friends, and only one way to make a living. The rum runner became a moonshiner.

"Only Owen balked at taking me back—after knowing me since kindergarten, after all I'd done for him. It was humiliating."

Eventually, Owen relented and Dave and Doug scouted the area around Synder Creek. Above its junction with Waterfall Creek, for a half mile, it ran through a steep ravine covered with a wall of blackberries that appeared impenetrable. But if you knew the terrain, there were open areas perfect for growing weed.

The partners bought a house near Covelo and Doug moved in. Their nearest neighbor was a quarter-mile away, so no one saw anything— or smelled what they dried in the shed. They folded the houseplant company and launched Northern California Drip Irrigation Systems. But most of their lines, emitters, and pumps ran from springs deep in the woods to plots hidden in the ravine. Doug became a trapper running his lines, while Owen issued W-2s and Dave spread happiness from Arcata to Grass Valley to Monterey.

Bogen took a sip of beer. "The funny thing was, all those years of slaving away for my dad actually taught me how to grow. The terrain was steep and I wasn't in the best shape. At first, I was huffing and puffing. But pretty quick I became a ravine rat, and whenever I turned an ankle or got poison oak or cut up by blackberries, I thought about Paul in prison, and how lucky I was to be with Owen, even though he could be an ass."

Tropical Plants Direct had been a front, but it was a real business. The partners hauled tons of houseplants and made decent money wholesaling to nurseries and plant stores. But by the time they started growing, Owen realized that a paper front was good enough. They never intended the drip company to be a real business. So what happened?

The bands started buying homes and hiring them to irrigate their yards—Jefferson Airplane's mansion by Golden Gate Park, the places Bill Graham and Jerry Garcia bought in Marin, and Neil Young's in La Honda.

"For a couple years," Bogen recalled, "installing drip systems kept Owen jumping."

"What about *Grow It?*" Ed asked. "Olivia said Owen was against it, and when Dave did it anyway, he wanted him to write as Johnny Appleweed."

"Correct."

"How'd you feel about the book?"

"I saw Owen's point. If everyone grew, we'd be out of business. And there was a chance the book could bring the cops down on us. But I also saw Dave's point. The *Berkeley Barb* had articles about overthrowing the damn government, and the police didn't bother them. Besides, anyone can grow carrots, but most people still buy them. See, Dave was on a mission. He wanted weed legalized and if enough people grew, there was no way the government could stop it. He and Owen had a few spats, but I figured if Dave wanted to write about growing, why not? Then the book made good money and the cops didn't bother us, so after a while, Owen shut up."

"Correct me if I'm wrong," Ed ventured, "but isn't Covelo miles from Synder ravine? How'd you get all the gear up there?"

Bogen's smile looked like a skeleton's. "In a backpack. I drove in as close as I could on logging roads. Got a deadwood permit that allowed me to cut downed trees. I kept some logs and a chainsaw in the back of the truck for show. Hiked the rest of the way with the drip lines like bandoleers and the hardware on my back. I hiked my brains out, lost fifteen pounds, got strong, felt great. I came to love the ravine. It was way out there. Nobody bothered me. I even got into making blackberry pies and preserves."

Ed poured the dregs of the pitcher into his glass, and held up the empty, signaling for another. Bogen had downed most of it and seemed to be feeling no pain. Ed thought he just might open up. "Until that fateful day in '78, right?"

Bogen bit his lip. "What do you know about *that?*"

"Not a thing, really. Just what I've inferred."

"Such as?" Bogen's eyes drilled into Ed's. "Tell me."

Ed recapped Olivia's vague tale of big-time trouble pushing them to quit, then explained his own findings, that a landslide on Waterfall Creek had exposed the remains of three men wounded by gunfire in the late '70s, then executed.

"I'm guessing you branched out and had plants growing on Waterfall. They ripped you off and you didn't like that."

The pitcher arrived and Bogen poured and drank. Ed could almost see the gears grinding inside his bald head.

"*Absolute confidentiality*," Ed said as emphatically as he could.

"Easy for you to say…but it's my ass."

"No," Ed said as if singing a lullaby. "It isn't. Doug Connelly disappeared thirty years ago. You're Joe Bogen, a respectable business-man. You've never been near Mendocino. And as far as the police are concerned, whatever happened there *never happened*."

Bogen took a deep breath and sighed. He planted his elbows on the table and pressed his palms together as if praying for forgiveness. "I was always real careful to cover my lines, but the fuckers found one and followed it to our biggest plot. I must have had twenty-five plants there, big and bushy, ripe buds ready to harvest—at least two pounds a plant, so we're talking fifty, sixty pounds, real money. I came over the ridge and heard them whooping it up. They were hacking my beautiful plants, stuffing them into garbage bags. I figured I'd scare them off with a few rounds. But the fuckers fired back—with a rifle. I'm kicking myself. All I have is a lousy .38. The damn AK's back in the truck.

"I see them fan out. They're quiet, but I hear them moving through the underbrush trying to flank me, standard military tactics. My head's in the jungle again. I scoot up the ridge but I'm outnumbered, outgunned, and they're surrounding me. I'm quiet but not silent. They hear me and fire rounds that kick up dirt pretty close. I'm in deep shit. And they're gaining on me.

"But I'm holding two aces. I'm in great shape and I know the terrain. Between Waterfall Creek and the ridge, there's a rocky overhang covered by blackberries, but under the ledge, there's a hiding place. I scramble over there. Getting through the blackberries is a bitch. I'm all cut up. They hear me thrashing and follow.

"I'm crouched under the ledge. Two of them come up the ridge path, rifles scanning. I look down at my gun hand. It's shaking. Even with a clear shot, who knows if I can hit them...unless they're very close. I wait and breathe and try to calm down. When they're almost on top of me, I stand up." He mimed a pistol with his thumb and index finger, then bent his thumb twice. "Boom! Boom! Two shots, two kills. I want to climb up and get their rifles, but there's no time. The other guy's running up the ridge. I duck back down, but after the shots, he stops and drops. He's yelling to his buddies. Turns out one's still alive and crying for help. The guy down the trail doesn't move. He knows I'm nearby, but not where. He puts a hand to his ear, but doesn't hear anything except his buddy moaning. He crawls up the path on his belly. I wait till he's real close, then...boom!"

Ed clenched his jaw to keep himself quiet. *Let him talk.* Bogen toyed with his mustache, his breath coming in short, shallow bursts.

"Turns out all three are alive but they're wounded pretty bad. My truck's miles away. There's no way I can hump them down there. Meanwhile, if they live, they'll just come back for the next crop—and me, so..."

"Back of the head."

Bogen looked away. "It was the only way."

Across the dining room, two parents divided a large pie among four boisterous kids.

"Then I pull out their wallets. Fuck! *Badges.* DEA. I pull the bodies into the hiding place under the ledge and run back to the truck for a pick and shovel—and leather gloves and a jacket to deal with the damn blackberries. I bury them and tie the bramble so you can't see anything from the trail above or the creek below."

Doug got on the phone and Owen and Dave rushed up to Covelo. The dead guys were clearly thieves, but what else were they? Crooked feds? Rip-off artists impersonating feds? Their badges looked real. If they were DEA, Doug was a cop killer and Dave and Owen were accessories. Doug was looking at the gas chamber; Owen and Dave, twenty-five to life. They'd gone into the woods to escape men with guns, but illegal drugs attract firearms like honey attracts bees. They'd been in the business a long time, and now, in their mid-thirties, it had lost its luster. They'd made enough money. It was time to get out.

They emptied the house, closed the irrigation business, and split everything three ways. Doug said he was thinking about traveling around the world. Owen seconded that emotion, saying it would be best for everyone if he disappeared. They smoked one last bowl, hugged each other, and Doug drove away. That was the last he saw of his partners for thirty years, until the funeral.

Owen hired a lawyer who stayed on top of Mendocino warrants and missing-persons reports. No one reported three men missing. No local cops or CAMP or DEA agents were reported killed in the forest. No one found any bodies. And no warrants were ever issued.

"Owen sent word through Artie," Bogen explained. "After a year, I figured I was safe. I thought about coming back, but Owen said not to, just in case, and I was having fun abroad."

"Who do you think they were?"

Bogen shook his head. "No idea, but they weren't yahoos. The way they fanned out to surround me, they had tactical training. Beyond that?" He just shrugged.

"Can you back up a bit? After…what happened, what did you do?"

"Trucked my stuff to a storage locker in Reno."

"Why Reno?"

"Closest city to Covelo outside California. And in Nevada, people mind their own business. Like when I changed my tattoo to a pine tree. The guy just took my money and did it."

"How'd you change your name?"

"Artie's father had a friend who worked for the VA, something to do with the database. He was looking to retire, but didn't have much of a nest egg. I helped him and he helped me. The real Joe Bogen was ex-Navy, a guy my age who'd just died in a motorcycle crash. My man canceled his death and substituted my photo for his. He also gave me Bogen's Social Security number. I ordered a copy of his birth certificate, which got me a passport."

The new Joe Bogen flew to Tokyo, then traveled the hippie circuit through Australia, Indonesia, and Thailand. In Phuket, he met a German girl who wanted to ride the trans-Siberian railway. They boarded in Vladivostock and parted company in Moscow. Bogen drifted through Romania, Bulgaria, and Turkey, into Afghanistan, and finally into Iran.

"You said you were there—when again?"

"Fall of '79 to the end of '83."

Somewhere in Ed's memory a match flared. "Wasn't that in the middle of—"

"The Iran hostage business. Yes, but that worked out great for me. The U.S. and Iran broke off relations. No way the DEA could touch me."

"But you were *American.* Didn't the Iranians—"

"Actually, I was *Canadian.* You ever want a counterfeit passport, I know a guy in Kandahar, the Picasso of forgery."

"Where'd you live in Iran?"

"Ever hear of Bandar-e Anzali?" It was Iran's largest port on the Caspian Sea, the world capital of caviar and a center of the Persian rug trade. "I rented an apartment overlooking the harbor. Picked up enough Farsi to get by. Drank lots of coffee, smoked lots of hash. I bought barrels of caviar and tons of rugs and shipped them to Artie. Slipped some hash into the caviar. We did very well."

Eventually Bogen grew homesick. He returned to Reno to pick up his belongings, but had nowhere to go and never left. He didn't have to work, but figured he'd raise fewer eyebrows if he had a business, and laundromats practically run themselves.

"Where was Artie?"

"Austin, but I didn't want to move there. I liked his wife a little too much and didn't want to fuck up the friendship."

"You had no contact with Dave or Owen?"

"None. When they saw the badges, they were ready to kill me—for real. It didn't matter that I had the connection in Mexico, or saved their asses down there, or hooked them up with the Colombians, or grew killer weed in the woods. They just kept wailing, 'You didn't have to *do that.*' Bullshit. If I'd laid low and let them take the crop, they would have come back for the next one—with more guys and more guns. Dave lived a hippie delusion of peace and love and getting the world high. Owen talked like a gangster but was afraid of his own shadow. We were *outlaws,* for Chrissakes. When thieves clean you out—it doesn't matter who they are—outlaws can't call the police. You take care of business. That's what I did, what I *had to do.*"

Ed found it hard to reconcile Bogen's hard line with the shrunken ghost sitting across from him. He talked like a Mafia soldier but looked like he barely had enough energy to swat a mosquito.

"Okay," Ed said, "I see your point, but I also see theirs. They were scared to death of winding up like Paul Nightingale. I can see you fleeing the country and them saying good riddance. But by the time you came back, you were free and clear. I'm surprised you guys didn't reconnect."

Bogen snorted. "I was still pissed at them for booting me out, and I was scared that if they knew my new name and whereabouts, one day the law might lean on them, and to save their own sorry asses they might give up the cop killer."

Ed didn't expect that. "Why would the police 'lean on them'?"

Bogen's lips curled into a slow smile. "Because they were still in business."

Ed's face contorted. "But—"

"Let me guess," Bogen interrupted. "Livvy and Paul and Ken all swore on a stack of Bibles that we totally shut down." Ed nodded and Bogen chuckled. "Then how do you explain *Grow It Indoors!*"

Ed reiterated Olivia's explanation of Dave's plants in the closet.

"Oh, sure," Bogen chuckled, "that was part of it—but only a small part. Once a dealer, always a dealer. It gets in your blood. I got out because I had to. I was looking at a death sentence. But once I was gone, they were off the hook. Of course they moved indoors. We were already talking about it before…what happened. We'd owned the warehouse for years, false wall and everything. All they had to do was string up grow lights in the secret room and they were in business—with no worries about men with guns."

"No one ever noticed the fake wall?"

"Why would they? The warehouse was sixty feet long with the main door at one end. We walled off the back ten feet and hid that door real well. No one ever went back there but us. The only people who ever visited were delivery guys, and they only got as far as the loading dock.

"Of course," Bogen continued, "once they converted the secret room for growing, they had a problem. Grow lights draw a lot of power. A sudden jump in the electric bill tips PG&E to a grow operation and they call the police. So I'll bet my right nut they installed solar to power their lights."

"What about the smell?" Ed asked. "I only buy an ounce at a time, but it stinks up the house so bad I have to keep it in a shed."

"We had that problem warehousing the Mexican and Colombian.

That was the reason we got a warehouse out in the wilds of Hunters Point. It backed onto the bay. We rigged up fans to blow out over the water and no one ever said boo. Of course, these days a good hydroponic setup includes odor-suppression. I bet they have a system. Dave grew a few plants at home to snow Livvy, but the action was at the warehouse. That's how he wrote the book."

"But Olivia said Dave and Owen hardly saw each other."

"So Owen didn't visit the house. They met at the warehouse."

"And Owen's hair salons? They're fronts?"

"*Obviously*. Haircutting is mostly a cash business. I imagine the salons make money. But I'll bet if you look at Owen's tax return, only a fraction of the gross comes from hair. And Dave's real estate? Buying property is a classic way to launder money. You go to a title company, open an escrow account, deposit a big down payment. You think anyone asks where the money comes from? Then you report rents, only some of it isn't rent."

"But Owen has a dozen salons, and Dave was on the Board of Supervisors. He was running for mayor! How would they have time to grow—and sell?"

"If you stay small like we always did, growing doesn't take much time—an indoor operation in that size room, maybe an hour a day, and a little more at harvest time. Neither of them had bosses. They could arrange to slip away. And selling's easier than ever. Medical marijuana operations contract to buy entire crops. I bet they only have two or three customers."

"Can you tell me where the warehouse is?"

Bogen shook his head. "I've already said too much."

The waitress brought the check. Ed grabbed it and produced a credit card. "So, what about you, Joe? After you sell your business, then what?"

"I'm not sure." Bogen gazed out the window toward Mount Rose. "Been thinking about moving to Tampa. Artie died last year—heart attack, very sudden. His wife, Jenny, moved there. We've been spending some time…and God knows how much I've got left."

Ed rose, and Bogen struggled to his feet. Ed started to thank him, but Bogen interrupted. "No, man, thank *you*."

"Any chance our conversation jogged your memory about Jackie's boy? His name?"

Bogen shook his head. "Sorry."

"If you ever remember…" Ed handed him a card.

47

As Ed drove through Reno, the glass facades of the huge hotel-casinos were aflame in the late afternoon sun. He was about to take the exit to 80 West when he had a thought. Hair salons are a cash business. *So are laundromats.*

Ed turned around, drove south, and remembered the exit. After a couple wrong turns, he eventually found his way to the gravel track. Bogen's pickup was parked in front of the house, and through a window, Ed could see images flashing on a big-screen TV. But this wasn't a social call.

Ed drove past the house and turned down a road in serious need of repaving. Forty yards past a cluster of Airstream trailers, he pulled up at a spot that provided a clear view of Bogen's garage. One look told him the man was growing. The roof was covered with solar panels. Earlier he'd noticed sunlight streaming through windows that ran the length of the side walls. But illuminated by the sun's dying rays, the windows closest to the back of the old barn looked different, as if they'd been painted black—to hide grow lights. The door to Bogen's grow room had to be tucked behind one of the rugs hanging from the false rear wall. Once a dealer…

Ed drove away confused. With only a little prodding and two pitchers of beer, Bogen had confessed to killing three men. Why wouldn't he admit growing?

Maybe because indoor growing had turned out to be no refuge from men with guns. The *Foghorn* had run stories about armed thieves kicking down the doors of grow houses. Bogen was just being prudent, protecting his crop.

Ed crested Donner Summit and rolled down toward Auburn. As night descended, he flashed on the last time Dave and Owen saw each other, when they clashed over the memoir and Owen stormed out. What if Bogen was right? What if they were still partners? Ramirez said Dave's memoir only got as far as 1971, when they were setting up in Mendocino. Ed couldn't believe Dave would even hint at how that ended or their move indoors, especially while running for mayor. So what had infuriated Pendleton? Ed had no idea.

But Bogen's story transformed Pendleton from obnoxious to understandable. His prickliness, his denials, and his hiring the PI—he wasn't merely a paranoid jerk refusing to discuss the distant past. He was a grower trying to keep his operation secret.

The afternoon Dave got shot, Ramirez had said Owen was at a check-up at General. He couldn't have pulled the trigger, but he'd spent many decades in a business that required guns. Nightingale and Artie couldn't be his only big-time connections. He had to know other guys with arsenals in their closets. And after forty years of bickering with Dave, maybe Owen decided he'd finally had enough. Not to mention that with his partner out of the picture, Owen wouldn't have to split the net. Pendleton had money. He could afford to hire someone who knew exactly what he was doing. One shot, one kill.

48

Ed hadn't seen the Thunderbird since he'd threatened Pendleton with headlines. But as he kept one eye on the road and the other on the silver Lexus ahead of him, he had to concede grudging respect for the PI. Following a car in traffic was harder than it looked.

It took Ed three tries to tail Owen to the city's gritty southeast corner. The warehouse stood above the Bay shore overlooking the ruins of San Francisco's shipbuilding industry, rusted cranes presiding over rotted docks in dirty water that emitted a fetid stink. The warehouse was utterly anonymous, without sign or street number. It was one of a dozen identical, squat, corrugated metal shells lined up shoulder to shoulder along abandoned railroad tracks. Except for Pendleton's car, the area was as deserted as the moon.

The way the warehouses were configured, Ed couldn't see the roof, so he wound his way up the hill to the housing project that was being renovated. Gazing down, he could see a large array of solar panels glistening on the roof of one warehouse.

Ed drove down the hill and noted Pendleton's license number. Back home, he Googled the DMV. It didn't take long to find the address.

49

Mill Valley felt ten degrees warmer than the Mission. The house was a modest 1950s ranch redone in twenty-first century splendor. Behind a wood fence and a thick wall of junipers, the front yard looked like a European park, sheltered and manicured with an oddly shaped bird feeder hanging from a Japanese maple.

Ed pressed the button, then turned away from the door. When it opened, he whirled to face Owen Pendleton. "Thanks for calling off your goon. I appreciate it."

Pendleton moved to slam the door as Ed said, "Imagine this headline: 'Local Philanthropist Runs Huge Pot Farm in Hunters Point.'"

The door stopped closing and opened an inch. Pendleton's expression said that if he'd been armed, Ed would end up in a body bag.

"You'll never guess who I ran into in Reno last week. Your old buddy, Doug Connelly—I mean, Joe Bogen. He told me all about solar arrays and the false wall at your warehouse and how moving indoors meant that you and Dave didn't need him anymore. A two-way split instead of three. And now, with Dave gone, all the income's yours. You must be coining money."

Pendleton froze. "Fucking Doug. He finally got his revenge."

"Listen," Ed added quickly, "I don't care that you grow. Your secret is safe with me. *Absolute confidentiality*. I have a card. For all I know, I'm smoking *yours*. I just want to talk about Jackie Zarella, that's all—just Jackie. Give me twenty minutes and you'll never see me again."

Pendleton scowled but opened the door. "Twenty minutes and

you're out of my life?"

"I swear."

Pendleton stepped outside and nodded toward a bench in a corner of the yard. He wore a starched shirt, sharply creased khakis, and loafers. As he sat down, Ed heard a faint whirring from the direction of the Japanese maple. A pair of hummingbirds hovered by the feeder.

From a pocket, Ed produced a one-hitter, a baggie, lighter, and a big fat brownie in plastic wrap. He held them out. "Peace offerings."

Pendleton's scowl softened into a simple frown. "Let's see the weed." He opened the baggie and glanced inside, then returned it to Ed. "Nope. These threads are yellow. Ours are more gold."

"Then let's research the competition."

Pendleton snorted and Ed loaded the barrel. As Pendleton lit up and exhaled a cloud, Ed fiddled with plastic wrap.

"How'd you know I love brownies?" Owen asked.

"You were eating one in your office."

"I don't like being pressured."

"And I don't like being followed by guys who flash guns at my wife."

Pendleton shifted from sitting with his back ramrod straight to leaning back and crossing an ankle over a knee. "All right," he said, his icy tone starting to thaw. "Let's get this over with."

Ed handed him the unwrapped brownie. He did not say thanks.

"When did you first meet Jackie?"

Pendleton took a bite and chewed. His eyes scanned the yard. Now there were four hummingbirds. "I forget. But we were living in the Haight—Dave, Livvy, Doug, and me—and Doug moved up in '66, so it had to be around then. Maybe early '67."

"She was photographed at the Be-In with Doug, so it had to be before January '67."

"Fine. So sometime in '66."

"What did you think of her?"

"Not much. I didn't trust her—and I was right."

"You're referring to the bust."

"So you know about that. Yes."

"Do you remember her boy's name?"

"No, as I already told you."

"What do you remember about her?"

Pendleton shrugged. "She wasn't around long. She was a runaway, like so many kids back then, a skinny little waif with a backpack and sleeping bag, only she also had the kid. She had a hunted look. She was dirty. Her hair was a mess. What Doug saw in her I'll never know. At the time, I figured easy pussy, and from what Doug and Dave said, that was true, but—"

"In the photo, she looks like a hippie cheerleader."

"After she cleaned up and got a haircut and some clothes that fit, she was reasonably attractive and devoted to her boy, but he was a brat."

"Joe—I mean Doug—said Dave took Jackie to bed and Olivia knew, but—"

"Hello?" Pendleton rolled his eyes. "It was the sixties: dope, rock 'n roll, and fucking in the streets. Dave and Livvy were married, but it was an open marriage, like some gay relationships, a primary lover and secondaries. That was a big reason Dave liked distribution. He was the candy man, rolling doobies and sharing tastes. Between the weed and his good looks and charm, he warmed a lot of beds. Livvy played around, too, nowhere near as much as Dave, but—"

"Doug said she had a fling with Jerry Garcia."

Pendleton nodded. "Other musicians, too. She had a groupie streak. And when Dave was off making deliveries, every now and then, she and Doug fooled around."

"Yes, he mentioned that. But Jackie moved into Doug's room."

Pendleton stretched out on the bench and gazed at a stand of calla lilies surrounding an avocado sapling. "I haven't thought about that house in years." He inhaled, then sighed. "Doug had the attic, two rooms. They were sort of hidden, up a steep stair behind a door in the back of the upstairs hall. It was classic Doug, the desperado in his secret lair. There was a dormer with a little alcove. That's where they put the kid."

"According to Olivia, Jackie turned you in."

"The bitch. My only arrest. Still pisses me off."

"How'd you know she—"

"Because she was a *fucking idiot*. She'd sell anything to anyone. She sold speed off a blanket on Hippie Hill for all the world to see."

"Paul Nightingale told me it was a dirty bust, no warrant, and the cops threatened to get one backdated unless you came up with fifteen grand in cash."

"You talked to Paul?" Pendleton almost smiled. "How is he?"

"Good." Ed filled him in, then asked, "Why'd you think it was Jackie?"

Owen shrugged. "Everyone said—friends, people on the street, at the *Oracle*. It made sense. Jackie was careless and we didn't really know her."

"Doug's convinced Jackie didn't rat on you. He said a dozen other people could have."

Pendleton savored a bite of brownie. "Sure, but we heard she was dirty, and I didn't like her hanging around, and Livvy wasn't happy about Dave fucking her, so it was easy to point fingers."

"Were you aware that after the bust, Doug and Dave continued to supply her?"

Pendleton made a sour face and shook his head. "No. Idiots."

"Doug also said that two cops let Jackie keep dealing in exchange for sex. You know anything about that?"

"No, but I'm not surprised. I've heard stories. Sex and drugs make the world go round."

"Doug thinks the cops killed her after she threatened to take their arrangement to the *Foghorn*."

Pendleton shrugged. "Who knows? Anything's possible."

"What about the Be-In?" Ed pulled out the photos. "I hear you opted out of the picture-taking."

"Damn right I did." Pendleton sneered. "Mike turned on the charm, tried to talk me into it, but—"

"Michael Bowen, the *Oracle*'s art director."

"That's right."

"So you were friends?"

"Hello? Who do you think paid the *Oracle*'s print bill? We did—the dealers. They had no advertising. Every time they went to the printer, Allen hit us up. And we gave: us, Owsley, several others."

Ed held his breath as he nudged the conversation ever so slightly from Jackie to Pendleton. "Really? Why? What was in it for you?"

"It never hurts to have friends, especially in an illegal business. In a pinch, I wanted supporters who could raise a ruckus if we got threatened with prison."

"I understand you weren't happy that Dave wrote for the *Oracle*."

"Of course not. It was like he wore a sign: 'Dope Dealer. Bust Me.' I insisted he use 'Johnny Appleweed.'"

"But he published *Grow It!* under his own name."

"Which was really stupid. Even back then, Dave was a politician fishing for name recognition. But what could I do? I ran the business, but I didn't control him."

"Didn't Jackie move out before the bust?"

"Yes. She was conveniently gone by then, another reason we suspected her."

"How long did she live with you?"

"I forget. A few months. Underneath that dreamy exterior, what Jackie really wanted was a husband, a station wagon, and a white picket fence. Doug wasn't going to provide that. Dave was married. And I was gay. So she went looking elsewhere."

"And found a speed dealer."

"Apparently."

"What do you remember about her death?"

"Not much. We heard a girl got shot on Hippie Hill. The next day, we saw her picture in the paper."

"Any idea why she was killed?"

"Just what we heard—that she owed a meth dealer and didn't pay up."

"When you heard, did you care?"

"Not really. I was still furious about the bust. But Doug was distraught. He went on and on about how much he loved her—which was news to me."

"So you were furious with Jackie, and then she got killed."

Owen's eyes drilled into Ed's.

"I'm not accusing you—"

"Sounds like you are."

"No, but one person I interviewed—"

Owen looked like he'd just sucked a lemon. "Let me guess. Livvy."

"She didn't exactly *accuse* you. She just said she...wondered."

Owen shook his head as he finished the brownie and licked his fingers. He was stoned. He'd had a chocolate sugar fix. And his tongue had loosened. "She never liked me."

"Why? Your paranoia?"

"Oh no, she *loved* that. I kept her husband out of prison."

"So?"

Pendleton's lips curled into a tight smile. "She was afraid I'd woo Dave back into bed."

Ed's eyebrows jumped to the top of his forehead.

"Livvy didn't mention that, did she? When she met Dave, he and I were lovers."

50

Dave and Owen? Ed felt his head spinning like a cartoon character taking a punch. They'd moved away from Jackie, but he hoped Pendleton would keep talking. "Another hit?"

Owen reached for the paraphernalia and worked the lighter. "Smooth," he said, exhaling. "Fast-acting and stony. But mine's better."

"I'm sure it is," Ed said, loading himself a hit.

"Dave was bi," Owen explained, "but he leaned straight. We fooled around, but I knew he'd eventually go for girls. As soon as Livvy got her hooks in him, we were done. Which was fine—we were better partners than lovers. But Livvy always saw me as a threat. She felt she could keep her man over any other woman, but what could she do if Dave went gay? Day to day around the house, we were civil. And in the business, she always supported me. But she never cared for me. She even accused me of killing Dave, the cunt. The cops were all over me."

"Any idea who might have killed him?"

"No, but he was running surprisingly strong for mayor. If I had to guess, I'd say it was politics that killed him."

"Who? Conservatives who hated the idea of legalizing weed and prostitution?"

"No, CAMP or the DEA or a prison guard."

"Whoa, you think *cops* killed him?"

"I do. Marijuana prohibition pumps billions into law enforcement. Dave's legalization efforts were starting to gain traction. If weed is ever legalized, a lot of cops and prison guards lose their jobs."

"You think he could have won? Become mayor?"

"Maybe. But it would have ended there."

"Why?"

"Let me tell you about Dave." Owen's smile reminded Ed of an iguana. "He was a hippie stoner who didn't know the difference between a balance sheet and a triple-beam balance. But he *really was* Johnny Appleweed. He spread a lot of seed, and I'm not just talking cannabis. San Franciscans don't hold their politicians to personal purity, but outside Gomorrah by the Bay, it's another world, and he didn't stand a chance of winning higher office."

"If he was such a philanderer, why'd Olivia stay with him?"

"Because she loved him. And he loved her. In his own way, he was devoted to her."

"Earlier, you called Dave 'the candy man.' From the song?"

"People called him that before the song. That's how what's-his-name came up with it."

"Tommy Smith of Magic Bullet Theory, the guy who broke Dave's nose."

Pendleton grimaced. "That's right. A prize asshole."

"What happened?"

"Tommy was a decent musician. But he was a drunk—a stinking, pathetic drunk who deluded himself into thinking he was the vanguard of the proletariat. But his idea of communism was that the world should take care of Tommy while Tommy took care of no one, least of all himself."

Ed recounted what he'd heard about hip capitalists.

"That's right. When I told Dave to cut Tommy off, the Diggers decided we were the enemy."

"How'd that play out?"

"Snide remarks when we stopped by the store, so we stopped going. Then snide remarks on the street. Then Tommy punching Dave."

"Did you feel hurt?"

"Dave did, Livvy, too, but not me. I never went for any of that 'Age of Aquarius' shit. I was a businessman, and from the start I had Tommy pegged as a parasite."

"What'd you think of the song?"

"Musically, I liked it—good beat, cool guitar licks. But I didn't want *any* attention on our operation, so I was glad when it faded and MBT crashed and burned."

"Earlier you mentioned Doug's revenge. What's that about?"

"Telling *you* that we went indoors. Sticking it to me after all these years."

"You might be interested to know that behind his house, he has a big barn with a false wall and a roof full of solar panels—oh, and a cash business. laundromats."

Pendleton snorted. "He told me about the laundromats. I should have guessed."

"Olivia swore that since '78, you and Dave had virtually no contact. She was very convincing."

"She ought to be. She never knew."

"Really?" That was hard to believe. "How did Dave keep it from her?"

"It wasn't difficult. He grew a few plants at home and told her that's how he wrote *Indoors!* Meanwhile, we had the warehouse. And it worked like a dream."

"Why didn't you tell her?"

"Dave wanted to, but I said no. Livvy started drinking and drunks can't keep their mouths shut." Ed recalled that at the store she had smelled of alcohol, before lunch.

"But Olivia said you and Dave didn't really get along."

"We were partners. You ever been in a partnership?"

"I'm married."

"Then you know. Sure, we argued. Who doesn't? But we were together forty years. And we made tons of money."

"What about your last argument with Dave? What was that about? When he threw you out—"

"Did Livvy say he threw me out? The bitch. She took too much acid and she's still hallucinating. He *didn't* throw me out. I left in a huff after he refused to show me his precious manuscript. Some shit about 'journalistic integrity,' whatever *that* is."

Pendleton shook his head, his expression a mix of grief and exasperation. "Dave was a great guy and I loved him, but he was a dreamer and a grandstander. That's a bad combination when you're in an illegal business. Of course, he wasn't stupid. All those years, he kept his lip zipped just fine. When he announced for mayor, everyone said he had no chance. Then suddenly, he started looking like a winner. Major players were coming around, telling him he could use the mayor's office as a springboard to who knows what.

"It went to his head. He had this crazy notion that legalization was just around the corner and when it happened, wouldn't it be cool to be mayor and tell the world that Johnny Appleweed had been growing all along? He saw himself as a cuddly criminal like the madam who became mayor of Sausalito. His commitment to security slipped and I got nervous. The police would have come in their pants to pop Dave Kirsch, and if that happened, I was toast. We had a sweet thing going. I just wanted to review his damn book to make sure the stars in his eyes didn't blind him and fuck us both."

"According to Olivia, you left the house in a rage…a possibly murderous rage."

"Which is why the cops were all over me—"

"Until they discovered you were at General."

"So you know I'm a long-term survivor."

"When did you get it?"

"No idea, but as soon as the test came out, I got the bad news. I'm sure you recall, back then, being positive—it was a death sentence. I wrote my will, bought a plot. Then I *lived*—me and about forty other guys. No one knows why, so they study us. It was beyond amazing. A real second chance. It taught me how precious life is. That's when I got into philanthropy."

Pendleton paused as if collecting his thoughts, then said, "I didn't kill Dave. I *loved* him. Livvy acts like he and I were cats and dogs while the two them were Romeo and Juliet. You should have *seen* them. They had some doozies. One time Dave threatened to leave her and Livvy threw half the china cabinet at him. And come to think of it, you know what that fight was about? Jackie and her boy."

"Do tell."

"Dave always wanted kids. That's why he and Livvy got married. Then she cooled on the idea. They were too young. The world was a mess. And I don't think she was too keen on her children's father being a dope dealer. They argued about it. Then Jackie moved in and Dave got to play daddy. He loved it, and pushed Livvy to toss the pill, but she wouldn't. So he started boning Jackie and talking about running off with her and adopting the kid. I knew he was bullshitting, but that's when we had to buy new dishes. Then they kissed and made up, and not long after, Jackie moved out and Livvy got pregnant."

"Why did she start drinking?"

"Why does anyone? I always thought it got her through the nights she slept alone and Dave didn't."

"Speaking of alcohol, you might be interested to know that I talked to Tommy Smith. He's in rehab down the Peninsula. A relapse after twenty years of sobriety."

"Figures. His denunciation of Dave reeked of AA."

"What denunciation?"

"In the *Foghorn*, a letter to the editor after Dave declared for mayor. Tommy, the alcoholic evangelist for sobriety, called Dave a 'drug fiend,' and other nasty things. Personally, I think Dave would have been a good mayor—or at least fun, like Harvey was."

Ed was surprised. He hadn't seen Tommy's letter—he rarely read letters to the editor. By and large, they represented the outliers, people on the far ends of the curve, who either adored an article or detested it and couldn't rest until they told the world why. But this one might be worth searching the archive.

Pendleton was as high as the tree tops. Ed decided to take another chance. "You know, Doug's dying—"

"He is?" Owen pursed his lips. It was news to him.

"Stage four headed for five."

Pendleton shook his head. "Sad."

"He wanted to get a few things off his chest…like what happened on Waterfall Creek."

Owen's eyes turned reptilian. "That has nothing to do with Jackie."

"Understood. But as far as the law's concerned, it never happened at all—as you know. Thirty years is a long time. Dave's dead. Doug Connelly disappeared in '78, and now Joe Bogen's dying. No bodies, no badges, no warrants, nothing."

Pendleton shifted uncomfortably. "There's no statue of limitations for—"

"For what? Nothing happened."

Ed pulled out the one-hitter, but Pendleton waved it off. "Look,

Doug is my oldest friend and I'll always love him like a brother, but that doesn't change the fact that he was a trigger-happy asshole. Mexico, all right, that was self-defense and no one got hurt. But Mendocino? He didn't have to…*do that.* He should have let them take the damn plants. Cost of doing business. But no, he had to be Gary Cooper in *High Noon*."

"So when he called you…"

"What do you think? I was ready to throttle him. Dave too. He killed *cops*—at least that's what we thought—which meant all three of us were looking at a death sentence."

"He told me they'd just come back for the next crop—with more men and more guns."

"Maybe. But we could have prepared, moved our operation deeper into the woods. What he did put our necks under the guillotine."

"So you dissolved the partnership."

"We kicked him out of the fucking country and made him promise never to return."

"What did he say about that?"

"He screamed bloody murder. Reminded us for the millionth time how he saved our asses in Mexico. But what else could we do? For everyone's sake, he had to disappear. Even before Mendocino, Dave and I were fed up with his outlaw shit. We'd been toying with moving indoors, hiding the operation so well that no one would ever suspect. Fortunately, Doug was terrified and left. I didn't see him for thirty years, not until Dave's funeral."

Pendleton laced his fingers and contemplated his knuckles, deep in thought. The hummingbirds flitted around their heads, then flew away. "After the funeral, Doug downplayed his cancer. He didn't look good and he leaned pretty heavily on a cane, but he was upbeat and said the chemo was working. You say it isn't?"

"Not me—his medical record, which my hacker found while digging up his address. He's selling his business, getting ready to go."

"After the funeral, a bunch of us got high on the patio, then I looked around and he was gone. I didn't get his number. Do you have it?"

On the drive home, Ed wondered if he'd misjudged Pendleton. Like Nightingale had said, get him stoned, and underneath the chainmail armor lived a person who seemed almost like a decent human being…

Or not. The man had beefs with Doug, Jackie, and Dave. The first went into exile and the other two wound up dead. And there was no forgetting that with Dave gone, all the money was his.

As Ed crossed the Golden Gate Bridge, he ran the numbers. Say two pounds per plant times forty plants per crop—even assuming they wholesaled everything to dispensaries cheap, the annual gross had to run into six figures. People have killed for a lot less.

Ed flirted with the idea of calling Ramirez. But he'd guaranteed confidentiality. And even if he weren't constrained, he knew what the detective would say. He had no hard evidence of anything—just suppositions based on memories warped by four decades.

51

Pendleton was right about Tommy's letter to the editor. Smith called Dave a "drug fiend" and a "menace to society," and claimed that if he won, the city would face "disaster."

But the letter was odd. After a crescendo of invective, you expect crashing cymbals, but it ended with a whimper, a milquetoast plea to vote for anyone but Dave. Ed knew what had happened. The letter had been edited, sanitized for a family newspaper. In all likelihood, the final graf had been cut and the editor had substituted the lame closing.

Now Ed was intrigued. What had Tommy actually written? He tapped a few keys to access the letter's complete editorial thread. It took a flashing PASSWORD REQUIRED to remind him that he no longer worked at the *Horn*. Now what?

Ed called Tim, whose password had also presumably been cancelled, but his friend was tech savvy and had intimated that there were back doors into the system. With Tim on the phone directing him, Ed tried A and B to no avail, but C worked and he was in.

"Dave Kirsch is a boil on the face of society. He should not be mayor. He should not be permitted to walk the streets."

The original had more of the passion Ed expected, but also something else, the faint aroma of a threat. Ed checked the date—four days before Dave got it and right about the time Tommy went on his bender. Maybe a grudge against Dave had pushed him off the wagon. Maybe it was a coincidence that Tommy was arrested on the edge of Golden Gate Park the day after Dave was killed there. Or maybe it wasn't. Tommy himself said he was a belligerent drunk. He'd gotten his arm broken resisting arrest. If he'd slug a cop, maybe he'd gun down an old enemy. Ed called Ramirez.

52

Ed was going blind reading midterm essays. Many of his students—college students!—didn't know a paragraph from an autograph. *Next time, multiple choice.* Then his phone chimed. *Saved by the bell.*

"Very interesting about Smith," Ramirez said, "the old assault, the letter, and his arrest near the park shortly after the homicide. Now I'll go you one better. When he was arrested, guess what the impound officer found in his trunk? A shell casing from a Remington 700, the rifle that killed Kirsch."

Ed drew a sharp breath and Ramirez heard it.

"But don't get your shorts in a bunch. Add it all up and the total comes to nothing."

"What?" Ed was incredulous.

"If I tried for a warrant, they'd laugh me out the door."

"Why?" Ed countered. "Means, motive, opportunity. He has a motive—the evangelist for sobriety saving the world from a dope fiend. He had the opportunity. He was in San Francisco and has no alibi for the time Kirsch got it. He's also a violent drunk, and he was arrested just a few blocks from the scene the day after. And now you've got a *bullet*. If that's not means, what is?"

"Nice try, but it's all salsa, no burrito. It's not a bullet, just a *shell*—one lousy shell. If it was a *slug*, I could get ballistics, but it's just a casing. The impound officer found it under the floor of the trunk. Smith said he had no idea how it got there, which could easily be bullshit, except that he bought the car used eight months ago—I checked with the

DMV—so maybe the previous owner was a hunter. The Rem 700 is a very popular rifle, millions out there. And when Smith was arrested, we had no idea he might be connected to Kirsch, so we didn't do any tests for powder residue. Even if the letter contains an implied threat, which is a stretch, I can't take it to the DA. And assaulting Kirsch forty years ago and then getting popped near the scene—like I said, interesting but a long way from probable cause."

"So what now?"

Ramirez sighed. "More of the same. I keep my ear to the ground and hope somebody tells me something I don't know."

53

Where else would the Diggers hold a reunion but Longshoremen's Hall, psychedelic central back in the day? As Ed approached the domed hexagon near the northern waterfront, he couldn't recall if he'd ever been inside. By the time he'd arrived in San Francisco, the rock scene had moved elsewhere, and these days, with shipping relocated to the Port of Oakland, the dockworkers union hardly used the place, which seemed adrift in a sea of hotels catering to tourists who wanted to stay near Fisherman's Wharf.

But when Ed opened the door, he stepped through the looking glass into 1967. The air was redolent with incense and marijuana. The illumination came mostly from a trio of hallucinatory light shows projected around the dome. A band featuring grizzled survivors of Quicksilver, the Charlatans, and Moby Grape crowded the stage and wailed through old hits. At tables around the perimeter, vendors hawked T-shirts, underground comix, and weed paraphernalia, and many of the several hundred attendees were decked out in period costumes. It might have been the Be-In, except for the paunches and gray hair.

Ed floated into the throng. A fat man in a Che Guevara T-shirt accosted him.

"Medicine?" he asked, offering a vapor gadget as he stood next to a No Smoking sign. "An exquisite blend of *sativa* and *indica*." Ed took a hit. As he exhaled his thanks, the man handed him a flyer advertising a dispensary in the Mission.

Moving toward the stage, Ed heard a distinctive laugh and noticed a black woman who could have been dressed for church.

"Carol Covington!" Ed yelled over the music. "Remember me?"

At first, she didn't, then the realization dawned. "The museum, right?"

Ed nodded and smiled. "Thanks for telling me about this! Incredible turnout."

"Yes, amazing! So many people I haven't seen for so long. Have you seen Tommy? He's here with Rita…somewhere."

As the band finished "White Rabbit," Ed spied Smith standing beside a woman who looked younger, a child of the seventies. Ed touched his shoulder and reminded him who he was. "So you got out."

"Last week," Tommy said, introducing his wife.

"How are you?" Ed asked.

"He's *fine*," Rita said a bit too brightly, snaking an arm around her husband's waist and drawing him close.

"I'm back at work, counting my blessings, and going to seven meetings a week."

"One day at a time," Ed said. "Cliché, but true."

Smith gazed at him with watery eyes. "It's *not* a cliché."

Ed worked the room, introducing himself, talking up the exhibit, handing out business cards, and gathering contact information for future interviews. Wandering behind the mixing booth, he came upon a forest of life-sized cardboard cutouts of the departed: Janis, Jerry, Jimi, Chet Helms, Bill Graham, Abbie Hoffman. Standing next to a cutout of Emmett Grogan was Al Miller, leaning close to a woman with short hair, long earrings, and big glasses.

"I thought you hated the Diggers!" Ed yelled over a drum solo as he leaned close to the professor.

Miller shrugged. "It's a reunion. On St. Patrick's Day, everybody's Irish." He introduced his companion, a petite brunette who looked more Beat than hippie. She was the creative director at Public Media Center, San Francisco's leftist advertising agency. "Leslie and I worked together in Draft Resistance. She came up with our best slogan."

"Oh, Al, please—"

"Come on, it was great. 'Girls say *yes* to boys who say *no*.' Don't you love it? Then the women's movement came along and we had to drop it."

Leslie blushed and Al flashed her a big smile. Were they flirting?

Near the bar, Ed noticed Olivia Kirsch trying not to spill a glass of red wine while being embraced by a woman in a leather skirt and fringed jacket. As she drifted off, tears slid down Olivia's cheeks. Then she noticed Ed and pulled out a tissue.

"We used to work together at Magnolia's," she shouted over a rollicking version of "Who Do You Love?" "We were reminiscing... about Dave."

"Must be hard being here."

"It is. But it's good, too. Everyone's been very kind."

"Mind if I ask you a question?" Ed yelled over the music, then the song ended, and he dropped the volume. "I talked to Doug and Owen. They both said you had a fling with Jerry Garcia. Is that true?"

Her eyes widened. "You talked to *Owen*?"

"I did," Ed said, omitting the reason Pendleton hadn't slammed the door in his face.

"I'm surprised," Olivia said. "He must have been *really* stoned." Ed smiled. "As for Jerry, yes, once. Dave dealt to the Dead. Jerry was adrift and confused and needy, and one night when Dave was away, I was over there and—"

"Why do you say 'adrift and confused and needy'?"

Olivia took a gulp of wine. "Because Jerry was basically a bluegrass banjo player who suddenly found himself on lead guitar in a rock band. He preferred acoustic music, but the rest of them wanted to blow the roof off everywhere they played. He and his first wife—I forget her name..." She closed her eyes, then opened them. "Sally? No, *Sarah*. Jerry and Sarah tried acid together. Jerry saw God, Sarah saw trouble. Soon after, they broke up and she took their daughter, so he was lonely. That night, I was over at the Dead's flat and one thing led to another."

"What was he like?"

"It's not like I knew him that well, but he was shy, introverted. He was uncomfortable around people, especially after the Dead got famous. I always thought that was why he got messed up with heroin. He couldn't take the pressure of being *Jerry Garcia*."

"Owen and Doug also mentioned that Dave got it on with Jackie."

"So you found Doug."

"I did. In Reno."

Olivia looked away and drained her glass. Then she looked back. "Once or twice."

"I understand that Dave really liked Jackie's kid."

"Yes, it got us thinking about a family."

"But you weren't into it."

"I changed my mind, and I'm glad I did. Our daughter Hope was born in '69."

"Pardon me for asking, but…did Dave ever threaten to leave you to play stepfather to Jackie's son?"

Olivia looked like she'd been slapped. "*Absolutely not.* Did Owen tell you that? He should stick to cutting hair. No woman could ever take Dave away from me." She turned her back and walked away.

Ed wandered toward the stage. As the band finished a funky rendition of "All Along the Watchtower," he ruminated on Dave's death.

Tommy might have killed him in a drunken rage. But could he aim a rifle while blind drunk?

Al Miller might have had it done to save his marriage or torture his ex. But he'd been out of prison forty years. Did he still have the connections to hire a hit man?

Olivia had the ancient riflery award and might have gotten sick of Dave's philandering. But it seemed like she would have made her peace with it by now, not to mention that losing him had clearly devastated her.

Owen might have arranged it to derail the memoir and keep all the money. But they'd always had a contentious partnership. Why kill him now?

Was there anyone else? Ed's thoughts drifted to Reno. Bogen claimed he wound up there by coincidence, but it put him in convenient striking distance of his old partners. Maybe he had a private beef with Dave. He was dying, after all. Perhaps he'd decided to settle an old score while he still could.

Then Ed recalled Jackie cuddling with Doug at the Be-In. She'd come to San Francisco for peace and love, but found mostly the opposite. Had she lived, would her boy have become such a huge success? Probably not. In all likelihood, her greatest gift to her son was her death. She was on Hippie Hill cradling him in her arms. She set him down on the blanket, and then stood up—

Finally, Ed flashed on Ramirez. The detective kept talking about ballistics, how he couldn't go to the DA without a match. Ed worked his way to the door, and stepped into a cool, foggy evening that smelled of saltwater, seals, and sourdough. It all came down to ballistics. Then he had a thought and pulled out his phone.

54

It was a warm, sunny Sunday and Sonya had been pestering them about the pedal boats, so the family headed off to one of their favorite destinations, Stow Lake in Golden Gate Park. The bucolic lake was a short walk and a world away from the bustle of the art and science museums, a donut-shaped body of water that served as a moat around verdant Strawberry Hill. From halfway up the hill, a fifty-foot waterfall tumbled noisily down to the lake.

Ed had written about the lake. Like everything in Golden Gate Park, Stow had been man-made back in the 1880s, carved out of a wasteland of hundred-foot sand dunes. But the lake's forested beauty disguised a more utilitarian purpose. It was also a reservoir. From its murky depths, a network of pipes radiated throughout northwestern San Francisco and helped maintain water pressure in the fire hydrants.

When Ed and Julie were dating, they'd spent several romantic afternoons on the lake. They were in a rowboat when Ed proposed. When Julie accepted, from his backpack, he pulled two carefully packed flutes and a bag of ice containing a bottle of champagne. They toasted their future and kissed, cheeks dampened by waterfall mist.

After Sonya arrived, the family often visited the lake for picnics, hikes up the hill, and boat rides. Sonya enjoyed the rowboats, but she truly loved the pedal boats and couldn't wait until her legs were long enough to reach.

That day had arrived, so she and Julie shared one. As they churned away from the dock, Sonya waved and shouted, "Daddy, look at me! I'm pedaling!"

Ed waved. *It's always a pleasure to look at you.* He arranged Jake in his car seat on the floor of a rowboat and followed the girls around the island. Jake rocked back and forth and waved his spoon as if he were a jockey wielding a riding crop.

Stow attracted flocks of birds that fascinated Jake. He flapped his arms and waved his spoon, crying, "Birdie! Birdie!"

Ed pointed to some and said, "Ducks."

"Duckie! Duckie!" Jake chortled. He had a rubber duckie bath toy, and seemed just as eager to squeeze the real ones. He reached for them, straining against his seat belt.

Ed pointed to larger birds and said, "Seagulls." The word was new to Jake and he called them "siggles."

"Daddy!" Sonya shouted, pointing. "The turtles! They're fine!"

Sonya and Julie had pedaled to the edge of the lake, to a marshy area filled with tall grass and waterlogged tree branches. When Sonya was four, Ed had pointed out the congregation of turtles that lived there, mentioning that the species was endangered around the world but carefully protected at Stow. Ever since, no trip to the lake was complete without Sonya checking on the turtles.

"You hungry?" Julie called to Ed. They'd packed sandwiches, fruit, and juice boxes.

"Getting there," he replied. "Let's go around once more, then eat by the waterfall."

"But I'm *hungry*," Sonya whined. "I want my sandwich *now*."

Jake echoed her, chanting, "Sammich, sammich."

"I thought you wanted to *pedal*," Julie said.

"I *do*, but—"

"Let's go around once more," Julie said, "then have lunch."

The pedal boat churned off as Ed worked the oars, spinning the rowboat around and following. In the distance he heard a firecracker, but the moment the thought registered, an unseen hammer smashed his shoulder and suddenly his arm was on fire. Another firecracker, another hammer blow. His arm felt numb, hot, and wet. He fell backward. Looking down, he saw two holes in his jacket. Its gray fabric was turning bright red, and the color was spreading.

Ed screamed and collapsed in the stern. Julie turned and shrieked.

Then Sonya was howling, and Jake was crying, and people along the promenade were shouting and running.

Ed looked up and saw clouds spinning. A blowtorch was searing his shoulder. He couldn't move his arm. He heard splashing and yelling. Jake was wailing. A familiar voice screamed his name, but he could not reply. The last thing he remembered was gazing up to see if Jake was all right. *You never know what a magic bullet might do.*

55

Was he underwater? Ed strained to lift his eyelids. Through a thick fog, he spied the bottom half of a duck, webbed feet and gray wings framing a white belly. He'd seen this same duck before but couldn't recall where.

Then he remembered something slamming into his shoulder and searing pain and hitting his head as he tumbled backward. He couldn't feel his shoulder now. He couldn't feel anything except a swollen tongue filling a parched mouth like a charred log in ashes.

He tried to move but couldn't. With an effort, he cranked his gaze past the duck and saw another one—feet, belly, and wings, but this bird had its head in the water and its eyes met Ed's. The duck didn't move. It just stared the way Julie did when he said something that annoyed her. He heard labored breathing and realized it was his own. But he was under water. How could he breathe?

The fog cleared and Ed realized he was not submerged, but in a bed gazing up at a ceiling decorated with the bottom halves of ducks for the amusement of people on their backs. Then he remembered where he'd seen these ducks before. At the dentist.

Ed heard a noise, a chair scraping the floor, and suddenly he was peering through a wide-angle lens at a huge round face framed by black hair flecked with gray.

"You're awake," Tim said. "Welcome back."

Then Tim's face disappeared and Ed heard footsteps. From a distance, he heard his friend call, "Nurse! He's awake!"

More footsteps and Tim reappeared. "They gave you a sedative.

You've been out cold for—" He glanced at his watch. "—twenty-six hours." Tim produced a phone and spoke quietly into it, half turned away from the bed. "He just woke up…Woozy…Okay, see you soon." Then to Ed: "Julie and the kids are on their way."

Ed inhaled and smelled roses and floor polish. He turned his head and heard himself groan. Out the window, trees rustled in the afternoon breeze. When he looked back, Tim's face was gone, replaced by the pinched features of a rail-thin redhead dressed in white. She primped a bouquet in a vase on a table by the bed. "Three bouquets and an orchid," she said. "Mister Popularity. Do you know where you are?"

All Ed could manage was a moan.

"Saint Mary's. You got shot. The ambulance brought you here. Would you like something to drink?"

Ed's mouth felt full of sand. His tongue was a rock on the beach. The nurse fiddled with something beneath him and Ed started as the head of the bed rose with a mechanized whirr. She held up a plastic bottle and threaded a straw between his lips. He sucked and immediately gagged and coughed and spit.

"Careful. You're still sedated. Take little sips."

Ed tried again and swallowed. He tried to sit up farther but failed. He tried to speak but was still underwater with the ducks.

"Doctor is on her way," the nurse said.

Ed flashed on Stow Lake and panicked. Gunshots! Jake! His good arm flailed. His hand found somebody's arm and pulled. Tim's face loomed over him as large as a rising full moon. In a thick whisper, Ed croaked, "F-fa-fam-lee."

"They're fine," Tim said. "They'll be here soon."

Ed let go and sank into the mattress, exhausted. "Sh-shooter?"

"No arrest," Tim said, "and as far as I know, no suspects. The cops have security outside your door for as long as you're here. But when you get home…you'll have to cross that bridge."

Tim fiddled with his phone, then held the screen above Ed's face. "You're page one: 'Foghorn Columnist Wounded in GG Park Shooting.' Below the fold, but still. Want to read it?"

Ed closed his eyes and cranked his head left and then right.

"Want me to read it to you?"

Ed worked up the strength to whisper, "No."

"Good choice," Tim said. "It's totally predictable, except they identified you as 'staff,' not 'freelance.'" He sighed. "That's what happens when you fire all the copy editors."

Ed dozed. He was awakened by distant bells and buzzers and the aroma of coffee and French fries. He heard footsteps like soldiers marching, then saw an unfamiliar face, a woman with thick glasses and crimson lipstick whose make-up couldn't hide her age.

"Good afternoon, Mister Rosenberg, I'm Doctor Stevens."

Ed cranked up his concentration as she explained that he'd been shot twice, once in the triceps, once in the pectoral muscle. The triceps would heal. But the bullet that pierced his pec had nicked the lung, which raised the possibility of pneumothorax—air in the chest cavity—which might collapse the lung—very bad, hence the chest tube, to drain air and fluid. But barring infection, he should be home in a few days. With physical therapy, he should be good as new in a few months.

Trying to follow her exhausted Ed and he fell into a fitful slumber. He dreamed he was back in high school, in a noisy, crowded hallway lined with metal lockers, kids joking, pushing, shoving. He was on his way to a big test, but had no idea where or what he was supposed to know. Then he was staring at duck feet. In the distance, he heard familiar voices.

"Daddy!" Sonya shouted, running up to the bed. "I made you a card, see?" She unfurled a construction paper scroll filled with hearts, flowers, and rainbows.

"Careful, Sonya," Julie warned. "Don't touch Daddy. Don't touch anything."

"Thank you, honey," Ed said in a hoarse whisper. "It's lovely."

"What's this?" Sonya asked, pointing to the tube snaking out of Ed's side.

"A chest tube," Tim said, "to drain fluid from around your dad's lung."

"Why?"

"Because one bullet hit his lung."

Sonya asked, "Is that bad?"

"It's okay," Ed croaked. "Little while, good as new."

"You said shootings are *rare*," Sonya sputtered, folding her arms across her chest like a teacher confronting a delinquent.

"They are," Ed whispered.

"No they're not! Mom's boss. Then Mom—almost. And now you. That's *not* rare."

"Sonya," Julie admonished, "Daddy's tired—"

"Who shot you?" the girl demanded.

"I don't know, honey."

"Why'd you get shot?"

"I—"

"She's obsessed," Julie explained, "and very anxious."

"Am *I* going to get shot?"

"No—"

"How do you *know*?"

"Daddy's tired," Julie said. "We'll talk more about this later, okay? Tim, the snack bar sells fruit. Would you be a dear and take Sonya?"

"Sure," Tim said, extending a hand to the girl he'd known since Julie was pregnant. "But you know, Sonya, they also have ice cream sandwiches—"

Sonya's eyes widened. "Ice cream!" The two of them skipped out the door.

Jake squirmed on Julie's hip. Ed peered at her face and wished he had the strength to tell her she'd never looked more beautiful. Tears formed in his eyes. He reached out and squeezed her hand. He drew a deep breath and worked his lips and tongue, "Th-thank G-God you're okay."

"Thank God *you* are," Julie replied.

Julie set Jake down with his spoon and a toy truck, then leaned over Ed and kissed him deeply. "For a minute there—" Then she started to cry.

"It's okay." Ed squeezed her hand. "I'm still here."

It all came out in a rush Ed struggled to follow. When she heard the shots and saw him fall, she thought the worst. An off-duty firefighter and his girlfriend were in a rowboat nearby. The girlfriend called 911 and the firefighter rowed to Ed, reaching him just ahead of Julie and Sonya. He reassured them that Jake was fine and that Ed's wounds didn't look life threatening. Then he instructed his girlfriend to hold the D-ring on Ed's bow while he rowed them in. When the boats reached the dock, the ambulance was pulling up.

"In my entire life," Julie whimpered through her tears, "I've never been *so scared*. If you…" She wiped her eyes and blew her nose. "I don't know what I'd do."

"No need to think about that."

Julie inhaled sharply and forced a tear-stained smile. "I've made a decision," she said, clutching Ed's hand in both of hers. "I've stopped drinking." Ed's eyebrows arched. "I made a deal with God. If I have you safe and sound, I don't need alcohol."

"B-but you don't believe in God."

"I know, but—"

"No atheists in pedal boats, huh?"

Julie laughed and wiped her eyes. "Something like that."

"How are you going to do it?"

"Cold turkey. I haven't had any since—"

"What's that? One day?"

"One day at a time."

"So you're joining AA?"

"No, I'm not an alcoholic."

That's what they all say. Then Ed said, "Fine, but maybe you could use some help."

"If I need it, I'll get it. But last night, I poured everything down the drain—except one bottle."

Ed's eyes asked the question his mouth couldn't form.

"The champagne in the fridge—for when one of us gets a job with benefits."

"Ah," Ed murmured. Then Ed had a disturbing thought. She might want him to reciprocate and abstain from his favorite medicine. "I hope you don't expect me to stop smoking weed."

"Cutting back wouldn't hurt," she replied, "but no, I don't expect you to quit. I'll probably smoke more myself."

"Speaking of which, any chance you brought some?"

Julie's face fell. "You're in a *hospital*. You can't *smoke*."

"Fuck 'em. It's medicine. I have a prescription. Next time, bring me a bud and my one-hitter. Please."

Ed dozed and dreamed of Sonya peering at the turtles. When he woke, a man of around forty was striding into the room. He wore a suit and had thinning blond hair. His nose looked as if it had been broken more than once. He introduced himself as Detective Robert Molloy. He asked several questions, and Ed wearily nodded or shook his head. Then the detective asked if Ed could identify anyone who might wish him harm. He considered the question, then asked to speak with Detective Ramirez.

"Anything you'd tell him you can tell me."

"Where is he?"

"At Stow with the techs, dragging the lake for the slugs."

"What's the chance of finding them?"

"Slim to none. You wouldn't believe the muck down there."

Ed slept and dreamed he was a little boy sitting between his father's legs on the bench in a rowboat at that park on Long Island. His father was showing him how to row, two small hands on the oars covered by two large ones. They leaned back and pulled. Above him, young Eddie heard car horns. He looked up and saw birds in formation.

"Ducks?" he asked.

His father leaned forward, dipped the oars into the water, and they both pulled. "Canada geese."

56

On the morning Ed was discharged, he was still shaky, so a nurse rolled him out the door in a wheelchair. Julie was taking the kids to school and daycare and then had to shepherd a client through radio interviews downtown, so Tim volunteered for the pickup. At the curb, Ed tried to hoist his suitcase with his good arm, but could barely lift it off the pavement. Tim flipped it into the trunk and helped Ed fold himself gingerly into the passenger seat.

Ed felt as though he'd been sprung from jail. The morning was sunny and cool but warming quickly. Seagulls wheeled overhead. The sky looked impossibly blue, the trees impossibly green. He took a deep breath, inhaling until his shoulder ached. It felt wonderful to breathe air perfumed by the Pacific instead of disinfectant. Ed closed his eyes and thanked his lucky stars for his survival and his family's safety, and for having a friend like Tim.

"Thanks for doing this, man."

Tim glanced over his shoulder and pulled away from the curb. "Beats working."

But Ed also felt like a fledgling rudely pushed from the nest. Where he was going, there was no armed guard at the door. He'd asked the guy at his hospital door, a retired cop, what he charged. A bundle. And even if they could afford it, that was no way to live. But not having a bodyguard left Ed feeling vulnerable and frightened. Someone didn't like him, and next time they might have better aim.

He willed the worst case from his mind and focused instead on the friend who'd schlepped all the way from the East Bay to fetch him.

"So?" Ed asked, "did you enroll at Oaksterdam? Or are you a plumber's apprentice?"

"Neither," Tim replied, maneuvering around a bus. "I'm actually considering something else...becoming a handyman."

"Whoa," Ed said. "What brought this on?"

Tim flashed an impish smile. "My neighbor."

Tim lived in Piedmont, an exclusive enclave of upper-crust homes completely surrounded by more modest Oakland. On weekends, Tim's affluent neighbors had watched him replace half the bricks in his front stoop, repair cracked concrete in the driveway, and build a screened porch off the dining room—all pretty much by himself. Now a neighbor's decorative shutters were coming loose. Tim ran into the guy one evening and the man asked how best to repair them. Tim was looking to fill his time and offered to do the job as a favor. The neighbor accepted—but insisted on paying the rate quoted by the previous handyman, who'd turned out to be an alcoholic flake. Tim demurred then finally accepted, surprised that his services could command such a rate. While in the middle of the two-day job, another neighbor saw him up a ladder with a screw gun and asked if he might be interested in wallpapering her guestroom.

"It's weird," Tim said. "I'm getting work and I'm not even in business."

"So you've decided? You're a handyman?"

"Who knows? At the moment, I'm just trying to keep busy. I have no idea if I'll stick with it, but so far, it's fun. I Googled 'handyman Piedmont Oakland.' There are some, but not many. There's probably room for me. I'm taking it slow, but I'm thinking of having business cards printed. What do you think of: 'HELPFUL HANDYMAN. For jobs too big for you but too small for a contractor. Free estimates. Reasonable rates. References.'"

"I like it. May all your dreams come true."

57

That afternoon, Sonya came home in a foul mood. Before her parents could even ask, she whined, "It's *no fair*! They're not going to change *anything*. He says it's *good*. But he *doesn't care*."

"Wait a minute," Julie asked, "what's good? Who doesn't care?"

Sonya dug through her backpack and produced a piece of paper folded in thirds, which she thrust at her parents. It was a letter from the assistant superintendent in charge of curriculum and instruction. He wholeheartedly congratulated Sonya on her critique of the DAP program's treatment of marijuana, then mentioned "financial priorities," "federal regulations," "contingent funding," and "Congressional oversight of the Department of Education." In closing, he urged her to send copies to San Francisco's representative and California's two senators.

Ed and Julie looked at one another, each hoping the other would speak first. Ed suddenly felt tired and weak, and slumped in a kitchen chair. Julie cleared her throat. "Well, honey, he complimented the fine work you did—"

"But it doesn't mean anything! Nothing's going to change! It's *no fair!*"

"You're absolutely right," Ed said wearily. "The federal government gives the district a ton of money, but it comes with strings attached, and this bozo is saying that one of them is teaching the DAP program exactly the way you got it." Ed sighed. "The district is knowingly lying to kids about weed—for money. And that's fucked."

"Oooh, Daddy, bad word."

"I know, honey, but it's bullshit."

"Maybe you *should* send your report to Congress," Julie said. "Maybe they'll change the program."

"In your dreams," Ed said.

Julie shot him a look and Ed executed a quick pirouette. "Mom's got a point, honey. The school district can't change the curriculum, but Congress can."

"How?"

Julie told Sonya to print out three copies of her report. They would send hard copies to their representative and senators, and also e-mail it.

"I'll help you find the addresses," Julie said, following Sonya toward the stairs.

"I'm sorry, honey," Ed called wearily after them, "sometimes the adult world makes no sense." He wasn't sure if he was talking about her report or his life.

58

Even with pain medication, Ed had trouble sleeping, and by late afternoon, after physical therapy, picking up the kids, and using his good arm to transfer loads from the washer to dryer, he was beat. He didn't have the strength to climb the stairs and start dinner, so he collapsed into his office chair and returned to editing an interview with a former hippie couple who'd started out hawking homemade granola at the Be-In and now, with their adult children, owned a Petaluma-based company that sold organic breakfast cereals and snack foods through health stores nationwide.

The doorbell rang, but Ed couldn't face the stairs. He heard feet scurrying above and lunged for the intercom. "Sonya! Don't answer it!"

They couldn't afford a guard, but they'd upgraded their locks and bought Ed a Kevlar vest. It was expensive and uncomfortable, but with no arrest and no leads, why take chances? Still, Ed worried about his family's safety. If someone wanted to *really* hurt him—

Ed struggled to his feet, dragged himself across the garage, and hit the button. As the door rose, he stepped outside and scanned the street. Nothing unusual. He craned his neck up to the front porch and saw the back of a dark-haired man in a sport coat. "May I help you?"

"I hope I'm not disturbing you," Detective Ramirez said, smiling down at him, "but I have news."

Ed gestured into the garage. Ramirez descended the stairs and followed him inside.

"You couldn't call?"

"I wanted to tell you in person." Ramirez noticed the pool table and touched the felt. "Nice. I didn't know you played. How's your game?"

"At best, fair." Ed nodded toward his sling. "And with this—"

Ramirez scooped a ball out of the reservoir and bowled it toward a far corner. It rattled in the gate but refused to drop. "I always wanted one."

"You play?"

"A little."

Ed smiled. *That's what every hustler says.* He handed the detective a cue and the triangle, and pointed at the chalk.

Ramirez racked up, shot the break with a smooth stroke, and sank four before overcutting a tough shot to a side pocket. "Guess where I just came from? Booking the shooter who killed Jackie Zarella and Dave Kirsch and almost killed you."

"Really." Ed's eyes widened. "So I was right? Olivia?"

59

"Yes," Ramirez said. "Olivia."

Ed suddenly felt woozy and leaned on the pool table for support. "Well, what do you know…"

"You okay?" Ramirez took a step toward him, but Ed held up a hand. "I'm fine."

Then he realized that he actually was. He felt weak and lightheaded and his shoulder throbbed, but now his family was safe. No one would hurt them now. He was safe, too. Ed's sigh could have blown a fog bank all the way to Hawaii.

Ramirez chalked up and sank a long cross-table shot. "When you called and said I should check the ballistics of the slug that killed Kirsch against a cold case from forty years ago—" He grimaced. "Let's just say it wasn't my highest priority. But when a slug in *your* shooting matched Kirsch, I dug into the archive, and *bingo*. So here's my question: how'd you know?"

"I didn't," Ed said. "It was just a thought. I was at a party and ran into Olivia. She said no woman could ever take Dave away from her. It wasn't so much what she said, as *how* she said it."

"Go on."

"They both fucked around, but Dave a lot more. For this project I'm doing, I talked to people who knew them in the sixties. I got an earful about their affairs. But I heard of only two cases where Dave ever threatened to leave her—Jackie way back when, and just recently, with Cindy Miller. When Olivia said no woman could take Dave from her, she didn't sound like the long-suffering wife. She sounded more like the ranch girl with the rifle keeping the varmints out of the vegetables. I thought maybe Olivia did Jackie to keep Dave, and then, when he started making noises about leaving her for Cindy, she finally got fed up and did him, too."

Ramirez sank a long straight shot. "You've got a future in homicide investigations, but that's not quite what happened. When I got the match, I rubbed Olivia's face in it. Told her the weapon that killed her husband had also killed Zarella and wounded you, and what did she know about it? I was ready for a line of horseshit, but she broke down crying and confessed. She seemed relieved. The thing is, she didn't mean to kill Kirsch. She was aiming for *Miller*. That's why she was so distraught. She killed the *wrong guy*. She was out of practice and her eyesight isn't what it used to be. In my office, she reeked of alcohol, so maybe she had a few before aiming at Miller—and you. Her drinking may have saved your life." Ramirez just missed a long rail shot.

"And she went after me because I was asking too many questions."

"Right. After missing Miller and killing her husband, she came unhinged, and then you showed up asking about her previous victim. She got spooked and saw only one way out."

"You'd think that after missing Cindy, she would have gotten a better sight or laid off the booze."

"You'd think," Ramirez said, "but I'm guessing she's an alcoholic, so she couldn't think straight. The arrest is news today, but the explanation doesn't happen until the press conference tomorrow at the Hall. Ten o'clock. You should be there—otherwise you'll have every reporter in town camped out on your front porch. The mayor'll be there. He's giving you a commendation and a check for $25,000."

"Money? Great! But why?"

"Don't you remember? The dispensaries put up a reward."

Ed's heart leaped. His family was safe—and now they were safer.

"What about you, Tony? You matched the ballistics. What do you get?"

Ramirez sank a sweet cross-table cut shot. "I get to clear three violent felonies, including a forty-year-old ice cube. Good for the stats. In the department, my dick grows two inches and nobody fucks with me—for a while."

"What about her?"

"Depends on the DA. He might try for special circumstances, but San Francisco juries never go for death. I'm guessing life without parole."

The enormity of it all suddenly crashed over Ed like high tide in a hurricane. His family was safe. He was safe. And he was about to cash a big check. But two people were dead and he'd barely escaped being number three. Suddenly his gut cramped and his Kevlar vest itched. He had to sit down on the basement stairs.

"You okay?" Ramirez asked.

With his good hand, Ed unbuttoned his shirt. "Could you give me a hand, Tony? I want to get this damn vest off."

Ramirez help him peel his shirt away, then gingerly worked the vest around Ed's bad arm and helped him back into the shirt.

"Thanks. Now I could use some medicine. Do me a favor, would you? In my office—" He nodded toward the door. "On the right, the middle shelf, behind *The World Rushed In*, there's a bong and baggie and lighter. Would you, please?"

Ramirez obliged. Exhaling, Ed felt better almost immediately. Then he remembered his manners. "You want?"

Ramirez smiled and shook his head. "Thanks, but not while I'm on duty."

60

Ed escorted Ramirez to the garage door and said he'd see him at the press conference.

As he watched the detective walk to his car, he shook his head. Who knew that his shot in the dark would hit the target, let alone the bull's eye? And the reward! What luck! He'd never learned Gene Simons's birth name, so no jackpot. But the consolation prize would certainly help him sleep more soundly, and Julie, too. He couldn't wait to tell her.

Ed was about to close the garage door when a UPS truck pulled up. The man in brown waved and hopped down holding a box—probably some catalogue item Julie had ordered, he thought. But no, it was for him. The return address said Reno.

Ed shuffled into his office and used his good arm to cut the box open. He found a purse, some clothes, and a note: "Sold the business. Moving to Tampa. Came across this box of Jackie's things. Forgot I even had it. Thought her son would like it. Joe."

The clothes looked like thrift store rejects, but the leather purse was in decent shape. Ed opened it and found a comb, brush, pen, lip balm, some tampons, a dog-eared copy of *The Teachings of Don Juan*, a ticket stub from a Lovin' Spoonful show, and a receipt for $3.27 from Mendel's Far Out Fabrics.

Ed was about to stuff everything back in the box when he heard the faint sound of paper crinkling. He rooted around the purse and discovered a small zippered pocket in the lining. Opening it, he extracted a faded snapshot of a little boy seated between two young adults, a hippie gal and a guy whose long hair did not entirely cover a tattoo. Turning it over, Ed read the spidery writing: "July 4, 1968, Golden Gate Park with Doug and Forrest."

Ed stopped breathing and stared at the name just as the intercom came to life. "Dinner's almost ready," Julie said. "Would you set the table?"

Ed couldn't take his eyes off the name.

"Ed?" Julie called. "You down there?"

He leaned into the intercom. "On my way."

A surge of adrenaline propelled him up the stairs and over to the refrigerator. He reached inside and pulled out the bottle.

Julie's eyebrows asked a question.

Ed's grin was as broad as a circus clown's. "The exception to your new rule. Not a job with benefits. But something just as good. Maybe better!"

AUTHOR'S NOTE

The major characters and Magic Bullet Theory are fictional, but except for a few details, the material about the hippie Haight-Ashbury is true. I am indebted to *The Haight-Ashbury: A History* by Charles Perry (Wenner Books, New York, 2005); *The Summer of Love: The Inside Story of LSD, Rock & Roll, Free Love, and High Times in the Wild West* by Joel Selvin (Dutton-Penguin, New York, 1994); and the DVD compilation of the *San Francisco Oracle* (available from Amazon.com).

The material about the evolution of the marijuana industry is also true, not only in Northern California, but throughout the United States. It began with importation from Mexico and the Caribbean, then importation from Colombia, followed by domestic cultivation, first outdoors and now increasingly indoors. Marijuana continues to be imported and grown outdoors, but indoor growing accounts for an increasing proportion of the U.S. supply. For providing this information, my deepest thanks to several individuals who prefer to remain anonymous.

The material about the evil weed's health effects is also true. Marijuana does not appear to be a significant risk factor for lung cancer. It causes about as much driving impairment as antidepressants and antihistamines. And it's the recreational drug least likely to cause emotional dependence and physical addiction. Scientific references can be found at KillerWeedNovel.com.

WHERE ARE THEY NOW?

Joan Baez (1941–) continues to sing on behalf of causes she supports. She lives in the San Francisco Bay Area.

Marty Balin (1942–), founder and co-lead singer (with Grace Slick) of the Jefferson Airplane, has released several solo albums and continues to perform with the band's current incarnation, Jefferson Starship. He lives in the Bay Area.

Jerry Garcia (1942–1995), lead guitarist for the Grateful Dead, succumbed to a heart attack while being treated for heroin addiction.

Bill Graham (1931–1991) was born Wolodia Grajonca to Jewish parents in Berlin. He and one sister were the only family members to survive the Holocaust. After the war, he moved to New York and then in the early 1960s to San Francisco. In the mid-1960s, he managed the San Francisco Mime Troupe, raising money for the street theater company by persuading local rock bands to play benefits. Eventually, he became a full-time rock promoter. He was killed in a helicopter crash while returning home from a Huey Lewis and the News concert at Concord Pavilion.

Allen Ginsberg (1926–1997) was the poet laureate of the Beats. Author of *Howl* (1955), which established the legal standard for obscenity ("redeeming social importance"), he also inspired and befriended prominent hippies and rock artists, among them, Bob Dylan. He was an early advocate of both gay rights and marijuana legalization. Shortly before his death, he gave his last public reading at a bookstore in the Haight-Ashbury.

Emmett Grogan (1943–1978) was a founder of the Diggers. He was a backup vocalist on Bob Dylan's recording of "Mr. Tambourine Man," and Dylan dedicated his 1978 album, *Street Legal,* to him. Grogan was the author of an autobiography, *Ringolevio.* He died of a heart attack complicated by heroin use.

David Harris (1946–), founder of the Draft Resistance, is a journalist and author. He lives in the Bay Area. He and Joan Baez are divorced.

Chet Helms (1942–2005) managed Big Brother and the Holding Company and persuaded his old friend, Janis Joplin, to move from Texas to become its singer.

Janis Joplin (1943–1970) was a blues and rock singer, first with Big Brother and the Holding Company, then as a solo performer. She died of a heroin overdose complicated by alcoholism.

Timothy Leary, Ph.D. (1920–1996), was a Harvard psychologist who, in the late 1950s, began researching the effects of hallucinogenic drugs (psilocybin mushrooms and LSD). Fired from Harvard in 1963, he became a lecturer, author, and, at the Human Be-In, a hippie inspiration. He was arrested and imprisoned several times for drug offenses. He died of prostate cancer.

Phil Lesh (1940–) was the founding bass player of the Grateful Dead. He continues to perform with Phil Lesh and Friends, the Other Ones, the Dead, and Furthur, named after Ken Kesey's bus.

Ken Kesey (1935–2001) was a novelist who called himself "too young to be Beat but too old to be a hippie." As a student at Stanford in the early 1960s, he sponsored raucous parties called Acid Tests that combined live rock music (often featuring future members of the Grateful Dead) with marijuana and LSD. With a group of friends called the Merry Pranksters, he took a cross-country bus trip chronicled in *The Electric Kool-Aid Acid Test* by Tom Wolfe. Kesey's novels include *One Flew Over the Cuckoo's Nest* and *Sometimes a Great Notion*. He died of a stroke.

Grace Slick (1939–), born Grace Wing, sang with the Jefferson Airplane and Jefferson Starship. She retired from music in 1988 and moved to Southern California, where she became a visual artist. Her drawings and paintings have been exhibited at many galleries.

Augustus Owsley Stanley III (1935–2011) was the namesake grandson of a Kentucky governor and U.S. Senator who opposed Prohibition. After LSD was outlawed in the U.S. in 1966, he became famous for producing large quantities of the hallucinogen. In the 1980s, he moved to Australia, where he lived until his death.

Wavy Gravy (1936–) was born Hugh Romney, but in 1969, blues great B.B. King renamed him. He was the hippie "clown prince," a founder of the activist commune, the Hog Farm, that helped organize the Woodstock Rock Festival, which Gravy emceed. For several years, Ben and Jerry's ice cream marketed a flavor called Wavy Gravy. Today he runs Camp Winnarainbow in Northern California. He lives in the Bay Area.

Bob Weir (1947–) was the founding rhythm guitarist of the Grateful Dead. Today he plays with Rat Dog, the Other Ones, the Dead, and Furthur.

ACKNOWLEDGMENTS

Thanks to Rob Kessler for perspectives on school-based drug education programs.

Kudos to the talented and generous editors who critiqued various drafts: Belle Adler, Randy Alfred, Dan Hubig, Clyde Leland, Larry and Pat Morin, Andrew Moss, Phil Ryan, Anne Simons, Ed Stackler, Annie Stine, and especially my brother, the indefatigable Deke Castleman.

As always, deepest thanks to my fabulous agent and friend, Amy Rennert of the Amy Rennert Agency, Tiburon, California.

Many thanks to my publisher, Pat Walsh, editor Marthine Satris, copy editor Michelle Dotter, and designer Dorothy Smith. Equal thanks to tech wizard Frank Colin, cannabis consultant Michael Gosney, and publicist Anita Halton of Anita Halton and Associates, Laguna Beach, California. And a tip of the hat to David Poindexter (1954-2013).

Finally, deepest love and thanks to Anne, Jeff, Kristen, and Maya.

ABOUT THE AUTHOR

Michael Castleman grew up in Lynbrook, a Long Island suburb of New York City. He graduated Phi Beta Kappa from the University of Michigan with a degree in English (1972), and earned a Masters in journalism from UC Berkeley (1977). He has lived in San Francisco since 1975. An award-winning medical journalist, he is the author of twelve consumer health and sexuality books and currently publishes GreatSexAfter40.com. He has published three previous Ed Rosenberg novels: *The Lost Gold of San Francisco, Death Caps,* and *A Killing in Real Estate.* Visit mcastleman.com.